STORIES FROM THE ROUND BARN

Stories from

THE ROUND BARN

Jacqueline Dougan Jackson

TriQuarterly Books
Northwestern University Press
Evanston, Illinois

TriQuarterly Books
Northwestern University Press
Evanston, Illinois 60208-4210

Copyright © 1997 by Jacqueline Dougan Jackson. Published 1997 by TriQuarterly Books/Northwestern University Press. All rights reserved.

Second printing 1997
First paperback printing 2000

Printed in the United States of America

ISBN 0-8101-5101-4

Library of Congress Cataloging-in-Publication Data

Jackson, Jacqueline Dougan.
        Stories from the round barn / Jacqueline Dougan Jackson.
            p. cm.
        ISBN 0-8101-5072-7 (alk. paper) — ISBN 0-8101-5101-4 (pbk. : alk. paper)
        1. Farm life—Wisconsin—Beloit—Anecdotes. 2. Dougan family—Anecdotes. 3. Dairy farming—Wisconsin—Beloit—Anecdotes. 4. Family farms—Wisconsin—Beloit—Anecdotes. I. Title.
        S521.5.W6J28 1997
        977.5'87—dc21
                                                                                    97-25488
                                                                                    CIP

CONTENTS

ACKNOWLEDGMENTS

Hundreds of people have contributed to *Stories from the Round Barn*, and to materials in a longer work in progress, *The Round Barn*, of which these stories will be a part. Their contributions span so many years and are so entwined with both works that it is hard to select only those persons who gave material for these particular stories. I've surely missed some. And I need to cite both the living and the dead, for so many who told me their stories have subsequently died.

Foremost is the family: Ronald and Vera Dougan, Trever Dougan, Joan Dougan Schmidt, Pat Dougan Dalvit, Craig Dougan. Also my grandparents, Eunice and Wesson Dougan, have contributed strongly through words and actions remembered by many people, as well as through their writings. The richest nonfamily source has been Eloise Marston Schnaitter, who rivaled only my parents and brother in stories and information. Others include Pat and Ralph Anderson, Ada Beadle, Geneva Bown, Ernest Capps, Gulbrand Gjestvang, Amos Grundahl, Bob Hart, Phil Holmes, Jim Howard, Margaret Wieland Ikeman, Dan Kelley, Marie Knilans, Richard Knilans, Milton Koenecke, George Lentell, Dorothy Kirk Lueken, Howard Milner, Roscoe Ocker, Lester Richardson, Kate Wieland Russell, Oscar Skogen, Helen Tapp, Russel Ullius, Fannie Viehman, and Betty Beadle Wallace.

Many of these stories were first published in *The Beloit Daily News*, and I thank editor Bill Behling, associate editor Larry Raymer, and Minnie Mills Enking. Others have appeared in *Brainchild, The Alchemist Review, The Writer's Barbeque,* and *TriQuarterly.* Several have been read over Wisconsin Public Radio's *Chapter-A-Day* by Karl Schmidt.

Those who have given support and valued critiques during the writing process include Peg and John Knoepfle, Ethan Lewis, Karl Schmidt, Phil Kendall, Joseph Tobias, David Bartlett, Paul Doby, Walter Johnson, Laverne and JJ Smith, Jean Ladendorf, Michele Woolsey, Sue Anders, Lloyd and Julia Hornbostel, the members of the Brainchild Writing Collective, Eva and Chad Walsh, Alison Sackett, Marion Stocking, Sandy Costa, Robert McElroy, Razak Dahmane, Luke Snell, Berniece Rabe, and my daughters: Damaris Jackson, Megan Ryan, Gillian Jackson, and Elspeth DeBow. Sangamon State University (now University of Illinois at Springfield) granted me three sabbaticals. Several of the above people have helped me with the researching, transcribing of tapes, typing, word processing, and proofing, as did Betty Bradley, Ruth Vogel, Marian Levin, Lola Lucas, and Charla Stone.

I have had considerable help in gathering photographs, from, among others, Eloise Schnaitter, Tom Kelley, Jim Howard, Ralph Flagler, Betty Beadle Wallace, Muriel Pollock and members of the Ned Hollister Bird Club, and the families of Henry Wieland, Roscoe Ocker, and Arthur Knilans. I owe the existence of much of this book to my grandparents and parents for saving so much material having to do with the farm and all its activities.

My appreciation goes always to my writing mentors: Chad Walsh of Beloit College; Roy Cowden, director of the Hopwood Program, University of Michigan; and William Perlmutter of St. John's University. Finally, thanks and appreciation to Reginald Gibbons of *TriQuarterly,* who wanted to publish the Round Barn saga, and who is proving unparalleled as an editor.

STORIES FROM THE ROUND BARN

I   PROLOGUE: THE ROUND BARN

There is the land. In the center of the land are the farm buildings. In the center of the buildings is the round barn. In the center of the barn rises a tall concrete silo. On the side of the silo are painted these words:

> THE AIMS OF THIS FARM
> 1. Good Crops
> 2. Proper Storage
> 3. Profitable Livestock
> 4. A Stable Market
> 5. Life as Well as a Living
>   —W. J. Dougan

The "Aims" on the round barn's silo.

Jackie could read these words before she could read. She said, "What do they say?" and her older sisters read them to her, or a hired man, or whoever was there. She learned them by heart without trying. She did not ask what the words meant.

W. J. Dougan is Grampa. He had the words lettered there, inside the barn on the silo, when he had just built the round barn. That was 1911, when Daddy was nine years old. Jackie sees these words every day. Sometimes twenty times, on a day when she and Craig and the others are playing hide-and-seek in the barn. Sometimes not for several days in a row. But add up the times she has seen them and the days of her life, and they will come out even.

Jackie is fourteen. She sits on the arm of Grampa's easy chair. She rumples his thinning hair and shapes it into a Kewpie-doll twist. This is a ritual, with all the grandchildren, ever since they were little. Grampa laughs with his stomach, silently.

An idea strikes Jackie. She takes a pencil and paper. These are always near Grampa, for Grampa is deaf. They are always near Jackie, too, for Jackie writes things down. Maybe she has this habit from writing for Grampa all her life. Being his ears. She writes, "Grampa, I am going to write you a book. I am going to call it *The Round Barn*."

Grampa studies the paper. He takes a long time to ponder it. Then he nods slowly. "*The Round Barn*," he says. "Yes, the round barn will have a lot to say." He crinkles all over his face and laughs silently. He is pleased, she can tell.

"I can write," Jackie says to herself, "what the round barn sees. Not just what I know it sees. But what Grampa knows it sees. And Daddy. The milkmen. The cows. All of us! For the round barn is in the middle of us all, and it sees everything. It is the center."

Jackie thinks, here are the circles of the book.

She draws a picture, starting with the silo and going out to the barn, and beyond.

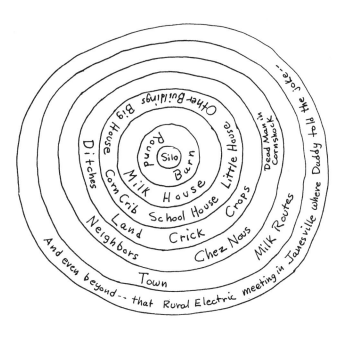

"That's it," says Jackie, "if it were just flat. But the book isn't flat, just as the barn isn't flat."

She takes another sheet of paper. She draws another picture. It looks a bit like the round barn, but without any hip roof. It looks a bit like three-dimensional tic-tac-toe.

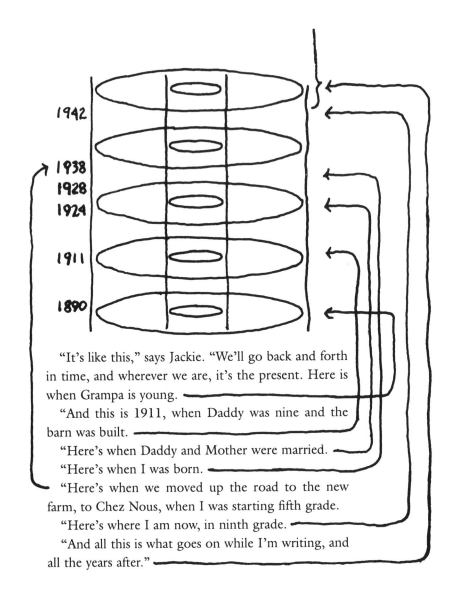

"It's like this," says Jackie. "We'll go back and forth in time, and wherever we are, it's the present. Here is when Grampa is young.

"And this is 1911, when Daddy was nine and the barn was built.

"Here's when Daddy and Mother were married.

"Here's when I was born.

"Here's when we moved up the road to the new farm, to Chez Nous, when I was starting fifth grade.

"Here's where I am now, in ninth grade.

"And all this is what goes on while I'm writing, and all the years after."

For the circles go out, concentric, in space. But they also go up and down in time. Like an onion. But not like an onion completely, for onion parts are too cleanly separated. They pop apart.

It's more like elm wood. Elm logs can hardly be split, for the fibers interpenetrate, from ring to ring, and bind all the circles together.

The story, the farm, Jackie decides, is like a log of elm wood. Everything, in all directions, in all dimensions, is bound together.

2   PREACHER FELLOW

It's 1906. Two Walsh brothers, farmers on the State Line Road, stand talking over a fence. Their lands adjoin and their back fields touch the Colley farm to the north of them.

"Have you heard that old Mrs. Colley's sold her farm?" asks one.

"Yep," says the other. "I give that preacher fellow two years."

The Reverend Wesson Joseph Dougan, Grampa, in the Juda parsonage before he left the ministry.

3   THE FIRST MILK ROUTE

It's May 1907, and Ronald's fifth birthday. He wakes before dawn. He looks out his window and sees a lantern bobbing toward the barn. His father is going down to milk Daisy and Bess and the eight new Guernsey cows that were shipped in from Fort Atkinson only last week. Ronald pulls on his clothes and follows. It's just starting to get light. It's fresh and clear outside; the air is balmy. A light breeze makes the windmill's wooden vanes whirr and rattle.

In the barn the cows are licking up their grain and munching hay. Grampa is sudsing Daisy's udder with a sponge. He sees Ronald enter the lantern light. "Happy birthday, cubby," he calls cheerfully.

Ronald watches while his father rinses the udder. He runs the sponge gently all over the four quarters and in the little upside-down pocket-cup the four tits surround, and then between and down the tits. Daisy's udder, Ronald has noticed before, is peppered with freckles. Bess's is creamy and unmarked. The udders on the new cows vary. All the time his father washes the cows he talks to them. "Coo, boss, coo, coo," he says soothingly. "Good bossy. Good cow. Let down your milk. Coo."

Then Grampa takes the milking pail. He lays a circle of gauze over its rim and fits a domed lid over the gauze. The lid has an opening in it, about a third of the surface. He puts the pail under Bess's udder and sets the little three-legged stool beside her. He sits on the stool and presses his head against the cow's side. Grasping the two tits farthest from him, one in each hand, he pulls down first one and then the other, in rhythm. The milk spurts into the opening of the sanitary bucket lid. Even through the gauze, Grampa makes the milk spurt with such force that it smacks into the pail and the metal sings. In a moment, as the bottom is covered, the song changes

*Ronald Dougan, age five, and his
brother Trever, age three.*

to a quieter one, milk splashing into milk. A little foam forms on the gauze around where the milk goes through. Grampa milks so well that the flow never pauses. While one tit is filling up, the other is shooting milk through the gauze.

Ronald squats on his haunches and waits. In just a moment now his father will say, "Open your mouth."

"Open your mouth," says his father.

Ronald opens his mouth as wide as he can and shuts his eyes, just in case. But Grampa doesn't miss—the stream of warm milk hits the back of his throat. Ronald chokes and swallows, and opens his eyes, laughing. Grampa laughs, too. Blackie the cat appears out of nowhere and opens her mouth. Grampa aims a tit at her, and even though her mouth is much smaller than

Ronald's, he hits the center of the pink gap. She sits down suddenly, licking her chops.

When the bucket is full Grampa empties it into a milk can. He finishes with Bess and then moves over to Daisy. Daisy keeps looking over her shoulder at Ronald.

"Come along," says his father. "She knows it's your birthday and says you're big enough to milk her now. Wash your hands."

Ronald washes first in the soapy bucket, then the rinse bucket. He dries with the clean towel on the hook on the wall. He sits down carefully on the milking stool. Daisy looms above. When he leans his head against her side, his hair butts against the lower curve of her firm belly. He can see every freckle on her udder.

"Some farmers milk wet and some milk dry," his father says. "That means some think a wet tit helps their grip. Some grip better with dry hands. In other barns, you'll see farmers spit on their hands in order to milk wet. But never, never will you see that happen *here!*" Grampa shakes his head and Ronald, pressed against Daisy, shakes his head too, but carefully. A cow's side is a strange, springy place to lean.

"Now hold the tits," Grampa instructs.

Ronald takes the two back ones. They feel firm and a little spongy, like a warm carrot with give. He squeezes. Nothing happens.

"You're squeezing the end so the milk can't get out," his father says. He holds a hand close to demonstrate. "You squeeze your fingers in order, starting with the top one, and at the same time you pull down. That moves the milk down and out the end. Then you let up, relax your grip, and the tit fills with milk for the next squeeze. And while you've eased up on that tit, you're pulling down the other. No, it isn't easy till you get onto it."

Ronald tries and tries. It's hard to squeeze his fingers in order. He feels very awkward. His father shows him again. At last Ronald produces a spurt from each tit, and then again. They miss the open part of the bucket lid, but

Ronald feels victorious. So does Grampa. "You'll make a milker in no time, laddie!" he says. He sits down, finishes milking Daisy, then moves on to the new cows.

It's full daylight when they finish. Grampa looses the cows from their stanchions and turns them into the barnyard. They amble toward the pasture. Ronald carries the empty wash buckets and the empty milk pail up to the house. His father carries the heavy milk can.

In the back room, the milkroom, there is new equipment. The milk cooler is a shiny metal grille that looks rather like a large scrub board but with the tub balanced on top. The coils of the grille are hollow and open above a tank at the bottom.

His father starts cold well water running through the coils. When the water starts to spill out into the tank, he climbs a broad stepstool and pours the milk into the reservoir on top. The reservoir has holes all along its bottom length. The milk drains out in a row of small streams above the top coil and ripples down the cold grille. Ronald watches till the first of the milk reaches the tray at the bottom and is funneled off into a can. Then he goes to the kitchen. A kettle of hot water is steaming on the stove. A frying pan of bacon is sizzling.

"Happy birthday, Ronald," says his mother. "You're up early. Trever's still abed."

Grampa comes in. Together he and Ronald eat eggs and bacon and flapjacks. His father tells how Ronald has marked the day by milking his first cow, and Grama clucks with praise.

After breakfast Ronald follows his father back to the milkroom. Now Grampa washes up the pails and milk cans and scalds everything. He turns the pails and cans upside-down on a rack. He takes six of the new glass bottles and sets them on the enamel-top table. He takes the can of cold milk and pours some into a pitcher. He then carefully fills each bottle.

Now comes what Ronald has been waiting for. Since the bottles arrived, his father has filled a few of them daily, pressing on the caps with his thumb. "For practice," he has said, twinkling, about the whole unnecessary process, for after the family has admired the new gleaming capped bottles, they uncap them and drink the milk. But now Grampa takes another piece of equipment, delivered just yesterday. It's a heavy metal hand-capper. It's already filled with cardboard disks from a long cardboard tube off the shelf. He positions the base of the capper over the rim of a bottle and presses down with the handle grip. With a ca-chunk, the bottle is capped. Ronald knows what the cap says, in deep golden yellow on white: "W. J. Dougan, The Babies' Milkman."

"There," says Grampa. "One day soon we'll have a bottler, too." He sets the bottles into a shallow tub of cold water.

Ronald trots behind his father out to the horsebarn. Grampa harnesses Molly to the buggy. He leads her to the hitching post by the back door of the house. He goes inside, and when he returns he's taken off his overalls and is wearing town clothes. His ear trumpet hangs around his neck. He's carrying the milk bottles in a wooden case covered with a wet flour sack. "That will keep them cool," he explains to Ronald as he sets the case on the buggy floor. "Do you want to come? Hop up, then."

Ronald hops up and sits with his feet resting on the edge of the case. Grampa hops up, too, says, "Gee up, Molly," and the horse starts out the drive. Looking back, Ronald glimpses his little brother's face in the window.

Grampa turns west on Colley Road. Molly is full of energy; she trots briskly. Ronald looks at the plowed fields. He looks up and down the railroad tracks where they cross the road. He listens to his father sing at the top of his voice:

> "Rock of ages, cleft for me,
> Let me hi-i-ide myself in thee!"

Ronald can't see how you can hide yourself in a rock.

They cross the tall red iron bridge over Spring Brook, and Ronald looks at the little stream; they cross the low black bridge over Turtle Creek and Ronald looks at the larger stream. A hill marks the end of the Turtle Creek valley. They go up it and are in town. Grampa drives to a house on the west side. He takes two quarts of milk, goes to the door, and knocks. Ronald stays close beside him.

"This is Dr. Thayer's. Look there in the shed. Do you see that round platform? He drives his new automobile onto that platform, and then he turns it so that the automobile is facing out again, ready to go when a patient calls."

The dais is empty. Ronald wishes that Dr. Thayer would drive up, both so that he could see an automobile and witness the magical performance.

Mrs. Thayer answers the door. "This is a red-letter day!" she exclaims, and smiles at Ronald. Ronald agrees.

His father gives the milk to Mrs. Thayer. She gives him two nickels. Grampa writes something in a book. He and Mrs. Thayer chat, Grampa holding his ear trumpet while she shouts into it. Then she gives Ronald a cookie.

Grampa drives Molly back to the east side and stops before another house. "This is where Harry Adams lives," he tells his son. Ronald looks at the shed to see if it, too, has a rotating platform, but it doesn't.

Mrs. Adams comes to the door. "Here is a day to celebrate!" she shouts into Grampa's ear trumpet. Again Ronald agrees. Grampa gives two quarts to Mrs. Adams, and she gives Grampa a dime. He writes in his book. Mrs. Adams gives Ronald a cookie, too.

They drive a few more blocks, and Ronald doesn't need to be told whose house this is. It's Aunt Ida Croft's, across from Strong School. They've brought Aunt Ida milk before, when they've come for Sunday dinner, carrying it in a covered pitcher or two Mason jars, but never in a milk bottle with a "W. J. Dougan, The Babies' Milkman" cap. He jumps from the buggy and carefully carries one of the two remaining bottles to the door. His father carries the other.

"Happy birthday, Ronald!" says Aunt Ida. She takes the bottles and puts them in the icebox. She and Grampa talk a bit. Ronald stands on a chair and looks into the beady black eye of the yellow canary. The canary teeters on a little perch in its cage and looks right back at Ronald.

"Here's a present for a big boy," says Aunt Ida. She's holding two packages, one large and flat, one small and square. To Ronald, it looks like two presents. He climbs off the chair and undoes the tissue paper. The large package is a checkerboard, the smaller one the box of checkers to go with it. She also gives Ronald a cookie.

Then Ronald and Grampa climb in the buggy and drive back through the streets to Colley Road. When they get to the edge of town Ronald sits between his father's knees and holds the reins. He feels important. He's old enough to milk Daisy; he's old enough to take milk to town; he's old enough to drive Molly.

"Ronald," says his father as they are crossing the crick, "do you know that this is a very special day?"

Ronald nods vigorously. It certainly is! And Mrs. Thayer and Mrs. Adams and Aunt Ida have all known it, too. He indicates his box of checkers on the buggy seat.

"Yes," says Grampa, "it's your birthday and you're growing sturdy in body and spirit. That's quite enough to make this a special day. But we've also just gone on our first milk route, and delivered our own product to our first three customers. From this day on we're not only farmers, we're businessmen. You are riding with 'W. J. Dougan, The Babies' Milkman'!"

Grampa laughs till his eyes disappear.

Ronald laughs and laughs, too.

4 FOOLS' NAMES

It is 1909. Ronald is seven. For his birthday, he has a new jackknife from Aunt Ida. Trever is jealous.

"I want a jackknife too," he declares.

Aunt Ida assures him, "When you're as old as Ronald, I'll get you a jackknife. Five is too little for one."

Trever has heard that story before. When he is seven, then Ronald will be nine, and Aunt Ida will have forgotten all about the knife. She'll be buying Ronald an air rifle, and telling Trever that seven is too young for an air rifle; she'll get him one when he's as old as Ronald. Trever knows he never will be as old as Ronald.

"Let me use your jackknife," he wheedles.

"No," says Ronald. "Five is too young to play with a knife. You'll cut yourself."

Ronald uses his new knife at every opportunity. He sharpens sticks, he tries to make willow whistles, he fashions parts for his red coaster wagon.

One morning at school he raises his hand. Miss Church excuses him and he goes to the boys' backhouse. While he's sitting there, his jackknife falls out of his pocket onto the floor. He picks it up, opens it, and begins carving an R on the inside of the door. He stays a few minutes longer than his business necessitates, to get a good start on it. At recess he finishes the R and starts on an O. O's are harder, because they are entirely curved.

Whenever he has to raise his hand during the day, and at lunch and recess, he works slowly and meticulously on the backhouse door. Sometimes he raises his hand when he doesn't really have to go. He's careful not to stay in the backhouse too long.

The other boys are much interested. They envy him his jackknife. They make bets on how long it will take him to finish his name.

Ronald is standing on the schoolhouse porch roof. Trever is sitting alongside him.

At last it's complete. The backhouse door is chiseled out in large, deep block letters. R O N A L D   D O U G A N. Ronald is satisfied with his workmanship. The boys are respectful.

That night after supper Trever shouts into Grampa's ear trumpet, "Ronald carved his name on the backhouse door!"

"Shut up! Shut up!" Ronald shrills.

"What?" says his father.

Trever shouts as loud as he can. "RONALD CARVED HIS NAME ON THE BACKHOUSE DOOR! WITH HIS NEW JACKKNIFE!"

Understanding breaks over Grampa's face. He looks sternly and sorrowfully at his elder son. "Ronald, is what Trever tells me true?"

Ronald hangs his head.

"I am disappointed in you," says Grampa. "You'll have to remove it.

Come along." He takes Ronald's hand. They go to the toolshed. "Select a plane," says his father.

Ronald looks at the three planes on the worktable. They are all large. They are all heavy. He takes the smallest one.

Grampa keeps ahold of his hand. Together they walk across the plowed furrows of the East Twenty toward the schoolhouse. Grampa takes long strides. Ronald has to trot fast. The plane in his other hand gets heavier and heavier. He cries. Behind him at a safe distance Trever capers and flings taunts.

At the boys' backhouse Grampa opens the door. There is the name:

RONALD DOUGAN

They survey it together. To Ronald the once splendid letters now seem to move and dance, to be red with the licking flames of hellfire, like the printing of the devil's whispers in one of his storybooks.

Grampa shakes his head. He says, "'Fools' names and fools' faces always appear in public places.'" He lets go of Ronald's hand and stands holding the open door steady.

Sobbing louder, Ronald begins to plane the letters. On the farm, he has always liked to use the plane, to run it along a board and have the sweet-smelling curl form behind and fall off. But he's never planed on a vertical surface before. It's terribly hard. He tries going from bottom to top. He tries going from top to bottom. He tries going from side to side. That's the worst, for the plane is heavy and keeps slipping.

His father gives no advice.

Ronald settles on bottom to top, crouching before the door in order to get more shove pressure. The wood curls fall down around his knees. Slowly, very slowly because he carved them so deep, the letters are erased. He has to come at some parts of them from all different directions. The plane grows so heavy he can hardly move it. Often it nicks and chips and is balky. He can scarcely see through his tears. Grampa stands silent. Ronald knows he will not be finished till nothing more can be seen. The swatch he planes gets larger and deeper.

Finally his father says, "There."

Ronald gets up, stands back, wipes his eyes and nose with his sleeve. The spot is now smooth and light-colored against the seasoned surface. No trace of R O N A L D   D O U G A N can be seen.

Grampa closes the door. He points to the mound of shavings left on the ground. Ronald scrapes them up and hides them between the bushes by the fence. Then he and Grampa start across the field again. His father still holds his hand, but now he walks more slowly, matching his stride to Ronald's, and he carries the plane. Trever is nowhere in sight.

In the middle of the field Grampa stops. "Look. There's an oat, just starting to come up." He kneels.

Ronald kneels, too. A little green shoot is pushing its way out of the furrow. The hull is still clinging to the blade.

"It's such an ordinary thing, springtime, and crops coming up," his father says, "yet every time a seed sprouts, it's a tiny miracle. Look down the furrows—all the seeds are pushing up. It was the rain yesterday."

Ronald looks, and in the slant evening sun sees the faint green flush of oat seedlings all over the field.

"Grow, little fellow," croons Grampa to the oat, touching it gently with his finger. "Grow strong and sturdy in the sun and the rain! Grow to make feed for the cattle and bedding for their stalls! Grow to do your little bit in the universe!"

Ronald thinks how little a bit it is, one oat plant! But multiplied by a field of oats, by fields and fields of oats, the granaries overflow, the strawstack is a golden mountain. He does not know why, but his spirits lift.

They stand up, return to the farm, replace the plane in the toolshed. Nothing more is ever said about fools' names.

5 BOOTS

Ronald is ten. It's summer. The round barn was finished last fall, and now the silo in its center is being filled for the first time.

Ronald watches. The horses pull the wagons of cornstalks onto the loft floor. The stalks are in bundles, piled in rows on the wagons. Two hired men, Percy Werner and Jack Ward, stand on the bundles and sling them to the loader. Grampa is the loader; he cuts the twine and feeds stalks, leaves, ears, into a trough with a belt rotating the length of it. The belt carries the stalks into the blades of the chopper. A fan blows the chopped stalks up a long tube into the top of the silo, where the silage then rains down, gradually filling up the great concrete cylinder. The chopper-blower is powered by a twenty-five-horsepower gasoline motor.

Inside the silo is a man with a silage pitchfork. He's not a regular farm-hand but an itinerant who wanted work, and W. J. hired him. Extra hands are often needed in the summer. His job is to spread the silage clear to the edges so that air spaces are eliminated and the silage will ferment properly. Ronald knows it's the fermentation that preserves the silage, and also gives it the sharp, sour taste that cows like.

The worker got into the silo by climbing up the wooden ventilation chute alongside it. There's a narrow gap in the silo's concrete from top to bottom; the metal reinforcing rods continue right through the gap and form rungs. Inside the silo the worker has a pile of wooden shutters that just fit the gap. As the silo fills, he sets a shutter into the gap and plasters the edges airtight with clay. Then the silage won't spill out the opening, nor will air get in. Ronald's early-morning job was to fill a bucket with clay from the crick bank and lug it to the barn. His job now is to be sure a second bucket is always ready.

Ronald watches the stalks moving along the belt into the chopper. He watches the knives grab them and the brief battle that reduces them to bits. It's a noisy process: the motor, the grinding whirl of the chopper and fan blades, the shooshy rattle as the silage is both blown and blasted up the tube. His eyes follow the tube to where it bends at the top of the silo and the end of it disappears through one of the little windows of the wooden superstructure. He's curious to view the complete trip, to see the silage falling down on the inside.

Through its narrow door on the barn floor he slides into the ventilator chute and climbs the rungs. He climbs past the most recently placed shutter and now can see the silage pouring down from far above. He climbs a little higher to get a better view.

Something is not right. The silage isn't spread out as it should be. There's a mound of it, a small pyramid which is steadily growing as the silage rains down. Is the man with the silage fork behind the pyramid, bent over? He watches a moment and sees no movement. But then he spots something—a pair of boots sticking out from under the pyramid. He skins down the rungs as fast as he can and emerges, screeching, onto the barn floor. He screams over the noise of the machinery. "Stop! Stop! He's buried up there! You're burying him in silage!" He pounds his father's arm. "Stop! Stop!"

The men stop the machinery. Jack and Percy crowd into the shaft and disappear up it. Ronald follows on their heels. He's in time to see them haul the worker out from under the silage by his boots. They pump his chest, and the man gasps and turns from blue to red. He's still alive; Ronald has saved his life. They pull out the last shutter, turn the man on his stomach, and thread him between the rungs out into the shaft. Percy above and Jack below lower him down the narrow column. Out on the barn floor, they prop him up against the hay. When he recovers sufficiently, Grampa fires him. It takes him a while to recover, though, for besides being nearly suffocated he's dead drunk.

At supper that night, referring to both the action of the silage and the action of the whiskey, Percy says to Ronald, "If you hadn't noticed him, we'd have had a twice-pickled farmhand!"

The next spring, when Jack is pitching down silage, he uncovers the empty bottle.

6   INCOME TAX

It is 1913, spring. W. J. Dougan has not been working outside at the planting, nor at manure spreading, nor even in the barn. All afternoon he's been laboring at his desk against the north wall in the back section of the parlor. It's a large rolltop desk. Once in a while, Ronald and Trever are allowed to roll up the top, so that it's magically swallowed inside the desk, and then they get to pull it down again. The desk has many cubbyholes along its back, which the boys are not allowed to explore. Each cubbyhole has different papers and receipts in it. The drawers at the side hold large clothbound ledgers held together with fat steel pins. All afternoon no one has disturbed their father at his desk.

Grampa at his desk.

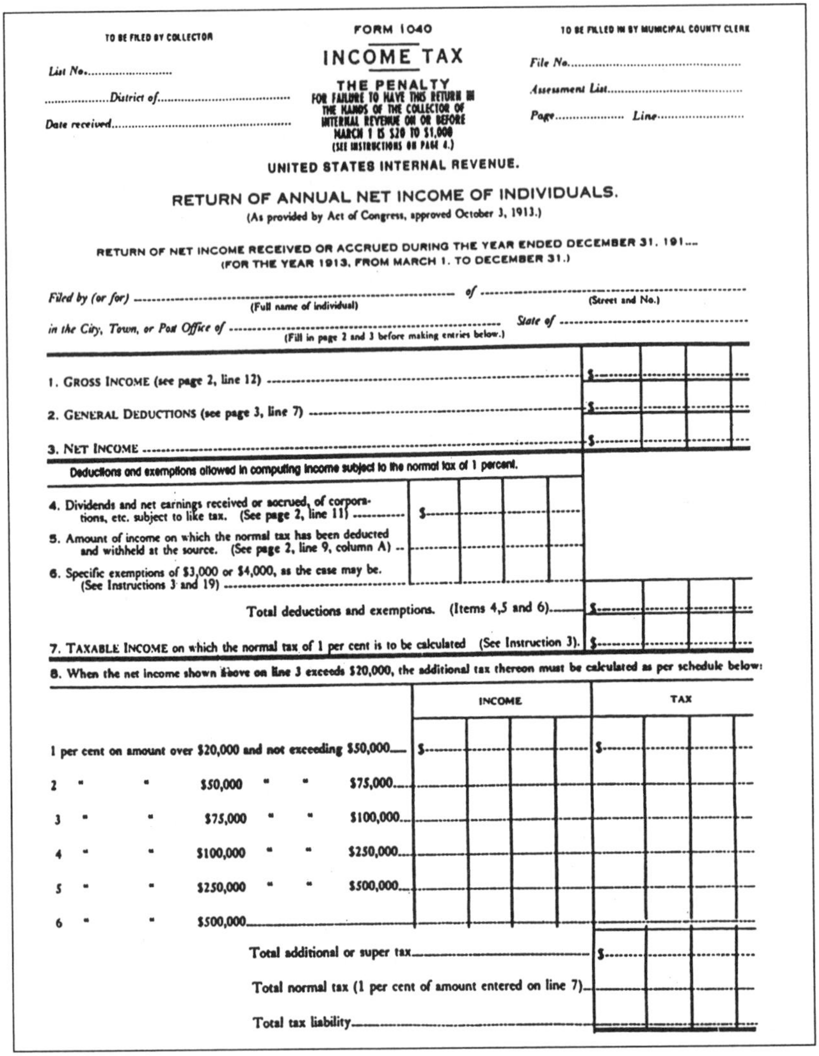

TO BE FILED BY COLLECTOR

List No.........................

..................District of....................................

Date received...

FORM 1040

INCOME TAX

THE PENALTY
FOR FAILURE TO HAVE THIS RETURN IN THE HANDS OF THE COLLECTOR OF INTERNAL REVENUE ON OR BEFORE MARCH 1 IS $20 TO $1,000
(SEE INSTRUCTIONS ON PAGE 4.)

TO BE FILLED IN BY MUNICIPAL COUNTY CLERK

File No..

Assessment List.....................................

Page.................. Line.........................

UNITED STATES INTERNAL REVENUE.

RETURN OF ANNUAL NET INCOME OF INDIVIDUALS.

(As provided by Act of Congress, approved October 3, 1913.)

RETURN OF NET INCOME RECEIVED OR ACCRUED DURING THE YEAR ENDED DECEMBER 31, 191...
(FOR THE YEAR 1913, FROM MARCH 1, TO DECEMBER 31.)

Filed by (or for) -- of --
(Full name of individual) (Street and No.)

in the City, Town, or Post Office of -- State of --
(Fill in page 2 and 3 before making entries below.)

1. Gross Income (see page 2, line 12)	$			
2. General Deductions (see page 3, line 7)	$			
3. Net Income	$			

Deductions and exemptions allowed in computing income subject to the normal tax of 1 percent.

4. Dividends and net earnings received or accrued, of corporations, etc. subject to like tax. (See page 2, line 11)	$			
5. Amount of income on which the normal tax has been deducted and withheld at the source. (See page 2, line 9, column A)				
6. Specific exemptions of $3,000 or $4,000, as the case may be. (See Instructions 3 and 19)				
Total deductions and exemptions. (Items 4,5 and 6)	$			
7. Taxable Income on which the normal tax of 1 per cent is to be calculated (See Instruction 3).	$			

8. When the net income shown above on line 3 exceeds $20,000, the additional tax thereon must be calculated as per schedule below:

	INCOME	TAX
1 per cent on amount over $20,000 and not exceeding $50,000	$	$
2 " " $50,000 " " $75,000		
3 " " $75,000 " " $100,000		
4 " " $100,000 " " $250,000		
5 " " $250,000 " " $500,000		
6 " " $500,000		

Total additional or super tax	$
Total normal tax (1 per cent of amount entered on line 7)	
Total tax liability	

Original Income Tax Form 1040 (1913).

Suppertime comes. Grama and Ronald and Trever and the hired men are waiting. Grampa is a few minutes late. Grama goes and calls him again

Grampa comes into the dining room holding a legal-size envelope. His face is severe. He puts the envelope beside his plate and sits down in his seat at the side of the table. Ronald feels uneasy. The hired men stir. All eyes are on the envelope.

Grampa bows his head. The others bow their heads, too, except for Ronald. He cranes his neck to see the address on the envelope, but Grampa has placed it face down.

Everyone waits for one of Grampa's usual weekday blessings, the one that starts "Bless the Lord, O my soul," or the one that starts "Praise the Lord, all ye nations, praise Him, all ye peoples." But Grampa pauses a long time, then clears his throat and says something new.

"Render unto Caesar that which is Caesar's, and unto God that which is God's. Amen."

Everyone looks up, startled.

Grampa picks up the envelope. No one moves to pass the platters of food.

"Our government has just instituted an income tax," Grampa says gravely.

Everyone nods. The income tax has been a topic of discussion before, at the table, and Ronald and Trever have talked about it in school.

"I have spent the day computing my income tax," Grampa continues. "I completed it just before supper, and I have written the check and placed it in this envelope." He holds up the envelope and studies it, then reads aloud the address.

He raises the flap and plucks out a large tan farm check. He surveys the check even longer than the envelope. Ronald can't see what's written on the check. Nobody can see it.

"For mercy's sake, Wesson!" cries Grama impatiently. "Get on with what you're going to say!"

Grampa can't hear her. He examines the check another serious moment, then casts a sudden mischievous glance at the assemblage.

"My income tax for this year is thirteen cents," says Grampa.

The table dissolves in laughter, with Grampa laughing the hardest of all. When order is restored and the dishes begin to move, Grampa looks around merrily.

"I am happy to do my share," he says.

7 THE NO-LEGGED FARMER

Ronald is eleven. He's in the buggy with his father, west of town.

"We're going to stop by and say hello to Mr. Wieland," Grampa says. "I like to visit with him when I can. He has a handicap, too, and turned to farming as I did. But his handicap is not the same as mine. He has no legs."

Ronald is astounded. He sticks his own legs out straight and shakes his head disbelievingly.

"How can he do it?" asks his father. "Well, you shall see. And he is fortunate—he has a good wife, and a flock of little lads and lasses to help him."

He tells Ronald that Henry Wieland had a successful bakery in Chicago. But he had an illness, called Buerger's disease, and the doctors told him he had only a year to live.

"And he decided," says Grampa, "for that short year he had left, to do what he'd always wanted to do. And so he sold his bakery and bought land in the Beloit area, and livestock, and started to farm."

Grampa tells how he heard about Mr. Wieland, right after he'd arrived, and had been one of his first visitors. He'd given him some help in selecting livestock after an unscrupulous farmer unloaded on him a half-dozen horses with heaves. He'd told Mr. Wieland of his own mistakes, and encouraged him. Mr. Wieland had had hard times. There were the horses lost. Then his crick fed Beckmans' mill, and the dam backed up, making a swamp of his pasture. He'd lost more animals to the swamp. And he'd had to have both his legs amputated, first one, then a year later, the other.

Ronald, looking puzzled, waggles one finger.

"One year, yes, that's what they said. But it's been four years so far and he's prospering, both in his body and in his farming. The doctors have changed their minds; they see no reason now why he shouldn't live to a ripe old age, provided he doesn't fall out of the haymow."

Ronald shows astonishment. "Haymow!"

"Yes," laughs his father, "the last time I visited, I saw him haul himself right up a ladder to the haymow!"

Ronald is goggle-eyed as they drive into the Wieland farmyard. He scrambles out, looking all around for the no-legged farmer, while Grampa hitches the horse to the gatepost. Mrs. Wieland comes out on the step and greets them. She says that her husband is in the barn.

Ronald follows his father through the Dutch door. He immediately sees the children. Nearby a girl his age is milking, and at the end of the aisle of cows a boy somewhat older is emptying a pail of milk into a milk can. A younger boy is in front of the cows, shoveling grain.

"How are you, my friend?" shouts Grampa.

Ronald sees an arm wave from between two cows as a voice booms, "Right here, Reverend!" Ronald follows to stand before Mr. Wieland. He isn't sitting on a milking stool but on a backless kitchen chair with all four legs sawed off at a few inches. He's a chunky, ruddy-faced man, and looks even chunkier, like Humpty-Dumpty, for he has no legs sticking out in front of him, only six-inch stumps. His denim overalls are stitched neatly over the ends and disappear beneath him.

"I've brought my lad Ronald to meet you," says Grampa.

Ronald tries hard not to stare while introductions are made. The children are named Katie, Fred, and Robert. Henry and Walter are out fixing fences, Margaret is helping in the house, and Lillian—well, Lillian is the baby.

"I have only Gussie here, and old Blossom left to go," Mr. Wieland says. He turns back to his work. Ronald notes how rapidly he milks. He finishes, lifts the partly filled pail, and shoves it ahead and under the cow. Then his hands grasp two blocks of wood that Ronald has not noticed till now, one on either side of his chair. They are two-by-fours with holes cut through them to make handles. With powerful arms Mr. Wieland launches himself

Henry Wieland with three of his grandchildren.

off his chair, scoots the empty seat under the cow, then ducking his head, swings himself under, too, grazing his shoulder on the udder. He plops down onto the seat in front of the next cow, adjusts the bucket, and begins to milk.

Ronald is startled. But Gussie isn't startled at all. She goes right on munching grain. Nor is Blossom disturbed by the unorthodox arrival.

Ronald has no eyes for the Wieland children doing their chores. His attention is riveted on Mr. Wieland.

"You have a wonderful father," Mr. Wieland says. "I don't know what I'd have done without his help and encouragement, every step of the way. He told me what to do about bloat, and to plant corn when the oak leaves are as big as a squirrel's ear. And that hickory burns hottest in a woodstove, but to watch out for corncobs; they burn so hot they can ruin your grate! But more than all that, he's been an inspiration. I always said, if the Reverend can succeed without his hearing, then I can succeed without my legs. It doesn't take legs to milk a cow. . . . Are you ears for your father?"

Ronald nods.

"These are my legs," says Mr. Wieland, pausing in his milking to make an inclusive sweep of his children. "They fetch the cows and carry the pails and shovel the manure."

Ronald nods some more. He does his share of all that, too, even though his father has two good legs and hired help.

Mr. Wieland gets the last milk from Blossom's udder by stripping down the tits as if they were rubber.

"Yes," he says, "your father is a fine Christian gentleman and a true friend."

He scoots under Blossom as he did Gussie, vaults the manure trough, and joins Grampa on the walkway behind the cows. Grampa hunkers down so that he's on a level with Mr. Wieland. They talk cows and crops and weather. Mr. Wieland writes on Grampa's pad.

Katie and Fred empty the buckets and stagger off with a milk can between them. Ronald is not tempted to follow. He hopes that Mr. Wieland will climb a ladder, but no ladder is in sight. While the men talk he picks up and closely examines the polished handholds that allow the farmer to swing along.

"Noticing my shoes, eh?" says Mr. Wieland. When he leans to one side to scratch a buttock, Ronald glimpses that the overall leg is folded back and forth and quilted to his seat, to make a pad. Everything about Mr. Wieland seems eminently sensible.

At last his father stands up.

"Will you lead us in a word of prayer before you go, Reverend Dougan?" asks Mr. Wieland, and writes the request on the pad.

Grampa takes off his hat and closes his eyes. Ronald takes off his cap, too.

Katie, running into the barn, halts and closes her eyes.

Grampa prays, "Our Heavenly Father, our hearts go out to Thee in thanksgiving. We thank Thee for life, with all of its opportunities, with all of its responsibilities. But most of all we thank Thee for Thy gifts of courage and love in the human heart. Amen."

Ronald is more used to his father as a farmer than a preacher, but somehow it doesn't seem strange to be praying in a barn with his father and Mr. Wieland and Katie. They all go up to the house. Mrs. Wieland serves them dishes of rhubarb sauce and cookies and glasses of milk. Robert shows Ronald the air rifle and jackknife he got as premiums for selling subscriptions to *Hoard's Dairyman*. Ronald tucks away the thought that he might become a subscription seller, too. Katie has him crawl into the downstairs closet to see her father's artificial leg. It's standing behind the coats and boots, alongside a small square seat with runners that her father uses in snowy weather. The leg is a metal contraption with leather straps.

"But he never used it," says Katie. "He said he did better without it."

Ronald has no reason to doubt it. Then he and Grampa leave.

"Whenever I start feeling sorry for myself I think of Mr. Wieland," says his father, "and that man's courage puts me to shame!"

At home, Ronald tells Trever all about it. The next day they saw off two-by-fours and gouge them out to make handholds. They take turns swinging along. It's not easy, for their legs keep getting in the way, and it's also very hard on the wrists. They find a kitchen chair with a split seat at the farm dump. They saw off the legs at four inches. They saw off the back. They repair the split.

Ronald carries the seat to the barn and sits cross-legged on it while he does his milking. It's awkward. He finishes Daisy, edges the pail to the side, slings the seat, and scoots underneath her.

Daisy is so startled that she kicks Ronald head over milk bucket into the gutter.

8   BAREFOOT

It is early October 1914. It's suppertime. Grampa sits midway on one side of the dining-room table. Grama is at the end. Ronald and Trever and the hired men are in their places. The hired men have showered, slicked back their hair, and donned clean shirts and trousers. Fried potatoes steam in a dish on the snowy tablecloth. There are pitchers of milk, slices of cold meat, bread and butter, fresh applesauce, creamed carrots.

Grampa has said the blessing: "Bless the Lord, O my soul, and all that is within me, bless His holy name. Bless the Lord, O my soul, and forget not all His benefits."

The food is passed. People begin to eat.

A dinnertime. Grampa is across the table, left, with glasses. Hilda, the cook, and Grama are standing.

Grampa looks around the table. He says, "I saw a sight today I have never seen before, and I hope I shall never see again."

Everyone pauses to pay attention to Daddy Dougan.

"I went over to Tiffany very early this morning, to buy a cow," Grampa says.

Everyone nods. They know where Grampa went, and that he returned with a cow.

"It was still dark when I got there," says Grampa, "and I saw a light in the barn. I went in, and saw a lantern way down at the end of the row of cows. Someone was milking there, so I walked down to see who. And as I got close, I saw it was a little lad, and he seemed to be milking in an odd sort of manner."

Grampa has everyone's complete attention.

"It was chilly this morning," says Grampa. "There was frost."

Everyone nods.

"The little lad was barefoot," Grampa says, "and when I got up to him I saw that he was balancing himself on the milking stool with one foot, and holding the other one over the bucket"—Grampa pushes back his chair and demonstrates—"and milking the stream of warm milk onto that dirty little foot! And when that foot was warm, he put it down on the stall floor and raised his other dirty little foot and milked onto that one!"

The gathering is thunderstruck. Grampa looks at their stunned faces and laughs silently. His eyes disappear.

Then everyone explodes into laughter. When the hubbub dies down, Grama declares, "Wesson, that can't be true!"

Wesson assures her it is.

Ronald shouts into his father's ear trumpet. "Did you say anything to anybody? Did you tell his father or mother?"

Grampa laughs and shakes his head no. "The wife asked me in for a cup of coffee and some coffeecake," Grampa says. He adds, "I drank the coffee black."

9 AGNES

It is May 1915. Grampa and Grama are on their way to town, to take the train to the orphanage at Sparta. As they leave they stop at the Marstons', their closest neighbors down the road. Lura Marston, and her mother Mrs. Smith, are the only ones in whom Eunice has confided about the many miscarriages she's had since Trever's birth eleven years ago. Eunice says to the Marstons' only child, "Oh, Eloise, we're going to get you a little playmate, just your age."

Eunice and Wesson have longed for a daughter ever since their own first child died within a few hours of birth. At Sparta they sign indenture papers

Ronald and Trever's new sister.

for a beautiful almost-six-year-old girl. She has light brown curly hair and a
sweet face. Her most striking feature is her eyes, unusually large and blue.
Eunice and Wesson are charmed. Her name is Agnes Groose. The papers
state that Agnes is to stay with the Dougans until she is eighteen, at which
time they must provide her with "two suits of good clothes" and fifty dollars, and she will be on her own. The papers also instruct that she be taught
a trade at which she will be able to earn a living.

Agnes has sisters and brothers at the orphanage, but Wesson and Eunice
take only her. They are not told anything about Agnes's parents.

*Eloise (on left) and Esther
playing dress-up.*

They return on the train. At the farm Agnes meets her new brothers, Ronald and Trever, and they show her all over the house and barns. She is quiet and shy. She has her own room upstairs. Eunice arranges her few possessions in a drawer.

That night Eunice holds Agnes on her lap before bedtime. Agnes cuddles against her. Eunice says to her, "We've wanted a little girl for so long! Ever since our own baby died. We're going to change your name to Esther, after that baby, and after Esther in the Bible."

Agnes's body goes stiff. She draws away from Eunice. She will not cuddle anymore. Hurt and upset, Eunice puts Esther to bed.

A few days later Eloise Marston is invited to a tea party. She arrives, all dressed up. Esther is dressed up, too. Eunice introduces the girls and brings in the tea.

There is a small table and chairs, and a cloth on the table. There is a small china tea set with a little teapot and diminutive cups. There are small sandwiches on a plate.

Esther presides at the teapot. "Won't you have some tea?" she asks politely. "Oh, *pardon* me," she says frequently, even when there isn't any need. Eloise is disappointed. Esther is so proper, so exaggerated. What sort of fun can she be?

When the party is over Eloise says, "Good-bye, Esther."

Esther leans forward, her eyes suddenly hot and angry. "My name *isn't* Esther!" she hisses. "It's *Agnes*, the name my mother named me!"

The weeks go by, and Esther turns out to be fun to play with after all. She loses her formality. Eloise decides that that first day was the result of the new situation, and the training of the orphanage.

Trever is delighted with a little sister. After all these years he now has someone who will look up to him and listen to him, and Esther is an avid listener. He sits on the flour box in the kitchen and tells her stories, while she fills the woodbox for him. She follows him around and admires his ability in running and throwing and shooting pigeons with his air rifle. Ronald is glad enough to have a sister, too, but he's thirteen and busy with other things. Esther's coming doesn't particularly affect him.

On her sewing machine Eunice stitches sturdy playclothes for her new daughter. She makes her a dress for church, and enrolls her in Eloise's primary class at Sunday School. She shows off her pretty little girl to all the other mothers. Esther smiles shyly at the attention.

Esther's new father takes her with him to see the piglets, and to watch the calves being fed. At night, he sometimes holds her in his lap and they look at a picture book together.

Esther settles so well into life on the farm that it isn't long before it seems as though she's always lived there. She and Eloise are best friends, and share a desk at school.

When Christmas comes, Esther receives a large and beautiful doll from her foster parents. She names the doll Agnes.

10 GOOD FOR SOMETHING

Ronald is fourteen. He's finishing his freshman year at Beloit High. Trever is going to Strong School, across from Aunt Ida's. Every day Ronald drives himself and Trever to school and back in the new Dodge. One afternoon in mid-June he pulls into the farm and parks the car by the back entrance to the house. Trever gets out with his books. Ronald stays in the car, in his good school clothes, his collar still on, reading.

It's hot. Beyond, at the side barn, Grampa is directing the first haying. A loaded hay wagon stands alongside the lower part of the barn, its mounded hay reaching almost up to the wide open end of the haymow. Men are busy on the load and in the mow. Chuck Hoag is in the roadway, driving the team that provides the power to lift the hayfork.

Ronald has admired Chuck ever since he arrived. He's a husky young man, curly-headed, broad of chest, a student at the university, getting his M.A. in agricultural economics. He's down from Madison for a year-long internship on the farm. He's writing his thesis on the farm's economics. He's keeping data on all the processes. Chuck Hoag is everything that Ronald would like to be.

Today he's stripped to his waist, his body glistening with sweat and streaked with grime, his hair dusty. As soon as the huge tines of the fork are embedded in the hay on the wagon, Grampa yells, and Chuck drives the team toward the road. The ropes the horses pull tauten and strain, the pulleys roll, the hayfork grips and with its great burden slowly rises up to the track. It switches onto it in a right-angle turn, and with a swish swings into the barn. Chuck drives the plodding horses past Ronald and the Dodge. When the next yell comes, signaling that the hay is now over the spot where it's to be dropped, Chuck calls "Whoa!" to the horses. He himself stops

Ronald's high school graduation photograph.

right beside the car's open window. He glances at the reading Ronald, turns the team, and returns to his starting place. A second time he drives as far as Ronald, glances in, and returns. The third time, as he turns, he speaks.

"Do you think you'll ever amount to anything?" he says.

Three springs later Ronald is seventeen and a senior. He receives his yearbook. His picture is in it, along with pictures of all the other graduates. Under every face is the name of the student, the grammar school, a nickname, and other data. At the last comes a brief comment about the person, written by somebody on the yearbook committee: "A lad with quiet ways," or "Dignity and reserve are two of the graces she possesses." Ronald turns the pages and finds himself.

In his picture he is solemn, small of face and fine of feature. He wears round, metal-rimmed glasses that make him look owlish. His high white collar is up to his chin. Under his picture it reads, "Arthur Ronald Dougan, District School," and then "Doogy," a name he's never heard anyone call him. His place and date of birth follow: "Oregon, Wisconsin, May 20, 1902." Next are listed his high school activities: Literary Society, Thespian Club, Debate. Last comes the little squib: "Not only good, but good for something."

Ronald remembers Chuck Hoag and wonders, good for what?

II DAN KELLEY

It's 1916; the milkhouse has just been built. There is a second floor to it, reached by a steep staircase, almost a ladder, that can be raised and lowered. Not all the farmhands live in the crowded house anymore; Mother and Daddy Dougan—as everyone on the place calls them—have moved several men to the bunkhouse above the milkhouse.

Dan Kelley drives the bobsled.

Dan Kelley is one of these. He's eighteen, a Roman Catholic. One Sunday he returns from delivering his route. It's about two o'clock and he's bought a paper. He is sitting in the bunkhouse, reading the news, and doesn't hear someone come up the staircase. Suddenly there's a crash and his paper is kicked out of his hands; he is narrowly missed by Daddy Dougan's boot. Grampa's face is severe. He bunts the newspaper down the stairwell and climbs down after it.

Dan is in shock. Then he's furious. He seethes to Ronald, who happens by, "I guess I'm not supposed to read a paper on Sunday! I guess I'm only supposed to be reading the Bible! But Daddy never told me I couldn't read a paper on Sunday!"

Dan Kelley in front of the milkhouse.

Ron says, "When we were younger we couldn't even throw a ball on Sunday."

A few days later a milkhouse worker says, "Daddy's looking for you."

Dan is apprehensive. "Why?"

"You went out of here with so many bottles of cream and you've come back with one not accounted for."

At that moment, W. J. puts his hand on Dan's shoulder. "What happened to the other bottle of cream, Dan?"

"I drank it," Dan says.

"What did you do that for?"

"Because I was hungry."

"All right!" says Grampa. "If you're hungry, take more. Take all you want."

Nothing else is said. Dan figures that sort of evens things up. That, and when something terrible happens a few months later. It's a winter day; he is back from the route, eating a late dinner at the kitchen table in the main house. Daddy comes to him, his face concerned.

"I can see a big fire to the north of us, Dan," he says. "It looks like your place. You go get something warm on; I'll saddle one of the horses, and you go home. And if you don't want to come back tonight, that's all right—we'll double up on the work tomorrow."

Dan can tell, as he gallops across the fields toward the smoke and flames, that the fire is indeed at his home. When he gets there, everything is gone, but his family is safe. He helps out there for several days before returning to his job. Daddy Dougan is almost totally forgiven.

12 GRAMPA'S BLUE MEMO

It is late November, 1923, and Grampa is in a crisis of faith. Here is the background.

He'd had misgivings about allowing Ronald to attend a North Shore private university instead of the Ag School at Wisconsin, where he'd first been enrolled, and those misgivings seem justified. The fraternity is Ronald's main interest. Grampa writes him, in his sophomore year, "I am sorry you are not able to retrench in the useless and harmful and wasteful expenses. If you realized that it meant quitting school if you cannot get on without these flowers and parties and eat and dance times you would think twice before following the crowd." By his junior year Ronald is earning much of his own money, but at what cost? His grades are undistinguished. He has no idea of what he wants to do with his life. He shows little interest in attending church.

And a year ago, he and forty other Northwestern boys were carted off to jail in a raid on a "Bohemian" speakeasy named The Wind Blew Inn. Grampa had to pay the stiff fine, and appear in court with all the other fathers and sons. The newspapers, even out-of-state ones, made hay of the story, with many puns on how the police blew in and blew out again with all the college youth in their paddy wagons. Ronald's name, usually misspelled, was in all the Chicago papers, but kind Providence omitted it from the front-page writeup in *The Beloit Daily News*. Grama writes to her son, "When we saw this in the Beloit paper our hearts stood still till we had read it through, fearing your name would be in it."

And, a month later, he is caught smoking. His mother writes:

> I asked Papa if you had smoked any since you went back and he had
> to tell me the truth. I cannot see how you can do it. Your father has

done so much for you and loves you so and you know how he has always despised the habit and felt men were so much smaller who do it. I should think you would want to tower up in his eyes and do nothing that would keep him from admiring you in every way. . . . The dear unselfish wonderful dad. He is carrying such a heavy burden and practically all alone. He cannot keep that beautiful optimistic spirit up always against everything. He told me so long as he could keep his grit he could make it go but if he loses that it is all up with him. Ronald you must be his support. He is the very best friend you have on earth and you must keep his love and respect. Oh my precious boy, if I could know you would stand firm against the cigarette or any smoking, I would be the happiest woman on earth. Papa and I would rather have that assurance and have you stand firm from principle than have the grandest home money could buy. . . .

So far, Ronald's college career has not made his father happy, especially when he thinks back to how hard he himself struggled to put himself through school, to get a solid education.

But there are other factors. There's a mini-depression in the early twenties, and Grampa is sick with financial worries. "I must pay taxes this month and many other bills. I will be $1500 behind on meeting running expenses and necessary bills the last of this month." He's upset about his help—they are not of the caliber he's used to. They come and they leave. Then there is Grama. She's suffering from some nervous malady, has insomnia, is dizzy, and spends weeks down at Aunt Ida's or in Chicago at the home of friends. Even when she's at home, she spends much of her time resting on the couch. Grampa is in charge, with the help of the hired woman, Hilda, extra hired help, and Esther, now fourteen. He's glum about the state of the house. He finds it hard to be in charge of everything.

When Ronald, twenty and a restless first-semester junior, thinks about dropping out of school and working for a while, his father is quick to offer him a job:

If you decide to do this I will start you in the barn as assistant herdsman. You help do the work in the morning then study and check up records in the PM. After about two weeks of this you will be familiar with the herd and hardened to physical work so I can put the other assistant to other work. In April I will want to take you out of the barn and put you onto the farm. Helping to prepare the field and put in the crop. By next winter you will be able to assume some management.

I do not want you to think of ending your schooling, but to plan to return after a year or so to your studies with a definite aim, then take the highest training in your chosen line.

At my Institute talk yesterday, a businessman asked, "Do you plan to continue in your present work as a life work, or to stick for a time then give up like so many do just as they are getting where they can accomplish something?" A year ago I could have answered his question positively and with all assurance that I should continue to the end of life and that I should be ever improving and progressing. Yesterday I thoughtfully and candidly answered, "*I don't know.*"

As it looks to me at present, the big problem is bettering the life in the home. Relieving the congestion and confusion, and making it possible to keep the family spirit.

I can manage the work so as to secure leisure and life for both the help and ourselves but the constant presence of so many at the table is distracting. There is only one thing we can do about it, with our finances as they are at present. That is to refine the home under the present plan. Change service at table somewhat. Have one of the helpers wait on table, possibly serve plates from kitchen and lay emphasis upon neatness of all to come to table—quiet and time for eating, wholesome inspiring conversation etc. All of these can be gradually brought about and make our meal hour a delight instead of a horrible nightmare.

We have help enough both inside and out to make the work run smooth. Mother and myself can and do get much time free from our duties. I more than the average businessman and Mother more than the average housewife in the city who cares for her own household. Our work is so organized that this is possible. Probably we could make and save more money if we stuck closer to our job, but that is not the question. The big problem is, can we manage the work and business so as to find life and stick to the job as a satisfying life work.

Such a work should fascinate one so that he would regret any circumstance that would necessitate his leaving it. I often ask this question: Would we leave the job with regret, or with anticipation and pleasure? I feel that Mother's only regret would be the cut in income and I rather think she would even welcome poverty if she could have her family to herself.

In my case there is a delight in the work itself. I like the responsibility of keeping things going. I enjoy especially the problems of the crops and the herds. Up to last spring I always entered into the cropping season with a peculiar joy of anticipation. A sense of confidence in the assurance that there will be a seed time and a harvest. Last spring I seemed to have none of this joy of the true husbandman. It worried me not to realize it. Of late the old sense of assurance and joy in my job has gradually returned.

I do not know but the cause of this is some real fellowship with Trever, also the part I am taking in the Junior Club work of the County. Trever helps me well in writing down the discussions and he is really interested in this work. He says he has the best time with me. It is not the idea that I expect to make him a farmer by these means but that we can talk together and that I can get through to his thoughts and feelings that gives me real pleasure.

How about your job possibility in France? I fear it is like my Tennessee speaking trip. Mine will not materialize this year at least. $280 is more than they can handle alone. If you finally decide to come home I will give you the best chance possible to fulfill your desires. You will be able to earn $40 or $45 per mo. after the first two weeks.

Remember, whatever you choose to do I will stand by you and help you to the utmost of my ability.

Ronald's decision is to stay in school for the second term. Then the offer to do social work in a war-ravaged French town does come through, and he takes it, departing before the semester is finished, and leaving his low grades to show up at the farm after he's out of the country. That summer Grampa doesn't have his elder son's help on the farm, nor his younger son's, either, for Trever, instead of working shoulder to shoulder with his father, as Wesson had happily anticipated, takes a job selling fly spray.

Ronald's letters from France are filled with the exuberance of youth, a young man having his eyes suddenly opened to the wide world and being dazzled. Trever goes off to Wisconsin, joins the UW chapter of Ronald's fraternity, and acquires a car. Grampa writes, "Regarding your car, you are better off without it. Even if it cost nothing. What you need is to develop quiet strength and poise of mind and character. The car tends to develop just the opposite qualities. Walk and think and grow great. I do not want you to use a car in Madison. Sell out and walk."

Trever is happy-go-lucky, and unlike his brother, doesn't bother to earn money. Grampa's letters to him have a three-note monotony: tend to your studies, don't spend so much so frivolously, and lead a pure, manly life. Concerning the budget Trever sends home in the fall, Grampa writes wryly, "Your financial statement was ambiguous. Whether you need $25 for these purchases in future, or whether you have spent this and more, I cannot make out. I notice you are not planning to eat for a month."

Grampa is also discouraged about his hearing. He writes, again to Trever, how those he takes along to write for him either think the talks are not worthwhile, lose interest, and cease to write ("you and Mother of late"), or become so intensely interested themselves that they forget him ("Henry and Lester"). When he gives talks and speeches, he finds the communication with his hosts and audiences increasingly difficult.

So in late November 1923, Grampa sits down at his desk and in a letter to himself, written in pencil on scratch paper, takes stock of his life.

These have been my ideals:

1. To build a successful business that would give opportunity for life, as well as a living; to build a home that would be a model for conveniences, beauty, and a desirable place to live.

2. To inspire my family and entire household with high ideals and give them a happy life.

3. To live a straightforward christian life; to continue to grow mentally and morally; to be active in work and religious work; to have our home distinctively christian.

4. To so direct and inspire my children that they would choose the good and detest the evil, and would seek to serve, would be efficient, outstanding characters wherever found.

Regarding my feeling as to my failure in realizing these ideals,

1. We have worked hard and developed a successful business and built the house but by its own burden it is destined to fail in its ultimate aim. We have no pleasure in it now. It is not a desirable place to live. We take no pleasure in the work or the life. There are many reasons for this: failing health, unsatisfactory help, necessity of economy in order to meet obligations, and especially the lack of interest on the part of our lads.

2. In the latter part of this ideal I have failed. The very things I have provided for making my family happy have caused discontent and unhappiness. I have given leisure and opportunity for camp and recreation. This has created a restlessness and dissatisfaction with real life.

3. In all but the first clause I feel I am falling down. Our home is becoming just an ordinary nonchristian farmhome. My church and religious work is of no account, to keep the mind alert and conscience sensitive seems difficult. Even in the personal christian faith and practice I am falling far short of the example of the Master. He had courage to undertake the difficult. He had perseverance. He had hope. He was confident of ultimate victory. He knew what he believed. I don't. In these things I am not following and it seems impossible for me to rise above my present gloom. I resolve again and again that I will face difficulties, trust in the future and have courage to go forward, but I find it is only a transitory stimulus. I pray with the psalmist, "Oh God restore unto me the *joy* of thy salvation."

4. In respect to the fourth ideal I cannot speak all I feel. It pains me greatly to see my lads deliberately choose the evil and scoff at the good. They seem to have no moral convictions on right and wrong. Nor any high sense of service, not even a spirit of helpfulness to myself, their mother, or the home, let alone of service to humanity. With all their

advantages for education they are simply attracted by the tinsel and bright lights of the show and society. Missing entirely the worthwhile associations and studies that would develop mental and moral strength. As yet they are not outstanding characters, they are one of the crowd, really in the lower strata of the crowd.

These are the things that make me blue. Some of them can be overcome but at present I see no bright outlook. To sell and change business would not help much.

This is a bitter accounting. The returning joy and assurance Grampa wrote about to Ronald almost a year ago was short-lived. His depression now is considerably deeper.

In the explication of his first point, Grampa's words about the home are shocking. He gives reasons. This is the only place where he says "we"; he means Eunice when he speaks of *failing health*. Things have not improved with Grama. She writes to Ronald in France, "It is so hard for Dad to have me this way. He needs me so. But I am not much good till I get stronger." And Grampa writes, "I do not know when Mother will come home. I miss her greatly. Work is my only diversion. I do work like the dickens when she is away."

And then, *unsatisfactory help*. He writes Trever, shortly before his blue memo:

Henry is not coming back to the farm. He is going into city business again. I feel very blue over my influence on the boys. Four boys have come to me this year enthusiastic about farming. After a few weeks or months with me they have had enough of it (my own included). I wonder if my ideals of work and life are right. They surely are not attractive.

And *necessity of economy in order to meet obligations*. The depression is not yet over, and repeatedly Grampa's letters worry about money: "I've had to buy a new cooler." "I've had to take out another loan to tide me over." Grama's illness costs money and so does hiring help to take her place. Grampa speaks longingly of taking Grama on vacations, where he, too, would get rest, but these are out of the question.

But the last item, *and especially the lack of interest on the part of our lads*, is the real kicker, particularly in view of Grampa's severe and specific judgment of those lads in the explication of the fourth point. In the second point he speaks of family restlessness and dissatisfaction with real life. In the third, he is despairing of his own spiritual life. But in the fourth . . . ! "It pains me greatly to see my lads deliberately choose the evil and scoff at the good. . . . They are one of the crowd, *really in the lower strata of the crowd*."

But is this fair? Certainly not to Ronald, who by now is sending home increasingly mature letters from abroad. His college sins are old, and he has been serving humanity for the past six months. If bright lights are still attracting him, they are now the lights of the opera houses, theaters, and art museums of Paris.

But Trever! Trever is only fifty miles from home, and has tobacco on his breath. His mother writes,

> . . . I was so crushed in heart and spirit after you had gone. I thought I never could write but you are my baby boy in spite of what you have done and I love you but I want to be proud of you. I was so weighed down it seemed I could not get off my bed, to think you could make light of the things that mean so much to me and that you could do the things you knew would break my heart and hurt a kind loving father as you have. Can you trade a mother's love and a father's respect for things that are going to undermine your own character? "Honor thy father and thy mother . . . " I knew you were smoking for a long time. I knew why you would not let me kiss you. Along in middle of the summer I kissed you and smelled stale tobacco and I knew then. I waited for you to tell but you deceived me and when I asked you, told me an untruth. . . . You are naturally a fine boy and have high ideals and good principles but one sin leads to another and it does not take long to slide down hill. I

want to look in your eye and know it is as clear and true as it was two years ago. We used to be so near to each other; don't let a nasty little devil of a cigarette separate you from your best love. . . .

Both parents write Ronald about Trever's smoking and lying, but with the trans-Atlantic time lag of two weeks each way, it is after Grampa's memo to himself that he and Grama receive Ronald's reply:

Your letter about Trever came this morning. Of course your worrying makes me feel rotten because I know how badly you feel. Trever's case so parallels mine that I can see both sides of it. My thought about it won't be a great deal of comfort to you, but I think it is pretty level. Here it is for what it is worth.

Trever at the University of Wisconsin.

Smoking in itself isn't a crime for which a fellow will be eternally damned. It is the thinking it is so bad that makes it so. I admit that it is injurious to health, but I don't think any more so than a dozen other indulgences that are not so heartedly condemned. None of these things need to become habits, neither does a little smoking need to lead to a harmful excess. I think you and dad are stressing the evil of smoking so much that you are making it the chief fault a man can have. It isn't, and it doesn't need to lead to other faults. Even if Trever should continue, the matter will more or less settle itself, for he worships his body, and when smoking interferes with his chances in athletics, smoking will go. It is hard to make a kid think it wrong morally, when he sees good and great men all around him indulging though, isn't it?

His deceiving you about it is more or less natural, although it hurts. He is too weak to hurt you outright, and when he slips up while he doesn't think he is committing a crime, he knows you will think so, and attempts to hide it. Smoking isn't the great crime. A man can think straight, love and be true to his friends, and lead a life without violating friendship and honor and still smoke. Oh gee—I so want to express myself—make you feel better about it—and my words don't come well.

This is my point. Because smoking is a tangible thing that can be nailed down, don't you think you are making too much of it? It is much more to the point that he realize he should deal seriously with his friends—that he should develop a high code of honor—that he should get enough sleep to keep him alert, than that he should take any definite stand about the other question. Perhaps by making him think you think he is headed for a bad life by smoking as he has, a bit, you really do make him think so. That is bad!

As to other things—Trever has the right stuff, and the right background. Don't bother about him too much. He is off on a nineteen-year-old tangent, just as I was a year or two ago, with its attendant questioning of everything, its tendency to coarse language, and all. Sometimes I think nineteen is a fellow's oldest period. He knows everything! After a bit, he comes to and loses his high horse. . . .

But I'm really worried about you both. Please don't take things so hard. Know you have three pretty decent kids who are surely profiting by your teaching even when they seem to be the least.

So the trigger cause of the blue memo comes clear. Trever's smoking and deceit. This against a background of Ronald's remembered shortcomings, plus farm worries, help worries, money worries, and concern about Grama. There is plenty here to make Grampa blue, to cause him to take up his pencil and assess his life.

He doesn't know it yet, but in regard to his sons, it is the darkness before the dawn. In his next letter to Trever, he gives advice and encouragement on Trever's upcoming exams, then goes on to outline a talk on "Problems of Dairying" he is soon to give in Iowa. About the last point, "Problems of Recruiting Dairymen," he says, "I am going to hold out my ideas of the opportunities in the broader field of dairy work, i.e., not just actually milking cows, but research work, teaching, marketing, etc." He adds, "You know I am to speak at a big state meet in Illinois in February. I shall use this same thought."

At that Illinois talk, someone takes down the speech verbatim, as well as the question and answer period. Throughout the speech, Grampa counters gloom. In the last section he states that farmers, by their own gloom, are discouraging those in their sphere of influence from going into farming, including their own children. He concludes the speech by saying yes, there are problems in dairying, but there is no cause for despair.

One of the questioners asks, "I would like to hear what this gentleman has to say about keeping the boys and girls on the farm. That is more of a problem than getting a good sire."

Mr. Dougan: "I do not know." (Laughter.) "I have two boys. I have talked the higher ideals and tried to give them a vision of their opportunity. I thought that they were absolutely against the farm. One boy has a position in community work in France at present. His last letter was to this effect: 'I am thinking more and more about the farm,' and 'the picture and vision of the farm.' He said, 'Some people would call it kiddish, but I call it a vision.' If he works that out he will be a farmer, he will be a progressive farmer. The other boy is telling me that he is getting to think better of the agricultural course that he is taking in Madison. I don't know whether they will be farmers. We do not care especially whether our boys and girls are farmers or not. This is the thing we hold up to them: 'First be good and strong men and women.'" (Applause.) "'Then choose the vocation in which you can serve humanity.' We figure out the education to that effect." (Applause.) "I believe the farm is going to appeal to them."

There will be future discouragements in Grampa's life, future major crises. But so far as anyone knows, he never writes another memo that so questions his own spirit, or so despairs of his sons. Jackie's personal experience, in the twenty years that she knows him, is of the beautiful optimism Grama writes about. To Jackie Grampa is, in the words of a famous writer, "the apple tree, the singing, and the gold."

13   RONALD'S COURTSHIP

Ronald's courtship is like this:

He goes off to Northwestern to college. His grades are so-so there. He takes French his freshman year, gets a C first semester, a D second semester. He figures that's not so good, so his sophomore year he takes the same French class again. He gets a C first semester, a D second semester. He joins a fraternity. He joins the Glee Club but never sings after the tryout, just mouths the words.

He gets into various scrapes. He telegraphs home one Sunday morning and tells Grampa not to believe everything he reads in the *Tribune*. Grampa is bewildered. He drives to town, and with some difficulty manages to find a *Tribune*. He can't find anything in it he thinks Ronald means he shouldn't believe. They call a friend in Chicago who reads them the headline of the local Chicago edition: NORTHWESTERN BOOZE DEN RAIDED. Ronald Dougan's name leads all the rest, even though, he assures his father, he had just entered the den looking for a friend.

Late in his junior year he gets a chance to go to France and work for a year doing reconstruction work. It's after the war. On a fine May day in Evanston, he gives a fraternity pin to one girl in the morning and asks her to wait for him; he gives away another fraternity pin in the afternoon and asks the girl to wait for him; he gives a third fraternity pin to a third girl in the evening and asks her to wait for him. He skips off to France the next day without taking any of his final exams.

After three months at the Methodist Memorial in Château Thierry he's head of a Boy Scout troop and speaks French like a native. He's sent to the train to meet a dean of women from an Illinois college. He's in short pants and rope sandals. He is not eager to meet a dean.

Mother steps off the train. Daddy immediately changes his mind about deans. It turns out Mother isn't a dean, anyway, but had been elected president of her alumnae association. Somehow information had become garbled between Illinois and France.

At the Methodist Memorial Mother teaches English and piano and ballet. Daddy sets right to work courting her. They take picnics of long French bread and cheese over to the little village of Essomes; they hang over the bridge and watch the waters of the Marne flow by; they climb around the ruins of the old château, and from the heights of the huge hill it was built on, look down on Château Thierry and all the surrounding countryside.

Daddy proposes. Mother is in love, but there's a problem. He is twenty-one, she is twenty-eight. That's too much of an age difference, Mother thinks. And then, how will Grama and Grampa on the farm react? They will be aghast that their son, barely of age, is marrying an Older Woman. One they haven't even met.

Daddy doesn't think there's any problem at all. Every night he proposes, every night Mother refuses. She expects him to be crushed and disheartened in the morning, but Daddy shows up for breakfast as bouncy as a new pup. He's persistent and indefatigable. Finally Mother succumbs. She agrees to marry him. Daddy is jubilant. He writes dozens of pages home, telling his parents how they will love his bride, and asking for their blessing. He says he now has direction in his life, he will finish school with honors, and wants to go into the family milk business with Grampa.

Mother and Daddy celebrate their engagement by going into Paris for dinner at a special restaurant. They are blissfully happy. After the *escargot* and *escalopes de veau à la crème* and *fromage*, Daddy becomes serious. He says, "Vera, I have something to confess to you."

"What is it, Ronald?" asks Mother.

Daddy says, "I've been lying to you in order to win you. I'm not twenty-one, I'm nineteen."

"Oh, Ronald!" Mother cries. "Nine years! Oh, I can't marry you! That's too much difference! I can't. I just can't."

Daddy lets Mother carry on for a little bit. Then he produces his passport. It proves he's twenty-one. Mother is so relieved that she's only a little angry. After that, the seven-year difference seems like nothing.

They are married on May 3, 1924, at noon at the Château Thierry city hall, wearing their Sunday clothes. That's the civil ceremony required by French law. In the afternoon they are married again, at the Methodist Memorial, by the Reverend Doctor Joseph Harker, president of the Illinois college that Mother is not a dean at. This time Mother wears a white gown and Daddy a tuxedo, and there are many guests and cake and flowers. There's a cablegram from Grama and Grampa, giving their blessing.

After the wedding a picture is taken. The young woman in the picture is beautiful, slim, with brown hair and classic features. She wears a look of grave serenity. The young man is dashingly handsome; his look is just a tiny bit cocky, like a rooster on top of a manure heap. They are standing on the outside staircase, which has an ornamental wrought-iron rail. The staircase curves about a wall fountain down to the courtyard.

Jackie sees this picture all her life. It's enlarged and framed on Mother's dresser. When she herself visits Château Thierry, many years later, and walks into the courtyard of the Methodist Memorial, she stops quite still. It is a familiar place, where she has been before.

14 SLEEP, LITTLE BABY

The months before Ronald's wedding are trying ones for Grampa and Grama, once they tumble to what's going on. They haven't seen it coming. Ronald's first mention in October of "a charming girl from Chicago just arrived," in November that "the girl from Chicago plays the piano well," in December that "the American girl and I have an awful lot in common and our trips to Paris are no end fun," and in January a lengthy discussion of the problems of love and marriage, and how well Ronald thinks his parents have worked out their relationship—all this and more does not tip them off. Nor are they alarmed by parallel references showing their son grappling with the decision of a life work. Doesn't every young man with a year or so of college to finish worry about his future?

It's not until mid-February of 1924 that Ronald's January 30 bombshell arrives: "This letter is bound to be almost entirely about a girl. For the first time in my life I am seriously considering the possibility of settling down, finding my work, and preparing myself to be responsible for a home." And several pages later:

> Of course I am doing quite a bit of thinking about what I am going to do from now on. The first thing is to finish my schooling. After that, I don't know. I would like diplomatic service, and I am sure that I would like some branches of commercial work. Farming, though, is appealing to me more and more. . . . The idea of working into cattle breeding is attractive. . . . After I get my Northwestern degree why couldn't I work with you on the farm, and take the Ag course at Madison in a few years?

Grampa replies, "Yours is a sensible straightforward letter for one in your state of mind. There were no senseless ravings," and "You show a clear conception of the meaning of life and the significance of a choice of this nature." He asks, "But is Miss Wardner of the same mind toward you?"

The bulk of his letter concentrates on his son's schooling and plans: "Whether you go into farming, or politics, diplomatic work or literature or community service, two years at Madison, not confining yourself to the technical lines but to the broader principles of agriculture, will be the best possible preparation. . . . Some farmers would consider your picture of actual farming with its intellectual and aesthetic side as mere foolishness and impractical. I do not. You are grasping something of what I mean by the farm yielding *life* as well as a living. . . ."

Grama's response to Ronald's news is in a postscript: "Your letter made me feel sad and glad," and "I am glad she is not a French Catholic."

Ronald's next letter, six dense pages on farming, is written before he has received his parents' responses. Grampa's reply is fully as lengthy.

> Reading your farming letter I think I have something of the feeling my mother did when I told her I was going into the ministry. I thought she would be elated. However she seemed to hesitate and questioned my decision. She either felt I was not smart enough or that I was not good enough. . . . Your letter has a fine tone and shows a clear analytic mind. You surely do see the drawbacks to other lines of activity. You are not quite so clear on the advantages of farming. . . . Regarding your fitting into the managerial work here I do not know. You realize how much you have to learn in order to be a competent manager. However I fear, knowing you and Trever as I do, that you may find it irksome to take a subordinate position until you gradually and naturally step up. . . . You must learn the truth: Only by the *slow toilsome* process of self-culture does one achieve success.

His final words are: "If you become the right sort of man, get the right sort of wife, and have the right sort of habits and a high ambition, I guess we can work out the details all right."

Then things snowball. Ronald announces an official engagement; then he does not want to wait till he has his degree but wishes to be married in the fall, before the school year starts at Northwestern; then, it's more sensible for them to marry in France and enjoy together the European travel each had planned separately. Every letter pleads, with increasing desperation, for his parents' approval of his plans.

Grampa and Grama's alarm grows. Events are moving with such rapidity that they are left gasping. The time lag of the mails accounts for much of this. By the time a letter has steamed across the Atlantic, been pondered, answered, and received back in France, almost a month has passed. Meanwhile, they've been inundated by subsequent letters, none of which have had the benefit of Grampa's caveats, his sage advice, and his cry, "Go slow! Go slow!" It's as though he's shouting down an empty track where the train has long since disappeared around the bend, even its steam and whistle no longer within sight or hearing.

But the train comes to a screeching halt when Grampa sends a cable on March 22: "PLAN NOT APPROVED. DAD."

Ronald responds with twelve pages. "Whew, Dad, talk about the long arm of the law—it is as nothing compared with the sure reach of a cablegram. . . . But as to what I am thinking about most I tremble to write. . . . " He says that words on a page can't take the place of conversation with all its nuances, but that there are three things he wants his father to be very sure about. That neither he nor Vera wish to do anything that doesn't meet with his approval. "Your cooperation, intimate interest in our lives, and your father-ing mean everything to us." That in all their plans it is he who has taken the lead: "It would be utterly natural for you to think that I am being hurried a bit, urged a bit, but that is not the case." And further:

> The last thing. You and I have not seen a great deal of each other for two or three years. You cannot know how I have matured, how my out-look on life has changed, how I have come to welcome the responsibil-ities and routine that life has shown me. . . . My thinking is sound,

absolutely. I want you to direct me as you think best about school and work. You can count on me to hit either for everything there is in me. *Dad, I am a man!* I am thinking as a man. . . . Do you know what you can do for me as an engagement present, and what will most thoroughly set the world at rights? Go down to Western Union and send this cablegram: PLAN APPROVED—LOVE—DAD.

There is a time lag for these twelve pages, too, but when his father receives them, after the several letters of thoughtful planning (and sped-up wedding date) that were mailed to the farm before Ronald received the cablegram, he knows when he is licked. He cables his approval.

Now it is May 3, 1924. Grama is beside herself. She doesn't know if she's coming or going. She wrings her hands, wails, "Oh, he's so young, so young!" and "He's way out there all alone, getting married today all by himself!" She says, "It's just not possible that one of my little boys is old enough to be married!" She repeats over and over, to everyone and anyone, the lovely things she's heard about her son's bride, but always with the refrain, "But he's so young!"

Then she goes to an afternoon church affair. A friend brings a young woman to her. She says to Eunice, "This young lady knows the girl that your Ronald is marrying." Grama listens eagerly as the stranger gives a glowing description of Vera—what a wonderful girl she is, so artistic, so talented, so sensitive. Grama returns home much calmed and cheered.

Vera finishes out her year of work at Château Thierry; Ronald, already finished with his, drives a cab for tourists to visit the battlefields. Then they honeymoon in France and Switzerland and Italy. They sail from Naples, with stops in Sicily, Tunisia, and Gibraltar.

When they arrive in New York in August, it's shortly after noon. They loiter around until 2 P.M. before wiring the farm of their safe return, and the time they'll be coming into Beloit. They've forgotten that all businesses in the United States don't close down for two hours after lunch. They have

practically no cash, though a year later Mother, getting Daddy's coat ready for the cleaners, discovers a twenty-dollar bill in an inner pocket.

Aside from short rations, the ride to the Midwest is uneventful. As they approach Beloit they are excited and eager to see Grama and Grampa. They're also both a little nervous. Mother has on a brown silk dress with fur trim. She wants to look her best for her new in-laws. As the train pulls into the station, Daddy gets her a glass of water. The train lurches; he spills water all over her. Mother gets off the train stained and streaky. But Grama and Grampa welcome her, prepared to love her, wet or dry.

Ronald takes a trip down to Northwestern and talks to his former professors. They all agree to let him finish up his work and take the final exams he missed. All but one, his professor of Russian history. The professor listens to his tale and then barks, "Young man, I have never seen you before in my life!" Ronald loses his two credits in Russian history.

Grampa and Daddy decide it will be best for Ronald to take his senior year at Beloit College. There will be no travel expense. Rent for a room at Aunt Ida's, only a few blocks from campus, will be much less than in Evanston. Produce and meat can come from the farm, and Lester Stam delivers milk to Aunt Ida's house every day. Besides, the couple now know Vera is pregnant. Better to stay nearby.

Ronald sees chemistry as a useful major for the farm, as well as a study that interests him. He takes nothing but chemistry courses, except for world history from Dicky Richardson. He tries to make some money by getting out a college directory, as he had at Northwestern, but the president decides Ronald should be paid a small stipend for this and the college keep the profits, so he abandons the project. Delta Upsilon is not among the fraternities at Beloit. Ronald organizes all the nonfraternity men into an independent group. The Independents carry off the scholarship prizes, the athletic prizes, and win the homecoming float trophy. The fraternities are left blinking.

Aunt Lillian, Grampa's unmarried sister, lives at Aunt Ida's, too. Every morning she comes down to breakfast and every morning she says, "I never slept a wink all night."

One morning in March she comes downstairs. "I never slept a wink all night," she says to Daddy and Aunt Ida.

"Then why aren't you congratulating me?" asks Daddy.

"Congratulate? What for?"

"Surely you heard all the activity here in the night," says Daddy. "Vera went to the hospital, and little Vera Joan was born at three o'clock!"

Aunt Lillian clamps her jaw shut and in spite of the good news is sulky for much of the morning.

In June Daddy graduates with high honors from Beloit College, and he and Mother and Joan move out to the farm. They live there with Grampa and Grama in what is now called the Big House, while the Little House,

*Grampa, Mother, and Vera Joan in
front of the Little House.*

built several years ago beyond the milkhouse for a married herdsman, is
extended on its east side to include a fireplace and built-in bookcases, and
upstairs over this space, a sleeping porch filled with windows. Then they
move into the Little House.

Daddy goes into partnership with Grampa. He takes over the business end
of the farm. He and Mother buy an upright piano so that Mother can play.
Mother joins the Treble Clef music club and starts teaching ballet.

Every morning Grama comes over. She watches Mother work, and tells
Mother how she has finished all her own housework and baked five pies and
eight loaves of bread, all before nine o'clock. She plays with the baby, creep-
ing up on Joan on her hands and knees, being a growling bear. Joan screams
with delight and kicks her little legs.

At some time every day, Grampa also stops by to see Mother and the baby. One autumn day he takes a workday off and spends it entirely at the Little House. He follows Mother around, watching everything she does: bathing and nursing the baby, washing the clothes and diapers, putting Joan down for her nap, taking her outside. He watches Mother do her housework and make the meals. He watches her do her ballet exercises, using the back of a chair for a barre. He asks her to play the piano for him, and even though he can't hear with his ears, he puts his hand on the wood and feels the vibrations. Mother plays and sings for him the lullaby she has just written for Joan's first Christmas; he first reads the words, and then follows her lips as Mother sings:

> Sleep, little baby, the daylight is fading;
> Dim yellow stars the dark heavens adorn;
> Once, long ago, in a Bethlehem manger
> The little Lord Jesus was born.
> Lulluby, lullaby, sleep, little baby, sleep.
>
> Sleep, little baby, my arms are about thee,
> A circle of love which enfolds thee secure;
> So Mary cradled the wee baby Jesus,
> The little Lord Jesus, so pure.
> Lullaby, lullaby, sleep, little baby, sleep.
>
> Sleep, little baby, thine eyelids are drooping,
> Thy warm, tender body relaxing to rest;
> Jesus thus slept in the arms of sweet Mary,
> His dear little head on her breast.
> Lullaby, lullaby, sleep, little baby, sleep.
> Lullaby, lullaby, sleep, little baby, sleep.

Grampa's eyes are moist when Mother finishes. He says, "I can hear it, Vera."

Mother's lullaby for Joan's first Christmas.

Grampa does no farmwork all that day. He talks to Mother about many concerns of his; he asks about hers. Mother writes back to him, or he reads her lips. He has specially requested that she not learn the hand alphabet that Daddy and Grama use so rapidly. He wants to practice reading lips, and he wants to be able to look at Mother's face when they talk.

It's a happy day for Mother, for Joan, for Grampa. "You are a dear little mother," says Grampa in benediction when he leaves at evening to go over to the Big House. Mother smiles and feels blessed.

15 JIM HOWARD

Jim Howard grows up on a farm near Tonica, Illinois. When his father sells the farm in 1925, Jim runs an employment-wanted ad in *Hoard's Dairyman*. W. J. Dougan answers it, saying he needs a herdsman. His letter states that there is no drinking or smoking on the farm, that he himself is deaf and a former minister.

Jim doesn't drink or smoke, and sees no problem in working under a minister-farmer. He thinks, privately, that it might be difficult to work for a deaf man, but he's willing to try. He writes that he will accept the job, provided the Reverend Mr. Dougan will take a man with a severe limp: osteomyelitis at age five has left him with one leg twisted and shorter than the other. But his handicap has never interfered with his ability to do a full day's work. W. J. writes back to come ahead.

When Jim arrives, Mother Dougan gives him the room in the Big House that has the little balcony. He meets the other hired men. Grampa shows him the farm. He reads the words on the silo and wonders to himself whether the last Aim, "Life as Well as a Living," is for the family only or includes the working man. He meets Ronald, who has just begun working full time on the farm that summer, in business with his father. Ronald is a few years older than he, and talks rapidly to his father by spelling out the words with his fingers. So does Mother Dougan. Jim pats his pocket. He's already purchased a little notebook and pencil to carry with him.

After dinner W. J. Dougan takes him into his office. "I never tell a man when to get up," he says. "I tell him when I want him on the job in the morning. You can get up an hour ahead, comb your hair, curl it, anything you want—or you can get up five minutes ahead. But I want you in the barn at four o'clock, ready to work."

He tells him about his day off: "You can sleep as late as you wish, and have breakfast here," he says, "but I want you to be gone part of the day. Get away from *here!* Even if you have to go downtown and stand on a street corner! If you're away from here part of the time you'll be a better man for me when you're back. And also for yourself!"

He twinkles. "But you won't have to stand on a corner. There are church activities and Grange activities, and I have a membership at the YMCA for every man here, so you can swim and play basketball."

Jim nods. A day off, every seven or eight days, even without Y privileges, seems very liberal. He's been used to having only one a month at his former job. Nor does the work schedule seem unreasonable: milk from 4:00 to 6:30 A.M., breakfast, then an hour's rest. Clean the barn and other chores till noon, then dinner and another hour off. Milking and cleanup from 3 till 6, then supper and off for the evening, except for putting the cows to bed—though Jim doesn't know what "putting the cows to bed" entails.

W. J. says, "These are my criteria for cleanliness," and tells of the spotless white cap and apron he is to wear at every milking; of how the cows are brushed and shaved and washed; of what the steps are in clearing the manure, washing down the sidewalks and gutters, and spreading lime. He says that the walls are to be whitewashed regularly.

Jim's salary will be fifty dollars a month, including room and board. That, too, seems liberal. He knows that his employer has just returned from Chicago, where he gave a series of radio lectures over WLS, and received a Master Farmer award from *Prairie Farmer* magazine. He is a bit awed to be working for a Master Farmer, and is filled with respect. He determines to do his best.

The former herdsman stays on for a week to break in his successor, and then Jim is in charge. Not only does he respect W. J., "Daddy," as he is called by everyone, but finds that Daddy Dougan treats him with respect. He never tells him, "No, you're doing that wrong, do it this way." He never seems to be checking up on him. In the mornings when Jim pushes the two-wheeled cart with its four cans of milk on it from the barn to the milkhouse and sees Daddy's head peeking from the small window of his bedroom in the Big House, he never feels he's looking out to spot loiterers, or count how many loads they are getting up. It's only Daddy surveying his world before emerging.

When the weather gets cold enough for the cows to stay inside, W. J. instructs Jim on putting the cows to bed. At 9 or 9:30 the two return to the barn. The cows are all lying down. They've eaten, they've knocked hay out of their mangers. W. J. and Jim get them all up. They sweep the hay back into the mangers, get more hay. A lot of the cows, once on their feet, make droppings. Not all the manure falls into the gutter. They scrape the walkway, tidy up around each cow, and shake up her bedding. All the while Grampa croons to his lassies. He also talks to Jim.

"You'll be surprised at how much cleaner the cows are in the morning, and how much more they'll eat, than if you just abandon them from 6 o'clock at night till 4 o'clock the next day."

He gives Jim other advice. "As Mr. Hoard says, 'The cow is a mother—treat her as such!'" And, "Every day, go around in front of each cow. Watch how she eats. Look her in the eye. See if it's got a bright sparkle or if it's losing luster. Then you know how that cow's feeling today. Go back around behind her, look at her droppings. From them you'll know how she's going to be feeling tomorrow."

Jim thinks everything Daddy tells him makes a lot of sense. He's also impressed with the routine of the Big House. The meals are served in the dining room, by Mother Dougan, Ronald's sister Esther, who is fifteen, and Hilda, the hired helper. The farmhands and Hilda eat with the family. Mother Dougan bakes all the bread, pies, and cakes, and spreads a lavish board. Breakfast is never merely bacon and eggs, but bacon, eggs, hotcakes, sausage, toast, jam, applesauce or another fruit sauce, fruit juice, milk,

Wesson Joseph Dougan, 1925; Eunice Trever Dougan, 1925. These portraits were hung in the University of Wisconsin Agricultural Hall of Fame. Wesson and Eunice were the first farm couple to be jointly honored by the university.

cream, and coffee. Dinners at noon make the table groan even more than breakfast. Suppers are simpler, but equally satisfying. At meals, W. J. doesn't sit at the head but at the middle of the table. He always says grace. After supper he reads aloud from the Bible, and from a commentary; the boarders stay for this lesson. Before bedtime Jim habitually polishes off a quart of milk: the day-old milk returned from the route is in a box inside the cooler door, and is free for the taking by the farm workers.

As a boarder, Jim has his bed made every morning, and his sheets and clothes laundered weekly. Mother Dougan and Hilda toil over the big washtubs in the men's washroom off the kitchen; in order to wash or to use the toilet in the closed room at the rear he must thread his way around tubs and women, and in the wintertime, clotheslines laden with overalls. More lines are stretched in the cellar near the furnace, and sometimes he helps hang the clothes or carry a basket. In fair weather, the clothes are hung outside to flap in the sunshine between the elms on the Big House lawn.

For his rest period, he can stretch out on his bed in his room or sit in the men's parlor off the dining room, where the radio is tuned in to WLS, and there are magazines, books, and papers to read. There is also a Victrola and records.

Out in the barn, when shorthanded, W. J. sometimes works along with him, taking the place of someone with a day off. Frequently, especially on Sunday afternoons, visitors from town come to see the milking. W. J. gives a mischievous glance at Jim, takes a cow leader, catches a cow through the nostrils, and exposes her gums. "This poor lass has no upper set of front teeth," he says. "She was born this way." The visitors cluck with surprise and sympathy; they don't know that all cows are born like this. Daddy Dougan doesn't give away the ruminant joke, nor do Jim or the other barnhands.

Jim works a year on the farm. He and the other barn workers make a smooth team. Every week they scrape the barnyard. Every three months they whitewash the cowbarn walls. Jim learns to swing all the way around the barn on the manure trolley track, hand over hand. Grampa sees him and says, "Hi! I didn't know this was the big top!"

Then Jim leaves for an operation that improves his hip. He returns to a roommate. Glen Gile acts a bit strange, and tells wild stories, but Jim reasons that every man is entitled to his peculiarities.

But Glen's strangeness increases. He gets it into his head that Mr. Griffiths, the oldest farmhand and trusted friend of Daddy Dougan, is losing his mind. Jim and the others laugh it off, but Jim feels uneasy. Then Glen decides that it's Daddy Dougan who is going crazy. He states that Daddy has a lot of worries with the farm, and with his flirtatious sweet-sixteen daughter, and with his harum-scarum college son, Trever. Jim and the others laugh this off, too, but Jim feels more uneasy.

On a summer night Jim and a milkhouse worker, Micky Baker, are sitting on a bench in the washroom off the kitchen, idly talking of this and that. Glen comes in. "I'm going to shoot Daddy Dougan," he says casually, and trots up the back stairs, slamming the stairwell door behind him.

Jim and Micky are speechless. They hear the floor creak and in a moment, Glen returning down the stairs, one slow step at a time. The door opens a crack; they turn mesmerized and see six inches of shotgun barrel ease out. Panic grips Jim's throat, but with the panic comes action. He reaches up and grabs the light cord. In the sudden darkness he and Micky sprint toward the front of the house, snapping off lights as they go. They find Mother Dougan in the dining room.

"Get Daddy out, quick!" Jim orders. "Glen's loco, he's coming with a shotgun to shoot him!"

Eunice asks no questions. She rushes to Wesson, working at his desk in the front room, and spells that they must go over to Ron's place instantly. Wesson stumbles to his feet. "Is it a fire?" he cries, and follows her out the front door and down the sidewalk to the Little House. No one worries about Esther; she's staying the night with her chum Eloise down the road. Hilda is also away, visiting her sister.

Jim and Micky run to the cellar and hide behind the furnace. Overhead they hear Glen prowling back and forth in the empty house.

"I've never hurt anyone in my life," chatters Micky, clutching a coal shovel, "but if he comes down here, I'm gonna kill him!"

Over at the Little House Wesson is hustled upstairs and into Mother and Daddy's bedroom. He sits in the dark. Vera calls the police. Ronald goes outside and listens to Glen shooting up a cornfield. Then Glen comes to the garage, starts his car, and leaves. The police arrive a few minutes later. They are provoked that Glen has been allowed to get away.

"How do you argue with a shotgun?" asks Ron.

Jim Howard and Dave Clark.

"He'll probably come back. Then call us again," say the police.

There's no sleep for anyone. Wesson, though he protests, remains in the dark in the uppermost corner of the Little House. Eunice stays with him. Ronald and Vera watch at the darkened downstairs windows.

Jim hasn't yet put the cows to bed. "Come with me, Micky," he begs. "What if he comes back while I'm out in the barn alone?"

Micky refuses to budge. Jim wavers, almost lets the cows be, but in the end he rushes down, practically kicks the bewildered beasts to their feet, and beds them more quickly than they've ever been bedded before. Then he and Micky watch from the front windows of the Big House.

About midnight Glen returns. Ron calls the police. Glen puts his car in the garage, goes upstairs, and gets into bed.

The police arrive quickly. "What's the best way to take him?" they ask.

"Every morning I call him about four o'clock," says Jim.

"Well—call him!"

From the top of the stairs Jim squeaks, "Glen, time to get up!"

Glen opens the door. Jim steps back, the police step forward, and it's all over.

That is the last any of them ever see of Glen. They hear he's been committed to the state mental hospital at Mendota. Everyone is sorry, but they're glad he didn't shoot Daddy Dougan, or anyone else. W. J. shakes his head. "Poor fellow," he says.

Jim stays on the farm for another year. Then he leaves and goes to ag school. He marries, and works as farm manager on a succession of farms in distant states. He eventually becomes a supervisor for Carnation Milk. He keeps in touch through Christmas cards and an occasional letter.

Some twenty years later Jim is in the area and drives out to the farm. He finds Grampa talking to Ronald in the barn. "Hello, Daddy," he writes on his pad. "I couldn't go by without saying hello to 'The Babies' Milkman.'"

Grampa and Ronald greet him warmly. They catch him up on some of the changes—the cows now almost entirely Holsteins; the improvements in the milkhouse; the growing hybrid seedcorn business with its buildings located at Ron's farm up the road; the Rock County Breeders' Co-op.

On the barn ramp, Jim says to Ronald, "Your father never preached to me, yet working and living with him was like a sermon every day." He motions toward the "Aims" on the silo. "My first day here I wondered if those words included me. I found out very soon they were meant for every person on the place. We were truly a family."

Ron reminds him of the Glen Gile episode, and spells the reminder to Grampa. Jim grins wryly and writes, "Daddy, I have tended a number of herds since you taught me, and that was the only time in my life that I almost didn't put the cows to bed!"

Grampa nods and nods over the message. His whole body shakes with silent laughter.

16 NAMING COWS

At first the Dougan cows have cowy names. Jackie knows this because one of Daddy's most repeated stories is how, as a little boy milking in the side barn—then the only barn—he knew every freckle on Daisy's udder. How he looked out the barn door, envying the freedom of the sparrows as they pecked on the horse apples. The other cow it was his responsibility to milk was named Bess, who apparently had no freckles worth mentioning. Jackie studies udders, and finds not only freckles but spots and blotches and sometimes warts, though most are plain and creamy smooth.

But during the years when Jackie is in the round barn almost daily, each cow has her name over her appointed stanchion, on a metal plate. The names are J-16, L-3, P-7, or the notorious M-12, well known and avoided because she attacks little children.

Grampa makes this change in 1915, a few years after the round barn is built. He's enlarging his business and increasing his herd. The cows still bear cowy names: Marie, Beauty, Princess, Lassie, Easter, May, Fantine, Fern, Gladys, Elsie, Gretchen, Hester. But this is the year Grampa starts to name his herd more efficiently. He calls the year "A," and gives each cow a number. Marie is A-1, Beauty is A-2, Princess is A-3, till all cows, heifers, and calves are numbered. When he buys a cow, or if a cow calves in the remainder of 1915, that animal receives the next A number. The year 1916 is year B, 1917, year C. Each cow also has her new designation on a metal tab clipped permanently to her ear. This system allows Grampa to know at a glance when a cow came into the herd and also to look up that cow quickly in his records. Some cowy names last at least into the early thirties, but new cows are seldom named, and old names are gradually forgotten.

When Daddy becomes involved with the cows, around 1926 or 1927, he decides it's to the farm's advantage to register all its purebred Guernseys with the American Guernsey Cattle Club. He sends a list of the cows' names: E-4, K-7, G-3, and all the others.

The cattle club writes back. They are sorry, but the Dougan farm can't register their cows by number. It's required that each cow have a name.

Daddy studies the letter and shakes his head at the nuisance to the farm records of double-designating all the cows merely to have them registered. He expresses his irritation to Mother.

"Name them in French," Mother suggests.

"*Quelle* the hell *la différence*?" asks Daddy. "Bessie or Babette?"

"Name them their numbers," says Mother.

"A rose by any other name," shrugs Daddy.

Mother picks up Daddy's pencil, takes the list of cows, and translates each number: *E-Quatre, K-Sept, G-Trois, . . .*

"It seems a little obvious," observes Daddy, "as well as spare."

"Then add something more," says Mother. "Add 'of our farm,' or 'of our home.'"

Daddy takes the pencil and adds "*de Chez Nous*" to each name: *E-Quatre de Chez Nous, K-Sept de Chez Nous, . . .*

"Thank you," says Daddy. He kisses her. He says in French, "How smart I was to marry a woman smarter than I am."

He sends the altered list back to the cattle club. There's not a murmur at the other end. They register all the Dougan purebred Guernseys with their elegant French names. At the farm, these names go into the herd book. But each cow, on her metal plate and her ear clip, retains her simple numerical designation. All cows, grade and purebred, are equal in the round barn.

In 1940 Daddy and Grampa come to the end of the alphabet; the cows are finally Z-1, Z-2, Z-3. For the next year they switch, and the cows are 41-1, 41-2. They continue this in 1942. But the new system is cumbersome. Since all the A, B, and C cows from before 1920 are only sweet memories,

Daddy starts through the alphabet again. He completes another cycle and has started around yet once more before he sells the herd in 1969 and retires from milking.

17   CIRCUMCISION

There is a mysterious space in the round barn. It's a dim passageway between the cowbarn and the lower part of the side barn. There's a window in this passageway, but it's so encrusted with dirt and lime and splashes of whitewash that only a murky light filters through. Under the window is a ledge, which is the lid to the slacked-lime bin. A narrow staircase winds up the wall of the passage past the bin and window to emerge in the loft of the round barn. On the other side of the passage is the inside opening to the outside silo. So all this is in the passageway, before you get to the lower barn: the window, the ledge, the stairs; and on the other side, the space before the silo opening, and the yawning black mouth of the outside silo. The passageway is whitewashed.

Jackie's earliest memory is of this passageway. It's an odd memory, like a dream. She's in this passageway, and so is the family doctor, old Dr. Thayer. He has her baby brother on the ledge under the window. The baby is naked. The doctor's back is to her; she can't see her brother. The doctor is doing something to her brother's bottom: she knows he's cutting the skin and stretching it over the buttocks. The baby is bawling. That's the extent of the memory: a setting, an activity, a sound. Jackie knows this is a genuine memory, for she never tells it to anyone until she's nearly grown, and realizes she's always been puzzled by it. Then she tells Mother.

Mother is startled. She has an explanation. Jackie was less than two years old, Patsy three, and Joan five when Dr. Thayer came to the Little House to circumcise Craig. He did it on the dining-room table. Mother must have explained to her sisters, or perhaps the adults were talking. Little as Jackie was, she got the idea of skin, and cutting, and bottom. And when the doctor began, Craig started to scream. Mother hadn't realized this would hap-

*Patsy, Jackie, and Joan
on January 12, 1930, the day
Craig was born.*

pen; she'd rushed the sisters into their coats and taken them for a walk around the farm till it was over. It was January and the weather was cold; they'd stayed in the buildings. They'd gone to the cowbarn to see the cows, and then into the lower barn to see the calves. In the passage, Jackie must have heard a calf bawling.

Jackie nods. Calves always bawl in the lower barn; it's where they stay right after they're separated from their mothers. It makes sense of the memory. She finds it satisfying to verify this as a memory, to see how it became garbled.

She tells her sisters, and gains further confirmation. "Sure," says Patsy. "We sat out the circumcision in that passageway, on the steps up to the loft."

"And it was COLD!" adds Joan.

Jackie's enormously pleased to know she has remembered something from before she was two. Craig, of course, is glad that he doesn't remember anything about it.

18 GRAMPA DRESSES

At the Big House, Grampa and Grama have separate bedrooms. Grampa's is the larger, right off the hall, while Grama's adjoins his. There's a small cot in Grampa's room and sometimes Jackie sleeps there for her nap, or occasionally overnight. She likes to lie facing the wall and pick the ivy wallpaper off, to reveal bit by bit the rose pattern beneath. She likes waking up in the morning and in the semigloom watching Grampa prepare for the day.

It isn't Grampa's rising that wakes her, it's the unaccustomed noise. What you hear depends on which side of the milkhouse you sleep on. On the Little House side, the only early-morning disturbance is the chitter-chatter of a hundred sparrows in the thick ivy that covers the chimney from ground to roof. But on the Big House side, she can hear the clang of the milk cans coming up from the barn to the milkhouse, and the crash and clatter of milk-bottle cases being loaded into the milk trucks, and the trucks themselves driving out of the yard. And then, from the woodpile side of the Big House, comes the strident crow of the rooster, soaring into the sky, over and over.

Jackie watches Grampa dress through almost closed lids, so that he won't know she's awake. If he is ever naked, it happens in the bathroom or when she's asleep, for he always has on one-piece long underwear as he moves quietly around his room. He puts on his blue cambric work shirt and buttons it almost up. He steps into his one-piece overalls and pulls the straps over his shoulders. He fastens the straps to the bib not by buttonholes or snaps but with metal loops that fit around the brass buttons on the two corners of the bib. Then he sits on his bed to pull on his mottled brown cotton socks with the white toes and heels, the kind she has a monkey made out of, and then his heavy work shoes that are leather and come up over his ankles. His movements are deliberate, and Jackie can hear every one of his regular breaths, labored as though he were working hard.

Sometimes she decides to get up and follow Grampa to the bathroom for the next part of the ritual. She loves to watch Grampa shave. It's more interesting than watching Daddy, who uses a safety razor.

Grampa soaks a towel till it's steaming, then wrings it and packs it around his chin. Holding the towel in place with one hand, with the other he scrubs his wet shaving brush in the china cup of soap on the windowsill till it's thick with suds. Then he sets down the towel and lathers up his whiskers. The white mask softens his beard as he strops back and forth, back and forth his single-edge razor on the brown leather strap that hangs by the window. At last he takes the razor and starts slicing off the lather in long clean swatches. After each swipe he rinses off the piled foam under the hot faucet. He twinkles at Jackie from the mirror but doesn't speak. When all the lather has been shaved away, he uses the wet towel to wash any remaining soap off his face, dries his neck and face and ears, puts away his brush and razor in the medicine cabinet, and returns to the bedroom. There Grampa stands before his dresser and brushes his sparse hair with a brush with no handle, only a strap on the back for his hand. He buttons the top buttons of his shirt so that his damp long underwear collar no longer shows. He puts his pad of paper and a pencil in his shirt pocket. He puts on his gold rimmed glasses. "Let's go see what's for breakfast," he says to Jackie, but she already knows. She can smell the buckwheats and bacon.

She also knows why Grama has a separate bedroom. Grampa snores. It's an incredible noise, a noise like repeated rolls of thunder. Then there will be a sudden complete silence, no breathing, nothing. She lies in bed, holding her breath, wondering if Grampa will ever breathe again. The silence is interminable. Then suddenly there will come two or three quick snorts, followed by another onslaught of thunder that makes the whole room tremble. No wonder Grama is in another room. The wonder is that she isn't in one of the bedrooms that are way across the hall.

19 S.O.B.

It's 1932. In the side barn off the round barn, where the newborn calves are kept, there's a calf with a broken leg. Grampa thinks her mother lay on her. Daddy calls the vet.

Dr. Russell comes. He glances at the calf. "Shoot the son of a bitch," he says to Daddy, and leaves.

Daddy gets some narrow boards. He measures them long enough so that they'll make a walking splint. He sets the break and splints it. He binds up the leg. He calls a vet in Janesville and asks how long he should leave the splint on. Dr. Knilans tells him he'll come check the leg in three weeks, if Daddy wants him to. Daddy describes the splint and asks if it's all right for the calf to walk on it. Dr. Knilans says there's no way to keep her from it unless Daddy plans to hog-tie her.

Sure enough, before long the calf has struggled to her feet, hobbled to her mother and started to nurse.

Twice a day Daddy goes down to the barn and checks the splint and bandages, and inquires into the welfare of his patient. She leaves her mother, is weaned to a pail, is in with the other calves. When all the calves go out into the field behind the calfbarn, she goes too, and manages a stiff-legged gambol. Grampa laughs and laughs when he goes past the fence. Joan and Patsy, Jackie and Craig, like to watch her, too. She becomes quite tame. They let her suck their fingers.

Dr. Knilans examines the leg and advises keeping the splint on a few weeks longer. At the end of the allotted time, Daddy takes it off. The leg looks fine. The calf has no trouble walking on it, although she does have a bit of hitch in her gait that she never quite gets over. She grows into a healthy heifer and productive cow. She spends twelve years in the round barn.

Daddy and Grampa don't call Dr. Russell any more. When they need a vet they call Dr. Arthur Knilans in Janesville. He becomes the farm vet.

Somebody once asks whatever happened to Dr. Russell.

"I shot the son of a bitch," says Daddy.

20 DADDY CHURNS

It is 1933, the Depression. The farm is barely surviving. If it weren't for the milk business, it would not have survived this long. Yet the profit margin is so slim that it's questionable whether either the milk business or the farm will be able to make it. W. J. is writing letters to Neil Bosworth in Elgin, a banker and his cousin-in-law, about procedures for declaring bankruptcy.

It is evening; the milkhouse has been a man short all day. Work is running behind. The butter is not yet made for tomorrow's delivery. Daddy goes out after supper to make it.

He's alone in the milkhouse. He fetches the cans of pasteurized sweet cream from the cooler, opens the churn, pours the liquid in, and seals the hatch. The churn is shaped like an oversize barrel, on its side. He throws the switch; the churn rotates. Inside, the cream sloshes rhythmically.

All the butter-making equipment and containers have been previously cleaned, but Daddy now runs the steam hose into a vat of water till the water is boiling, and sterilizes the large stainless-steel pan, the wooden butter paddles, and the two-pound crockery butter tubs. He sterilizes the enamel-topped table with the boiling water, and arranges the tubs upside down along the back of it, pyramid fashion.

He listens for the change in sound that heralds the coming of the butter. He knows the sound from years of churning by hand, as a boy, in the kitchen of the Big House. It wasn't a job he enjoyed. Then, he could tell not only by the change in sound but by the change in feel.

After a while he hears that the butter's come. He stops the churn, opens it, and lifts out chunk after chunk of the golden butter floating in the buttermilk. He drops them in the pan. When he has all the lumps he slaps them together with the paddles into a huge ball. He rinses the ball in cold water, works it more, rinses it again, salts it lightly, and works the salt into the butter. He sets the mound of butter on the table. Then he fills the tubs one by one, pressing the butter down so there are no air pockets, and smoothing the top of the butter flush with the crockery rim. Over every tub he lays a circle of sterile parchment paper. He then wipes off the tubs, carries them to the cooler, and stacks them, again in a pyramid, on the shelf beside the cottage cheese. They are ready for the morning.

He returns to the churn with a clean milk can and starts emptying the buttermilk into it. Several quarts will be bottled before dawn for the few people on the routes who swear by fresh buttermilk. The rest will go down the lane to the pigs.

As the buttermilk pours out he sees a dark lump flow by and hears it splosh into the can. He stops pouring, takes a dipper, and grapples in the can till he secures the lump. He pulls it out. There in the dipper, lying in a pool of buttermilk, is a sodden drowned mouse.

Daddy stares at it. He feels sick. He can't believe it. He stares at it some more. He feels sicker. He nudges it with his finger. The mouse turns a bit in the pale liquid. It is intact; its little legs and tail are all there. Its eyes are half-closed, its teeth show slightly. Daddy thinks he might vomit. He takes the mouse over to the boiler, opens the furnace door, and throws it in. He returns to the churn, finishes emptying the buttermilk, caps the can, and wheels it into the cooler. He stands looking at the neat row of butter tubs. He says a single French word. "*Merde.*"

He returns to the churn, muttering "*Merde, merde, merde,*" moving like a zombie. He rinses the churn and scrubs it with a stiff bristled brush. He rinses it again, puts in hot water and a caustic solution, then starts the machinery and the sloshing churn rotates for the prescribed number of minutes. He rinses out the solution, refills the churn with clean water, adds the steam hose until the water is scalding, rotates the churn some more, then empties the rinse water. He turns the churn upside down to drain, cool, and dry.

He walks back into the cooler and looks at the butter tubs. He bites the skin on the side of his thumb. His mind is numb. He finds himself counting the tubs over and over.

He knows what he must do. He thinks of the cost of the cream, the price the butter will bring. He feels sick. He knows what he must do.

He knows what he must do, but he doesn't do it. He walks past the lilac bushes to the Little House, speaks words to Mother that he himself doesn't hear, reads a story in the *Saturday Evening Post* whose words he doesn't see, and goes to bed. He has nightmares.

He wakes up with the rattle and bang of the milk trucks loading; he hears the murmur of the milkmen's voices. Beside him, Mother's breath is quiet and even.

His stomach is knotted. He knows what he should do. It is still not too late. He knows what his father would do.

He lies staring at the dark ceiling.

21   GRAMPA BANDAGES

Jackie is four or five when she nearly severs the tip of her left thumb with a hatchet. The accident happens at the woodpile, out beyond the back door of Grama's kitchen at the Big House. It's entirely Jackie's own fault. Someone has left a hatchet embedded in the chopping block. This tool, unlike the ax beside the block, is Jackie's size; she can wield it, and has done so before. This time she tries to chop in half a narrow ribbon of metal she's found on the ground, perhaps a strip peeled from a coffee can by its key. With her thumb she holds it firmly against the block and hacks at it. The metal resists; she hits at it again, misses, and strikes her thumb. The thumb is saved but heals a bit mishapen, and with a scar. It serves her forever in telling her lefts and rights.

Years later, when she's grown, she can't remember who tended to the injury. She remembers vividly when she smashed the same thumb a year earlier in the Little House window seat: the excruciating pain, and Mother sitting her on the kitchen counter and bathing the thumb in an enamel basin of cold water. But the accident with the hatchet happened behind the Big House, so it could well have been Grampa who took care of her then, who applied the bandage.

She has abiding memories of Grampa putting on bandages, in the years before Band-Aids. The recipient can be a sister, a brother, herself. It can even be Grampa himself, for he's adept at putting on his own bandages. First he has to get hurt. Jackie likes to be nearby when Grampa hurts himself, for he always cries, "Ouchy! Ouchy! Ouchy!" before he heads for the men's washroom behind the Big House kitchen.

If it is a grandchild injured, she or he cries "Ouchy! Ouchy!" too, then trails behind, dripping tears and blood, and stands while Grampa rummages on the shelf above the long sink. He lines up all his supplies—cotton, a roll of gauze, a roll of adhesive tape, scissors, and the big red-and-yellow tin of Watkins' Petro-Carbo Salve, its colors arching out alternately, like sun's rays, from the lid's center. Petro-Carbo is used on people and animals alike. It smells powerfully medicinal and cures everything. Grampa rips a long stretch of tape from the adhesive roll and with the scissors carefully splays one end an inch or two deep. He sticks the adhesive to the edge of the sink.

Now he is ready for his patient's wound. While the injured one winces and tries to be brave, he washes the dirt and blood off the gashed finger slowly and thoroughly with cold running water, until it bleeds freely again. He then swabs it with cotton, applying pressure to stop the flow. He takes the end of the gauze roll and swipes it into the strong-smelling brown salve, lays the salve against the wound, and begins to wind. Round and round the finger he goes, layering the gauze up and down and over, changing hands so that the ribbon doesn't twist. He does not stint on gauze. When the bandage has achieved rotund proportions, he snips it off and takes the adhesive strip. With this he binds the finger, making sure that the two tails are spread diagonally so that they hold the layers of gauze fast to each other. He then cuts a final strip of adhesive and uses this to anchor the bandage to the uninjured skin at its base. All the while he gives the work his unwavering attention, breathing heavily, not speaking, but sometimes accompanying the job with his familiar throat-drone of concentration. The one being bandaged, and those watching, give the work their equal undivided attention. When the bandage is finished, it's a work of art. Everyone knows there can be no better bandage; no germ would dare break through one of Grampa's bandages to start an infection.

"There you are, cubby," Grampa says.

The one bandaged sports a baton of impressive proportions and workmanship and walks off carefully, holding it with respect.

Grampa, like all good workmen, puts his materials back in their containers, replaces lids, and sets everything neatly back on the shelf, before returning to whatever job he had been doing when the crisis occurred.

There are so many cats on the farm that it's pointless to name them. The house cats, of course, have names from kittenhood—Mittens, Malty, the cat Buff at the Big House. But the barn cats go nameless. Except that Joan and Patsy and Jackie and Craig always name them anyway, for it's fun to name. A nothing becomes a something with a name. One cat can be distinguished from another. Usually they name the cats after some characteristic: Spotty, Snowy, Boots, White Whiskers, Spitfire. And the Spotties and Snowies come and go, like the rhythm of the seasons.

One season they name the cats differently. Mother has been involved in music club work. She's an officer in the National Federation of Music Clubs. She gets letters from all over the state and country. The return names in the upper left-hand corners of the envelopes intrigue Jackie and her siblings. Letters come regularly from the same names. There are Vi Kleinpell and Maude Blackstone. There are Hinda Honigman and Jennie Schrage and Julia Fuqua Ober and Sadie Orr Dunbar. There is Quaintance Eaton, whom Mother says the blind pianist Alec Templeton calls "Shouldaulda" because of the song "Should auld acquaintance be forgot." There's a music to the names of Mother's music club friends.

Two adorable kittens are born in the barn. The four decide to call them Sadie and Maudie. Mother laughs when she hears. Sadie is especially fun to cuddle, for there's a song to sing to her, to the tune of "The Bells of St. Mary." Mother wrote the words for everyone to sing at a national convention, when Sadie Orr Dunbar was being inaugurated as president.

Jackie rocks Sadie in her arms and sings:

We're singing to Sadie,
We're loving you, Sadie,
For you are the lady
We've come to adore.

So to you, beloved,
We pledge our devotion;
Each heart and hand at your command,
Dear SA-DIE ORR.

It sounds funny, of course, to refer to a little ball of fluff as a lady, but when Jackie sings, "For you are the kitten we've come to adore," it spoils the rhyme.

There are other kittens born in the barn, and they are named Jennie and Julia and Vi. There's one sleek black kitten with no white on her, not even a whisker, and to this one they give the name they like best of all, Fernwood Scrimshaw. They don't call this kitten by her first name only, but by her whole euphonious name. They summon her, "Here, Fernwood Scrimshaw! Here, Fernwood Scrimshaw!"

Fernwood Scrimshaw grows up into a long, lean black cat. She gets mange on her neck. Daddy brings her into the house and doctors her. He doesn't want all the barn cats to become mangy. He rubs Petro-Carbo salve on her neck every day for weeks. He cures Fernwood Scrimshaw but in the process she loses all her hair in the affected area. It never grows back. Now she's a long, lean black cat with a long, lean black neck with no hair on it. In the process of getting over the mange she becomes a house cat, but she retains her barn habits.

One Sunday afternoon Fernwood Scrimshaw walks past Jackie with a sparrow in her mouth. The sparrow is cheeping and fluttering. Jackie grabs for the cat. The cat runs. Jackie chases her around the lilac bushes and onto the lawn of the Little House. She screeches, "Fernwood! Fernwood Scrimshaw!

You drop that! Drop that right now, Fernwood Scrimshaw, you bad cat!"

The long, lean black cat with no hair on her black neck looks even longer and leaner as she streaks up the choke-cherry tree and sits on a branch, looking down. The sparrow's wings are like whiskers drooping down either side of her mouth.

Jackie gives up and turns around. There's a strange car beside the Little House. A woman with a startled expression is standing on the front step with Mother.

"Jackie," says Mother, "I'd like you to meet Mrs. Fernwood Scrimshaw."

23 THE SHOW

The mantle over the fireplace at the Little House is long and broad. On it sits the large wooden radio. Often, Craig and Jackie, Joan and Patsy, sit there, too. Today they are listening to the late-afternoon children's programs. First comes the Singing Lady; she's not very interesting. Then comes Jimmy Allen, the airplane pilot. Then comes Orphan Annie, who advertises Ovaltine, and then Jack Armstrong, who advertises Wheaties, and finally Captain Midnight; what he advertises keeps changing.

In the middle of Jack Armstrong, Grampa bursts through the door. His face is glowing.

"Hurry! Hurry! Hurry!" he shouts. "Hurry and come, cubbies, or we'll miss the show!"

The show! Everyone is electrified. Everyone tumbles off the mantle.

"What show, Grampa?" they cry, but Grampa isn't paying any attention to their clamors.

"Get your coats!" he shouts. "Hurry!"

They grab their coats and run. "Grampa's taking us to a show!" Patsy yells to Mother.

Grampa's car is outside the gate. They pile in; Grampa leaps behind the steering wheel, grinds the car into motion, and they're off.

"What show?" they ask among themselves. "The movie in town?" But Grampa never goes to movies. Grampa turns east on Colley Road, away from town. No, it can't be the movies. What, then?

Clinton is east. Clinton has no movie theater, but maybe a different sort of show is going on there. A visiting carnival? A magician? Or maybe something closer, at the Turtle Grange. What kind of show would be going on at the Turtle Grange? Sometimes there are suppers there, but a meal isn't a show.

Grampa speeds up Colley Road, not weaving from side to side as much as usual. He's intent on getting to the show and he's watching the road.

"We don't want it to be over!" he cries, his face creased with merriment. "We don't want to be late!"

Craig and Jackie, Joan and Patsy, are wild with curiosity.

Grampa turns at the side road to the Hill Farm. That cuts out Clinton and the Turtle Grange. The four cannot imagine.

"It's something at the Hill Farm!" Craig cries. But Grampa speeds past the Hill Farm house and barn.

"Then it's at the woods! There's something going on at the cabin!" Patsy says.

But Grampa pulls over to the side of the gravel road and stops short, before they get to the entrance to the woods.

"Here we are!" he cries. "Get out!" He gets out himself and hurries over the ditch. He holds the bob wire up for them to roll under. Then Joan holds the fence up for Grampa to roll under.

"Here we are!" Grampa repeats, his face all crinkled and his eyes twinkling. "And we're just in time!"

The four stand, bewildered. They are in an ordinary field. There is nothing there.

They look all around for the show. They are on the spot that is the highest in the township, maybe in the county. You can almost see Clinton eight miles east. You can almost see Janesville, fifteen miles north. You can see Rockford, eighteen miles south. To the west you can see Beloit, the Congregational Church steeple and the water towers rising out of the trees, five miles away over the broad Turtle Creek valley.

They look up at Grampa, puzzled. He's facing town. His weathered face is aglow, not only with Grampa's usual joy, but with the sunset that is lying in great banners and streamers of orange and gold and tinted clouds with purple edges. And then they know.

"The sunset!" cries Joan accusingly, and points. Grampa nods and laughs silently.

"I saw it was going to be a particularly glorious one this evening," he says. "Let's enjoy it together." He sits down in the alfalfa, glowing.

Jackie feels distinct disappointment. Craig complains loudly. Joan grumbles. Patsy says it's a cheat. They can say all this without hurting Grampa's feelings, for he can't hear the harsh words and he isn't looking at their faces. He's looking at the sunset.

They sit down beside Grampa and watch the sunset, too. There's nothing else to do.

There isn't a tree or shrub or building to impede their view. The sunset is spread out before them from Rockford to Janesville. It slowly moves and changes. It increases to greater brilliance; the sun itself comes from beneath the streaming gold-rimmed clouds, lies on Beloit like a red egg, then slowly starts sinking behind it.

The four cease chafing and are silent for a bit, and then gradually begin pointing out things another may have missed. This cloud bank, that color, this gradual change. Their voices are soft. A kind of timeless peace steals over Jackie.

The last sliver of sun disappears but the show is not yet over. The clouds reflect, change, slowly diminish in brilliance. The pink fades to mauve; the mauve and purple mute to deep blue; the sky darkens; at the north edge of Beloit the bridge lights over Turtle Creek wink on, making a pearl necklace on the dusky throat of night.

Grampa gets up, the four get up. The show is over. They give Grampa hugs, to let him know they've enjoyed it after all. They climb in the car with Grampa and he drives back home.

"Thank you for going to the show with me, cubbies," he says, letting them out beside the gate.

They go into the Little House. It smells of supper.

"What was the show?" Mother calls.

"Well, Grampa took us to that highest point, by the Hill Farm," says Joan.

"And we went into a field and there wasn't anything there, not even a bird's nest," Patsy continues.

"And then it gradually dawned on us," says Jackie.

"No," says Craig. "It sunsetted on us."

24 CHEZ NOUS

It's January 1936. The Little House is too little. It's been too little for quite a while. Mother and Daddy know it. Grampa sees it, too. "Now this house is getting too small," he says.

Mother and Daddy look around for a house to move into. They don't tell Joan and Patsy, Craig and Jackie. They find one on the near side of town, in the Todd School district. It's large, old, and built of stone. Mother looks at the kitchen. There's a thin layer of ice completely sheathing the interior stone walls. Mother decides against that house.

A few months later they locate another one, just on the edge of town. It's a mile from the farm, across Turtle Creek, and a block off Colley Road. It's a gracious, spacious mansion, well-insulated, two blocks from Todd School, and boasts a rarity, a swimming pool. They are well pleased. They visit the owner; they visit the bank. Then they take the four children for a drive. They stop in front of the Sherwood Drive house.

"Why are we stopping here?" asks Patsy.

"To see what you think of this house," Daddy says.

"It's elegant," says Joan.

"It's big," says Patsy.

"It's got a *swimming pool!*" Craig and Jackie whoop in unison, as they spot it together.

Mother says, "I'm glad you like it. We're planning to buy it."

There is a stunned silence. Then all four burst into tears.

Mother and Daddy are astounded. They question the four. All agree, positively. They don't want to be town kids. They want to be country kids. They don't want to leave the farm.

"Who cares about a swimming pool?" weeps Craig.

"What's wrong with the cow tank?" wails Jackie.

Mother and Daddy tell the bank they don't want the house after all. But the Little House is still too little. They look around some more.

"Why don't you think about the farm we're renting?" Grampa says.

Mother and Daddy consider the Snide farm, where Daddy and Grampa have been farming the land because Peter Snide was ill. Now Peter Snide has died, and the property is for sale. It's a mile and a half farther up Colley Road, midway between the dairy and the Hill Farm, the farm Grampa bought about the time Jackie was born. It's set back from the road forty rods at the end of a long lane. The buildings are on top of a hill that marks the edge of the broad Turtle Creek valley. Some of the land is eroded: beyond the barnyard and a field there's a scraggly hickory and oak woods, and in the middle of it is the start of a gaping gully that winds through fields down to the crick in the Catalpa Forest. The weathered frame house is ugly and shabby. It sticks up like a sore thumb. A few misshapen trees surround

"Sore Thumb" before remodeling.

Chez Nous after remodeling and landscaping.

it. The barn is sound, but needs paint. The farm is still in the consolidated school district; the same school cab would pick up the four children at the end of the lane and drive them to their same town schools.

Grampa stands before the house with them all, looking out over the valley to Beloit beyond. The land wears the green flush of spring. A gentle sun is sinking into a pale pink cloud over the far distant Congregational Church steeple. The dairy is in between, but the round barn is hidden by the pine trees of the Blodgett farm.

"It has a beautiful view," says Grampa. "Every night you'll have a sunset."

"We can use more land for the corn business," says Daddy. "The processing buildings should go up here. We can remodel those sheds."

"We'll have to remodel the house," says Mother.

"We'll call it 'Sore Thumb,'" says Daddy.

"We'll call it 'Chez Nous,'" says Mother.

"What does 'Chez Nous' mean?" Craig asks.

"Our Place," says Daddy. "Our Home."

The four stand content. This is their home. The dairy, with Grama and Grampa, is nearby, and the Hill Farm is up the road, beyond. It feels right, all of a piece. There is not a single tear.

25 GOD'S FOOTSTOOL

The worst thing Jackie ever sees with her own eyes, and which will haunt her to the end of her life, is the dog.

Town people are always leaving things in the country. They are always leaving garbage in the ditches, and old washing machines. They are always leaving animals: well animals, sick animals, baby animals—especially sick and baby animals. They drive out to the country and leave cats in the ditch, boxes of kittens in the ditch. They leave litters of puppies. They drive slow and open a door and shove a dog out of the car and drive away fast, while the dog runs and runs after them till it can't run anymore. They don't care if the dog or the kittens or the pups die, they just want to be rid of them. Those that care a little bit make the drop near a farm, so that the kittens might be found. So that the dog will show up whimpering and wagging its tail at the back door. The town people must figure, "Any farm can use another dog or cat. Cats and dogs are no trouble on a farm." Once, in the night, somebody had driven right into the dairy and closed a dog inside Grampa and Grama's screen porch. They'd found it there the next morning, curled up on the mat. It had thumped its tail tentatively, had looked up with beseeching eyes. But that isn't the dog that is the worst thing Jackie ever sees.

She's eight. The family has a dog, Jip. Jip is a mongrel, tan and white. They all love Jip. Jip likes to lie under Daddy's feet at night when he reads, and have Daddy use him for a footstool. Grampa and Grama have a dog, too. Bounce is a rat terrier. Maybe Grama loves Bounce, but Bounce is not an easy dog to love.

One day Jackie and Craig are up on the flat part of the milkhouse roof. They notice a dog out on the road. It's walking strangely, in a weaving, erratic pattern. Its head hangs down. It's far away but even at a distance Jackie can tell it's just skin and bones. It seems to have something very wrong with it. A car comes by; the dog is near the middle of the road but doesn't shy away. The car swerves around it. The dog stumbles on.

"Let's go see what's the matter with it," Craig says.

Jackie feels uneasy. "Let's find somebody," she says.

They climb off the roof and go down the stairs. They go into the office. The dairy office is a room off the end of the Big House. Daddy is at his desk, working the adding machine. Jackie watches his fingers skip around on the numbers till he comes to the end of a column, gives a large crank for the adding up, and pauses.

"Daddy," says Jackie, "there's a dog in the road and something's wrong with it."

"It acts like it can't see and can't hear," says Craig.

"It's terribly skinny," says Jackie.

Daddy puts down his pencil and pushes back his chair. "Let's go have a look," he says. "Somebody's probably dropped it and it's sick."

They go outside. Grampa is just coming along the sidewalk to the office. He's in a hurry about something. Daddy spells to him, and he looks to the road, where the dog is still stumbling. He joins them. The four of them approach the dog.

Daddy keeps up a quiet conversation with the animal as they get closer. The dog stops, stands still, as if he hears the gentle words, as if he's waiting.

"He at least can hear," whispers Craig.

"Stay back, cubbies," Grampa says to Craig and Jackie. "The poor beast may have rabies. He may bite."

They get closer yet.

"Jackie, Craig, get back to the house!" Daddy orders suddenly. But it's too late. Jackie stands rigid. She has seen, too. There's no danger from this dog. This dog won't bite. This dog can't bite. His jaws have been sewn together with a thick cord, from lip to lip, all around his mouth. He can't open his mouth to eat, to drink, to pant, to bark. The holes in the dog's lips are lacerated and loose where the cord goes through, but the cord is tight. The holes aren't bloody. The cord has been in too long.

Grampa and Daddy don't send them away. Daddy kneels by the dog and strokes its head. Grampa stands with one arm tight around Jackie's shoulder, with his other arm tight around Craig's. Jackie is shaking against Grampa's body.

"Poor, poor little fellow," Grampa says. "Poor, poor little cubbies." His voice is stranger than Jackie has ever heard it.

Daddy cradles the dog's head in his hands, gazes into his face. "Look," says Daddy without turning around. His voice is as strange as Grampa's. "You can both look. Look at his eyes." With one hand he spells over his shoulder to Grampa.

They come very close. They kneel and look into the dog's eyes. Jackie sees the dog's pupils. There is a hole right in the center of each one. It must have been made by a pin or a needle. She feels vomit rise in her throat, and swallows hard.

Grampa's grip on Jackie's shoulder is even tighter. "He's been blinded, too," Grampa says.

"There are some people that slow torture is not good enough for," says Daddy softly. "I'm sorry that you children had to see this. But since you did, I wanted you to see it all."

Craig is crying. "We can save him, can't we, Daddy? You'll cut the string, won't you?"

Daddy shakes his head. "He's too far gone. And he's so hurt he may bite if I do that. I'll take him and give him a drink; I think I can do it with a straw. And then I'll drive him up to Janesville. Dr. Knilans will put him out of his misery. He won't have much longer to suffer."

He stands up, spells to Grampa. The dog stands with his head down.

"I'll take the cubbies," Grampa says. Daddy leads the dog by the loose hair on his neck to the dairy. Grampa takes Jackie and Craig across the road, alongside the garden beside the currant bushes, into the orchard. They sit down under an apple tree, one on each side of Grampa. Grampa keeps his arms around them. Craig cries and cries against Grampa's side. Jackie's horror is too deep for tears. She keeps shaking convulsively, pressed close to Grampa's work shirt.

Grampa croons to them, making little comforting noises. After a while he starts talking. He tells them about kind people and cruel people. He says cruelty to animals is one of the worst kinds of cruelty because animals are dumb creatures and are at the mercy of their owners. He says cruel people are usually that way because others have been cruel to them.

"But you'll be the sort who will hate cruelty and help cruel people to learn to be kind," Grampa says. "Because you are treated kindly, and loved, and every day you see animals being treated kindly."

Grampa's talking helps. Craig gradually stops crying. Jackie gradually stops shaking. Grampa says, "Yes, ours is a special responsibility. Those of us who have been given so much have a responsibility to give much."

He gets up. He finds three windfalls in the grass. "Here," he says, giving them each an apple and biting into one himself. Together they go through the garden to the Big House, get sugar cookies from the cookie jar, and go to the milkhouse for chocolate milk. They sit on the old well lid outside the milkhouse to drink their milk.

Craig takes Grampa's pencil and paper out of his work shirt pocket and writes, "Are there dogs in heaven?"

Jackie waits anxiously for the answer.

Grampa ponders the paper for a long time. Then his eyes crinkle and he laughs silently.

"Do you know what I think?" Grampa says. "I think that dog will trot right up to God's throne. And then he'll curl up—just like Jip does with your daddy—and let God use him for a footstool."

26 HALLELUJAH, I'M A BUM

The hired men's sitting room was added to the Big House before Jackie was born. Mornings the room is usually empty, unless Grama is using her sewing machine, but it's always filled with sound. The radio is there, tuned loud to *Ma Perkins* or *Stella Dallas*, so that Grama can hear the next episode while she's in the kitchen making pies. The soap operas always have organ music that quavers and swells up between scenes, and sweeps to a massive vibrato at the end, nearly drowning out the announcer asking what will happen next; you must listen tomorrow. Grama always listens.

Very early mornings, when Jackie and Craig have stayed overnight at the Big House, they get dressed in the sitting room. Jolly Joe, who advertises Cocoa Wheat, conducts dressing races between the boys and the girls.

The men—Al Lasse, Ken Liddle, Ernie Capps, Russ Ullius—gather in the sitting room before dinner and again just before supper. They listen to twangy country music over WLS, the Prairie Farmer Station, and read the paper, or just talk and kid around.

Ernie Capps is a source of fascination to Joan, Patsy, Jackie, and Craig; he has a rotten ear. Its skin looks like the skin of a spoiled apple. Ernie sometimes spends the evening at the Little House, if Mother and Daddy go out to Bridge Club or Dinner Club and Eloise is busy. Then they tease him about his ear. He's good-natured about everything, even when Craig vomits all over the bed one night and Ernie has to change the sheets.

Before the Big House had a radio, the four children learn, the hired men listened to a Victrola. They find this out by discovering the Victrola. It's been in plain sight all along, but obscured by the upright piano at the end of the Big House parlor, the area that was the men's sitting room before the new one was built. It's a graceful cabinet on legs, with a lid; a scarf is on the lid. A broad copper tray containing rock crystals and twisted mineral formations always sits on the scarf. The four have fingered the minerals for years; it's all you can do with them. They're a boring display. That's why it takes so long to notice that under the tray and the scarf there's a lid, and under the lid there's something interesting.

A musical evening, posed to accompany W. J.'s 1915 Hoard's Dairyman *article about happy hired men. Ronald is on left, Trever at back, and the Victrola on right.*

The Victrola is a new and fascinating toy. They all like the picture inside the lid: a little white dog sitting with one ear cocked to the fluted morning-glory-shaped loudspeaker of an ancient instrument. Under the dog are the words "His Master's Voice." On the side of the cabinet is a crank they have to crank up to make the turntable go. They select a record from the many stored behind the two sets of double doors of the lower cabinet, position it carefully on the felt disk so that the metal knob comes through the center hole, push the switch to set it rotating, then carefully lower the needle arm onto the outside groove. They are enthralled with the old-fashioned records, and quickly establish their favorites. Of plain music, there's the "William Tell Overture," but with no "Hi-Ho, Silver, Away!" and a part the Lone Ranger never plays—"At Dawning," with birds twurbling, and then a storm that crackles and booms. "Stumbling" and "Four Little Blackberries" are played by bouncy, tinny orchestras. Of comic dialogues, they soon memorize a dozen routines of "Two Black Crows," and can mimic the words and intonations of the dialogues down to the "woo woo woos."

The songs, however, are their very favorites. Harry Lauder with his thick Scottish brogue sings plaintively about a wee hoose in the heather, and "I love to get up in the morning, but I'd much rather stay in bed." There's a long dirge about Willie the Weeper: "He had a job as a chimney sweeper. He had the dope habit and he had it bad. Listen while I tell ya 'bout a dream he had." The violin then weeps an interlude before the ballad relates Willie's encounter with Cleopatra while he's floating down the Nile on the back of a seagoing crocodile. The four bawl along with the singer. And they join in with the thin nasal voice of another weeping dreamer:

> Last night as I lay asleeping
> A wonderful dream came to me.
> I saw Uncle Sammy weeping
> For his children from over the sea.
> They had come to him friendless and starving,
> Whence from tyrants' oppression they fled,
> But now they abuse and revile him,
> Till at last, in just anger, he said:
>
> If you don't like your Uncle Sammy,
> Then go back to your home o'er the sea,
> To the land from where you came,
> Whatever be its name,
> But don't be ungrateful to me.
> If you don't like the stars in Old Glory,
> If you don't like the red, white and blue,

Then go BACK! like the CUR in the story,
DON'T BITE THE HAND THAT'S FEEDING YOU!

They give all the power of their strong lungs to the last lines of that chorus.

And then they find the hobo songs. Even though it's the Depression, Jackie has never seen a hobo come to the Big House or the Little House and ask for a handout. Men do come seeking work, and Grampa sometimes gives them a day or two's employment. And she sometimes sees men sitting on top of the boxcars when a train goes by in the back pasture, down by the crick. Daddy reports, at the Little House table, that he counted 110 cars on a freight train. "They were all empty, and at least one man was in every car. All going somewhere. All going nowhere, the poor devils."

She's familiar with hobos through the funny papers. They don't seem like poor devils, there. They cheerfully walk along railroad tracks with their shoe soles flapping and their possessions in a red bandana on the end of a stick. Or they sit around a campfire cooking Mulligan stew in a tin can. But the songs on the records are sad:

> I'm ridin' the rails on a train goin' West,
> Never again will I roam.
> I'm ridin' the rails on a train goin' West,
> Goin' back to my ho-ome.
>
> The conductor takes the tickets,
> The engineer runs the train,
> The porter puts them all to bed,
> While I stick out in the rai-ain . . .

and

> I'm a broken-down tramp without money,
> My clothes are all tattered and torn,
> And I am so weary and lonely

That I wish I had never been born.
All through this wide world have I wandered
A-looking for something to do
But whenever I ask for employment
They say I am only a tramp . . .

The Hallelujah song is the only jolly one:

Hallelujah! I'm a bum.
Hallelujah! Bum again.
Hallelujah, give us a handout
To revive us again!

Oh why don't you work
Like other men do?
How the heck can we work
When there's no work to do?

Hallelujah! I'm a bum . . .

The four lustily shout, "Hallelujah! Bum again!" along with the record. Suddenly Grama strides into the parlor. Her face is red. She shoulders through their circle, cuts off the singer in mid-Hallelu by flipping up the Victrola arm, snatches the record in her floury hands, and smashes it over her knee. Then she stamps back toward the kitchen. The four recoil in shock. Patsy and Jackie rush after her, horrified, in time to see her lift the stove lid and thrust the shards into the flames.

They hurry back to the Victrola and hide "I'm Ridin' the Rails" and "I'm a Broken-Down Tramp" from Grama's wrath. Then they hasten to the Little House.

Mother explains. The record Grama smashed is a parody of a hymn that goes "Hallelujah, thine the glory, Hallelujah, amen," and ends up asking the Lord to "revive us again." It's a song written during an earlier depression—

as are all the hobo records they've been listening to—to protest the plight of the jobless workers. But only "Hallelujah! I'm a Bum" is written to a hymn tune. Grama cherishes the old hymn. She thinks the record is making fun of religion. That's what upset her so.

"How come she never broke it before, then?" Patsy asks.

"She's probably never heard it before. The hired men who bought the record must have known better than to play it around her."

Patsy shakes her head. "We've never sung that hymn in church."

"It's not in the Methodist hymnal," Mother says.

Jackie is relieved about the whole affair. She thought Grama had it in for tramps.

There are two tramp stories connected with the farm that Jackie doesn't hear till she's older. One is that Uncle Trever, her very own uncle, known to everyone as Pat, rode the rails for a while after college, early in the Depression. "I didn't have any job or any money," Uncle Pat tells her, "and so I'd hop a freight to get anywhere, hunting for work. There were other men on the cars, too. The trainmen knew all about us, but they'd look the other way. Little raggedy children would be standing beside the tracks with their wagons, and they'd yell and stick out their tongues at us, and throw apples. Those of us riding on the gondola, the coal car, would throw down lumps of coal, and they'd scramble to pick them up. We knew that's what they wanted. And then we'd eat the apples. They knew that was what we wanted."

The other story concerns Ernie Capps. One day he goes down to the pasture to get the cows and returns without them, out of breath. He's green.

"There's a man—where our lane crosses the tracks," he manages to gasp to Daddy. "He's dead—he's been cut in half by a train."

Daddy phones the police. The police have just gotten word from the railroad that a hobo fell off a train back down the line and could be hurt. They were trying to figure out where to look. Now they know.

"Are you sure he's dead?" the policeman on the phone asks.

"Are you sure he's dead?" Daddy asks Ernie, covering the mouthpiece.

"Look, Ron," Ernie says. "Part of him is between the tracks, everything below his waist, and the rest of him is outside the tracks, everything above his waist, and the tracks are so clean you could eat off 'em, not a speck of blood, a thousand wheels must have gone over those rails after he got hit. Now you tell me if he's dead."

"He's dead," Daddy says back into the mouthpiece.

"Oh," says the policeman. "We'll call the funeral home, then. We'll be right out. Can you supply some gunnysacks? And we'll need to know where to go."

Daddy doesn't care for the whole scene. He looks green, too. "Go get some gunnysacks," he instructs Ernie, "and they'll probably want the farm truck. We'll have to wait on getting the cows."

Ernie goes off, looking sick. In ten minutes two policemen drive into the yard. They deplore the situation. They take the gunnysacks, and do want the farm truck, rather than risk their car over the rough terrain. They want someone to come with them to drive the truck and show the way.

"Go show them, Ernie," says Daddy.

Ernie gives Daddy a baleful look and climbs in the cab.

"Do you have gloves? You'll probably need gloves," one of the policemen says to Ernie, as he and his buddy climb in the other side.

While they are gone, the Rosman-Uehling-Kinzer hearse arrives, and the two attendants take out a gurney and stand it at the back doors of the vehicle. Then they wait around with Daddy. Nobody says much.

Before long the police return. Ernie does most of the work of transferring the two bulging gunnysacks to the gurney. Daddy stands by with his hands in his pockets.

The funeral home men drive away. The policemen thank Daddy and leave. Ernie has already made an abrupt departure, a spurt of gravel under his tires, to hose the blood from the truck.

After a while Daddy seeks him out in the barn and thanks him.

"I don't see why me," Ernie complains.

Daddy doesn't know if he's speaking to the universe—why was he, Ernie Capps, the unlucky one to be first on the scene?—or to Daddy personally—why should it be Ernie Capps and not Ron Dougan who had to scoop up the mess in the pasture? Daddy suspects he means the latter.

"I guess," he mumbles, "it's one of the advantages of being boss."

Daddy knows that had his father been on the farm at the time, instead of in town on some errand, he would have taken the gunnysacks and gone himself. Grampa takes pride in never asking a man to do anything he himself wouldn't do. Daddy follows this policy, too, and spends more time than any hired man inside the bottle washer, or at the bottom of cesspools.

Daddy tells Jackie, "It was not my finest hour."

Jackie thinks back to the record Grama broke. Uncle Pat did revive, and went on to get good jobs. But there was no reviving the poor hobo who fell off the train. She knows that none of the men on the boxcars, or in the funny papers, had anything to hallelujah about.

27 DEHORNING

It's 1938. Russel Ullius is herdsman. They are dehorning calves in the side barn.

If left to nature, a calf will develop horns from the two little hornbuds on her forehead. But Grampa sees to it that the calves get a caustic salve when these buds are just little buttons, about half an inch high. The salve usually stunts the horns' growth. Some horns continue to grow, and these have to be removed when the calf is about a year old, to prevent harm to other cattle and to people.

Dehorning is not a happy procedure. The animal is held still with a halter, her head immobilized in a dehorning frame and with a nose leader. The horns are snubbed with a special miter saw, and then a cauterizing, healing powder is put on the cut surfaces. It's painful to the calf, as painful as having a tooth pulled without anesthetic, for there are nerves in the horn, and an artery which is sometimes large and squirts. If the artery continues to bleed, a calf can bleed to death. The vet has to be called.

Today, all the calves go through the agony, bawling with fright and pain, and are finally freed. But one is a bleeder. The herdsman can't stop it; Grampa can't stop it. They call the vet. Dr. Knilans reaches into the horn with tweezers, pulls out the artery, and ties it.

The animal is weak from loss of blood. "Give her a shot of gin," Dr. Knilans tells Grampa. "It will do her good. You can give her some more later on tonight."

Grampa drives to town and buys a bottle of gin. It's probably the first and last time he buys gin in his life. He returns to the barn, and he and Russel administer a good dose. It seems to do the calf good. They give her another dose that night. By morning the calf seems normal and is released from sick bay. Grampa takes the bottle and puts it on a shelf in the men's washroom behind the kitchen, back by the shower with the Petro-Carbo salve and other medicines. It sits there, gathering dust.

A year later Russel has a terrible cold. He can't shake it. Every night he goes to put the cows to bed, just dragging his feet. One night he returns from the barn, looks up, and sees the bottle. He thinks, "What's good for that cow is good for me!" He takes a hefty swig and goes to bed. He sleeps like a baby.

The next morning he feels more energy on the job. That night when he returns from putting the cows to bed, he thinks again, "What's good for that cow is good for me!" He takes another shot, and enjoys another peaceful sleep. The third night he takes a final dose and considers himself cured. "It's good for calves, and it's done me good," he says to himself.

Only a day later Russel is in the back room washing up for supper when W. J. comes hurrying through. He glances up at the gin bottle and stops dead.

"Well!" he exclaims. "*That* thing's gone down!"

Russel doesn't confess, nor does Daddy Dougan probe. The bottle continues to sit on the shelf at its current level, gathering dust.

28 SEEDS

Jackie is in fourth grade. It's spring, and Todd School is having a seed sale. It will last a week. All the earnings will go toward new playground equipment. The other schools in town are having seed sales, too. The students are supposed to take an assortment and go around their neighborhoods, selling the bright-colored little packets of radishes and carrots, nasturtiums and marigolds. If they sell all their seeds the first afternoon, they can bring more home the next day. There will be a winner in every room, and the winner will have a choice of prizes.

Jackie knows which prize she wants—the shiny pedometer that hangs on your belt and registers how far you've walked with every step. But she doesn't expect to win. She has no neighborhood to go around. There are only Grama and Grampa in the Big House, and the Marstons down the road. However, both the dairy and the Marstons always have huge gardens; they must require an enormous quantity of seeds. And one night she might be allowed to stay overnight at Aunt Ida's and sell around the Strong School area, if the Strong School kids haven't gotten to everybody first. She signs out a hefty number of seed packets to take home.

In the schoolyard, waiting for the school cab, she finds that Craig and Patsy have seeds, too. They compare their selections and argue about who gets to ask Daddy and Grampa and Mr. Marston first. When the cab comes with the big kids from junior high and high school, Joan settles it. She writes the three names on slips of paper. Jackie draws Daddy.

At the farm, Patsy heads back down the road to Marstons, and Craig runs to the barn. Jackie hurries to the office. Daddy is there, on the phone. Ruby, the office girl, is using the adding machine. She stops and looks over the seed packets.

"Will you buy some?" Jackie asks.

"Well, I don't know," Ruby says doubtfully.

Jackie lays out the seed packages in neat rows in front of Daddy, on top of his papers. Carrots, squash, cucumber, lettuce. The desktop takes on a riotous appearance.

Daddy hangs up. He picks up a package of beet seed and rattles it. "What's all this? Who gave you these seeds?"

Jackie explains that she's selling them to him, to the farm. That the whole school is selling. That all the schools in town are selling. That she might be able to beat out the Strong School kids if Daddy will take her down to Aunt Ida's. And that there are prizes for the ones who sell the most.

At the end of her sales pitch she waits, hopeful.

Daddy shakes the beets again. "How do I know if these seeds are any good? Are they better than the seeds I buy at Cox's?"

Jackie is puzzled. "Aren't all seeds alike?"

"No," says Daddy. "So unless you can convince me that these seeds are superior to the ones I get from my regular supplier, I should stick with him, shouldn't I?"

"They wouldn't have given us seeds that aren't good," Jackie protests.

"Maybe not," says Daddy, "but where's the proof? I've never heard of this seed company."

"But it's for a good cause! And they're only ten cents a packet."

Daddy shuffles the packets. "There's another reason I shouldn't buy your seeds," he says. "Suppose we were selling seeds instead of milk. Suppose our living depended on how many seeds we sold. Suppose our milkmen were seedmen, selling seeds every day on the streets of Beloit, and I paid them to do that, and paid for gas, and advertising, and all sorts of other expenses. Then suppose that one day every school in town gave every kid a hundred packages of seeds to sell, and suddenly every house in town is besieged not once but dozens of times, by appealing little children with pleading faces.

Selling seeds for less than we can sell them, and for a good cause besides. What chance would our ugly old seedmen have to make any sales?"

"Not much," Jackie admits.

"You see," says Daddy, "the market has suddenly been glutted with salesmen. Our five or six seedmen can't compete with five thousand seedkids. Especially since those seedkids aren't earning any salary. They're donating their services absolutely free!"

"But the school gets the money!"

"Not all of it," says Daddy. "The company that supplies the seeds takes a cut first; after that, the schools get what's left. That can be quite a lot, for as you see, the company doesn't have to pay for salesmen, and a lot of other expenses a local business has to pay for. They can give the schools a good deal."

Jackie knows when she's beaten. She stands silent.

"It's bad for the local seed companies," Daddy says, "and that's bad for the community. This sale won't drive Cox's out of business, but it'll hurt them. And if such a sale were to close a seed company, then next year there'd be no seed company here, and either the people would have to say to the schools, 'You better keep on selling seeds, now you've taken over,' or go out of town for their seeds, which adds the cost of the trip. Or order them all from the seed catalogues. I ought to go talk to the school superintendent, for getting kids to do this. Give him an economics lesson."

Jackie shifts on her feet. She wishes she'd never brought the seeds home. She starts gathering up the accusing rows. She knows Mr. Cox, and Mr. Cox's seed store. She wouldn't want to drive him out of business.

"Go look at the Aims on the silo," Daddy says, helping her. "Number 4 in particular." The phone rings. He puts his hand on the receiver, but before lifting it adds, "Besides, Mr. Cox takes our milk. It's a matter of loyalty. Now *allez brouter l'herbe.*"

Jackie knows this mild dismissal; it's French for "now scram," or, literally, "go graze somewhere else." She starts for the door. It's all very clear. She feels chagrined that she didn't realize it herself. She doesn't need to go look at the silo; she knows that number 4 is "A Stable Market." It's obvious that five thousand seed salesmen will create an unstable market. And that if Mr. Cox loses a lot of money, he might not be able to buy milk. And if a lot of people, for whatever reason, aren't able to buy milk . . .

"Do you have any zinnias in that collection?" Ruby asks. "I'd buy a package of zinnias. I always like a few zinnias."

Jackie ruffles through the heap and finds golden zinnias. Ruby gives her a dime. "Don't tell your dad," she says, winking.

Outside, Jackie sees Patsy coming back down the road. She can tell by her shoulders that she hasn't had any success. Craig straggles up from the barn, dragging his seed bag behind him.

"Did Grampa buy any?" Jackie calls.

"No," says Craig. "He says we buy all our seeds from Cox's."

29 AN EDUCATED MAN

Grampa's sister, Aunt Della, lives in Mason City, Iowa. Every summer she drives to Beloit to visit her brother Wesson, her sisters Lillian and Ida, and Ida's daughter Hazel. She usually stays at Aunt Ida's on Bushnell Street, for the farm is busy and full. Hazel, who teaches school, lives with her mother. Lillian lives there, too. Della adores her brother, as do Ida and Lillian, but the three sisters don't get along.

Ron is privy to these visits from boyhood on. "It's bad enough to have Ida and Lillian quarreling all day long," he says, "but when you add Della to the mix, it's *three* independent old ladies bickering from dawn to dusk! There's nothing they can't disagree on."

When Aunt Della's eyes get too bad for her to drive herself, she has her eldest Kirk granddaughter drive her. At the farm Dorothy has many talks with her great-uncle Wesson, she writing, he speaking.

Grampa and Grama sometimes drive to Mason City to visit Della. When Jackie is ten, they take her along. They stop at Galena on the way, and Jackie is struck by the houses clinging to steep hillsides, by the gloominess of President Grant's home and the ponderousness of its Victorian furniture.

They stay overnight at an old white-frame hotel on the bluffs of the Mississippi. Jackie is in the midst of writing a long continued story called "The Cloudlanders," which *The Galesburg Post* of Galesburg, Illinois, is publishing. Every week they run an installment. Just before she leaves on the trip the newspaper arrives. She opens it to see her story, but instead finds a notice on the front page: "Attention, Jackie Dougan! Authors must not let their publishers get ahead of them. Send in the next installment pronto!"

Jackie sits up at the little hotel-room desk with its gooseneck lamp throwing a pool of light on the hotel stationery. While Grampa and Grama go to bed, she writes out her next installment.

In Mason City she gets to know the rest of her Kirk second cousins. Polly is the youngest, in ninth grade. Jackie goes to school with her, and pours over her Latin book. She is able to figure out the first several lessons. She decides she'll take Latin when she's in ninth grade. Back at the Kirk house she says, "Latin really makes you think!"

Her cousin Dorothy says to her, "When I was in Wisconsin, Uncle Wesson said something to me about thinking. I wrote it down in my diary."

"What?" Jackie asks. "Can I read it?"

"I remember it," Dorothy says. "We were talking about my future, and where I wanted to go to college, and what I thought about life, things like that. And he asked me if I knew what an educated man was. I said, 'No, I don't.' He said, 'An educated man is one who has taught his mind to think. And his hand to act. And his heart to feel.'"

Jackie, too, thinks that is worth writing down. It's a description of Grampa himself.

On the wall of the Little House used to hang a painting of a little girl in a yellow dress, sitting and looking sideways. It had the title printed under it, "The Age of Innocence." Jackie used to scorn that picture, that little girl. Innocent! An age of innocence! Nobody was innocent, except maybe babies. That girl was probably just as guilty as anybody else, in spite of the yellow dress. And a whole *age* of innocence? As if you're good up to a certain age, and then get naughty?

Patsy had been younger than that girl when she'd leaned over and bitten Jackie on the arm, hard, for no reason at all, when they'd been sitting together on the stairs. Craig had been younger than that little girl when he'd suddenly pushed Jackie off the flat roof of the milkhouse, when they'd been standing together up there. Luckily she'd fallen in the middle of a lilac bush and not onto the ground, though even then she'd been badly scratched. Certainly Craig and Patsy weren't innocent even at an early age!

It's not until Jackie is nearly eleven that she realizes what that picture is talking about. It's March at Chez Nous; it's nippy and blowy outside. The others stay in the house after they walk up the lane from school, but Jackie gets into her jeans and goes out to the barn. The barn at Chez Nous doesn't have a rhythm like the round barn, for no milking cows are kept here. Its rhythm is an erratic one, when somebody roars up in the farm truck to feed the heifers and young cows. The barn is not cleaned daily; there are stanchions, but the stock aren't closed into them. They wander loose in the barn's midsection. Although Jackie likes the barn as a place, usually no work of interest is going on in it. But today she's noticed that a strange car is parked out by the barn.

The barn door is open. She goes in.

A man she doesn't know is kneeling on the cement floor. He has newspapers spread out and a little suitcase is open on the newspapers. The equipment looks like a vet's: a container of small bottles, a glass tube, full buckets of antiseptic-smelling water. She looks around. Sure enough, a lone cow is standing in a box stall.

The man looks up and smiles. "Hello."

"Hello," says Jackie. "What are you doing? Are you a new vet?"

"No," says the man. "I'm the artificial inseminator. I'm about to inseminate a cow. My name is Amos."

Jackie has never heard the term "inseminator" before. It sounds interesting. "My name is Jackie," she says. "Do you mind if I watch?"

"Not at all," says the man. "Are you Ron Dougan's daughter?"

"Yes," says Jackie. "What does an inseminator do?"

Amos indicates the little case of bottles on the floor. "There's semen in those bottles. Bull semen."

That's another word Jackie doesn't know. "Semen?"

The man sits back on his heels. "I'll explain everything as I go along," he says. "First, I'm here because that cow is ready to have her first calf."

Jackie looks critically at the cow. She is barely more than a heifer. "She doesn't look fat enough," she says dubiously.

Amos laughs. "She's not freshened yet. She's only ready to conceive a calf, for a calf to start growing in her. Her body is ready; she's in heat."

"Oh," says Jackie. "What's 'heat'?"

"Look at her vulva," says Amos. "There, under her anus. You'll see blood."

Jackie looks. She's never heard the names of cow parts before, even though she's often watched their functioning. But from the urine slit under the puckered BM hole issues a thin thread of blood. It trails down the cow's rear end. She realizes she's seen blood on cows before, all her life; usually at least one cow in the round barn has blood, and there is sometimes blood in the gutter, or in the barnyard, where the ooze from the manure pile has a bloody tint. It was just something that happened to cows some of the time, part of the way things were in the round barn. Now she's surprised that she never wondered why.

Amos goes on. "When we see the blood, we know the cow's body is ready to receive the bull, and have a calf. Up until recently we'd take her to the bull then, or bring him to her, and he'd inseminate her. Breed her."

"Oh," says Jackie. "How?"

"You know that big sac that hangs between a bull's hind legs? The scrotum?"

Jackie nods.

"It's got two testicles in it, big as apples, and they produce semen. Semen means seed. There are millions of sperm in every drop of seminal fluid. And it takes only one sperm to combine with one ovum of a cow—one egg—"

"Cows have *eggs*?"

"Well, yes," says Amos. He sits down on the barn floor. Jackie sits down, too. It's becoming a long and complicated conversation. "But they don't lay them, like hens. The eggs are almost microscopic. And when a sperm joins with one, deep inside the cow, then it's a fertilized egg, and it plants itself in the cow's uterus—her womb—and grows into a calf. And when the calf is ready, it gets born."

"Oh." Jackie ponders. "But how does the bull get his sperm *to* the egg?"

"He mounts her from behind, and thrusts his penis into her. . . . You know what a penis is?"

Jackie nods. She *does* know that. She's seen Craig and Daddy, and male dogs and bulls and horses. They all pee with their penises. And she's seen naked statues at the Art Hall, down at the college, throwing discuses and things, although most of them wear a leaf.

"Well, the bull shoots his semen in with his penis. It's called an ejaculation."

Jackie is astounded. More than urine comes out of penises! Cows have eggs! The world is filled with marvels.

"How does he know to do it? Mount the cow?"

"The smell of the cow when she's in heat. It makes him want to."

"Oh."

The artificial inseminator, Amos Grundahl, prepares to service a cow.

Jackie watches. Amos takes out a long rubber glove, talcs his arm, and pulls the glove on up to his shoulder. He soaps the glove. Then he takes a long glass tube and draws semen from the bottle into the tube. The tube has a plunger; it's a syringe. The semen is tea-colored.

"Now open the stall for me," he instructs.

Jackie does. Amos stands at the rear of the cow and crowds her close to the side of the stall. "First I'm going to put my arm down her anus," Amos says.

He works his fingers around the cow's BM hole, and then pushes his hand

and arm in. The cow startles, her eyes bug, she tries to lunge. Jackie recoils; she'd hate it, too, if she were a cow! Amos leans against the cow and presses her against the edge of the stall, forcing her to stand still. His arm is in the cow's anus almost up to his shoulder. She stands, eyes bulged, back arched.

"I did that so my fingers can guide the tube to the proper place," Amos explains. "The intestinal wall is right next to the wall of the vagina. I can feel the tube through the membranes and position it right at the mouth of the uterus."

He takes the glass tube and threads it into the cow's vulva. He works it gently in, like a long rectal thermometer, till the whole length of it is inside the cow. Then he presses the plunger, pulls out the empty tube, and pulls out his sheathed arm. There is manure in patches on the glove. He sets the tube in one bucket, rinses off the manure with cloth from the other, then peels off the dripping glove, inside out, and lays it on the newspaper.

"There," says Amos. "What else do you want to know about this whole process?"

"Now she'll have a calf?" Jackie asks.

"Well, a hundred million sperm are going to try their darndest. But sometimes she doesn't settle—doesn't conceive—the first time, and then I have to come back. That'll be the next time she comes in heat—about a month. If she conceives, she won't come in heat again till some time after the calf is born."

He starts putting away his equipment.

"But why?" Jackie asks. "Why do you bother? We have a bull. Isn't it easier with a bull?"

Amos pauses. "This is all pretty new," he says. "Our Rock County Breeder's Co-operative is only the second one in the whole country. We began a couple of months after one in New Jersey did. But it's going to revolutionize cattle breeding all over the world. Because now every little scrub cow in every poor farmer's barn, giving only a little bit of milk, can have a calf from one of the very best bulls in the country. And because of that bull's superior traits passed on to her, the daughter will give more milk than her dam. Her calf will be a better milker yet, better than her mother. The daughters down the generations will keep on getting better and better. Milk production, or whatever we're breeding for, will go up and up. It's awfully exciting. Your dad knows all about it; he's on the board that hired me. Ask him for more details."

"I will," promises Jackie. She finds it exciting, too. She hurries into the kitchen. Mother is peeling potatoes.

"I found out just now how calves get born," Jackie says. "It takes an egg and a sperm, and the bull puts the sperm in the cow with his penis, except Amos will do it now with a glass tube. He's the artificial inseminator. All our calves will have prize bull fathers, and get to be better and better milkers!"

"I thought you knew all about that," Mother says, astonished.

"How could I? This is the first time I ever saw Amos here."

"No, about how calves or rabbits or babies or anything is made. The egg and the sperm. Where *you* came from. Haven't you read the book?"

"What book?"

Mother lays down her potato and goes and gets the copy of *Growing Up* out of a bookcase. Jackie has seen the book all her life. It's by some doctor. She's even opened it a few times, but never read beyond the second page. You can tell immediately that the writing isn't a story, and the pictures are in brown and white. She's never read a good book yet where the pictures are in brown and white. And Joan and Patsy never once recommended she read it, or said that there was anything interesting in it about eggs and sperms.

"I never read it," says Jackie. "It looked boring."

"And after all the pets we've had?" Mother is incredulous. "Well, I thought we'd talked. I guess we better have a talk now."

"We don't need to. Amos told me everything."

"Everything? About people as well as cows? Did he tell you about menstruation?"

"*What?*"

"Then he didn't tell you. It's bleeding every month."

"Yes, he did tell me. That's when the cow's in heat." An apprehension grips her. "But people—they don't come in heat, do they?"

"No."

"Oh, good," says Jackie, relieved. She hadn't liked the idea of that thin thread of blood.

But then Mother tells her about menstruation. It seems to be the same as heat, for there is bleeding, and more than a thin thread, but just the opposite, because the menstrual period is the time when you can't conceive a baby. Menstruation is the blood that builds up in the uterus to feed the baby, Mother tells her. Then when no fertile egg comes, it sloughs off. All the rest of the time you can have a baby, if the sperm comes. Your body is ready and waiting.

Jackie is appalled. She learns Joan has already menstruated; she's just fourteen. Imagine! Joan could have a baby. Patsy has not yet begun, at twelve and a half. She, Jackie, will begin when she's old enough. Maybe twelve. More likely thirteen or fourteen. Sometimes even older. There are special things to wear, absorbent cotton pads that you throw away. Nobody needs to know. You can do almost everything normally, except go swimming. Some people say it's your sick time, but it isn't at all. There's nothing sick about it. It's perfectly normal.

Jackie feels ill already. She starts to turn off her mind.

"It's a nuisance," says Mother, picking up her half-peeled potato, "but it's only once a month, and it happens to all of us women, and if it didn't, we couldn't have babies. So when you're a little older I'll have Kotex for you, and a belt in your drawer. And you'll know it's perfectly normal, nothing to be alarmed about. Not like Grama."

"Grama?" Jackie turns her ears on again. "What about Grama?"

"Well, you know she was a tenth child."

Jackie nods.

"And her next sister up, Kate, was a year older than she was."

Jackie nods.

"Well, Grama told me that her mother never told her anything. And when she was twelve, she started to bleed. She was frightened to death. She hid it for three days. She stuffed her underdrawers with newspaper, and got more and more terrified when the bleeding didn't quit. She was sure she was dying. Finally, she couldn't stand it any longer and she told her mother. Your great-grandmother. And all her mother said was, 'You beat Kate.'"

"*What*?" cries Jackie. "That's *all*?"

"'You beat Kate,'" repeats Mother. "No explanations, no nothing. Oh, she fixed her up properly, with special rags. Women had to use rags then, and wash them out—so did I, at the start."

Jackie feels a rush of pity for her poor grandma as a little girl, without any Amos to tell her anything, without Mother. For three whole days thinking she was dying. She decides, since it's inevitable, she's glad Mother has told her. It would be horrible to have all that blood come as a surprise.

She ventures one more comment. "But what the bull does. It must be awful for the cow."

Mother laughs. "The cow likes it."

"*Really*? She didn't like what Amos did. She tried to get away."

"Amos isn't a bull. If cows didn't like it, and bulls didn't like it, there wouldn't be any calves. Or puppies. Or kittens. Or bear cubs. Or babies. It's really very pleasant. Nature's made it that way."

"*Really*?" says Jackie.

"Really," says Mother.

Jackie grabs a handful of cookies and goes outside. She calls the dog and heads down toward the gully. She doesn't see the weeds, the leaves. She's lost in thought. Her mind is boggled, reeling with new information. She realizes she actually knew a lot of it before, that every animal had to have a mother and a father, for instance, but she just never put it all together. She could have, but she didn't. Now it all fits in place. The girl in the yellow dress, *that's* what she's innocent about. Not what she doesn't *do,* but what she doesn't *know.* And the Virgin Mary. She'd never been bred till God bred her with Jesus, and that didn't count. And Mother and Daddy . . . imagine! Daddy must have done to Mother what the bull does to the cow!

She can't picture it, she's reluctant even to think about it, yet her mind insists. He must have done it four times, to breed her and Joan and Patsy and Craig. Grampa only had to do it three times. And . . . she tries to keep her mind from making the leap, but it's already over the gully . . . herself, someday. It's unimaginable! She couldn't let any boy—any man—how embarrassing! How . . . yet . . . yet . . . in order to get married, have babies . . . She kicks at the tawny grass in the hickory woods. She mustn't grow up, then there will be no problem! But she can't help growing up. It's like menstruation. It's inevitable.

But, still . . . now . . . with science thinking up all these things, couldn't it work with people? Her husband could have a glass tube! She tries to push the thought of people out of her mind, she tries to stick to cows. But people keep crowding in.

She stands among the hickory trees on the edge of the gully. Lassie sits down; she pats her. The hillside across the gully is so dark she can scarcely see the beehives. She chews on her last cookie thoughtfully.

A star winks out. She looks at it, and draws a deep sigh. There's really nothing at all that can be done. But why is she worrying? Babies, they're a long, long time away yet. And menstruation—that's a long time away, too. At least two years. Maybe longer. A comfortable distance. She doesn't have to be anxious about that yet, either. Except. Except for . . .

She reflects on her sister. What if Patsy is slow to start, and she herself is early? What if she beats Patsy, like Grama did Kate? Now wouldn't *that* be a big fat gyp!

She fixes a vengeful eye on the pinprick of light in the pale sky, and starts in on the familiar chant. She has challenge in her voice. "Star light, star bright, first star I've seen tonight . . . "

31 4-H PROJECT

It's January 1939. Jackie is eleven and Craig just ten. They've joined 4-H. They've always been aware of 4-H, aware that Grampa was one of the founders of Turtle's 4-H club, and that the fair's full name is the Rock County 4-H Fair. 4-H kids take their cows and pigs and sheep to the long barns and stay overnight in sleeping bags on wooden shelves up above their animals. They busy themselves all day trimming hooves and polishing horns and scrubbing pigskin. They hang the animals' blue and red and green ribbons on the uprights of their pens. Jackie has envied them.

Joan and Patsy have never been interested in 4-H; their attention is turned toward violin and other music activities. Jackie takes violin lessons, too, but being third fiddle isn't much fun. Her sisters tell her what to do.

4-H is different. She and Craig are on their own. Meetings are held at the Turtle Town Hall once a month in the evening. Daddy drops them off at their first session. They sign their names on an attendance sheet, and a pleasant woman whom they've seen before but whose name they don't know asks them what their projects are going to be. They say they are going to raise calves. She says, "Of course," and "How are your grandpa and grandma?" She gives them each a booklet. The booklets have soft black covers with a green cloverleaf that says "4-H."

On the stage, a big banner is hung with the four-leaf clover emblem. Each leaf stands for an H, and the H's stand for Head, Heart, Hands, and Health. Country kids are clustered in rows of wooden folding chairs. They talk and laugh and call back and forth. Jackie and Craig are country kids, too, but there's a difference. They go to town school, and except for Billy Umland who rides in the school cab with them, they scarcely know these kids. Billy, though, seems to know everybody and is throwing wadded notebook-paper balls back and forth with another boy. Jackie sits beside Craig and feels strange, like a not-quite-country kid. She has sometimes felt this way in town groups, too, only there it's the reverse. She's a not-quite-town kid.

The business meeting is brief, followed by a humorous lesson on parliamentary procedure, and then someone plays a musical saw. After that there are cookies and cocoa and everybody goes home.

Grampa brings two weaned heifer calves up to Chez Nous, and gives Jackie and Craig box stalls in the barn for them. They are grade calves, not purebred. He brings a sack of balanced calf ration and puts it in the feed and harness room to the left of the barn doors. He takes the project books they got at the 4-H meeting and writes on the finance page, in a column called "debit," the cost of the calves—each fifteen dollars. Jackie is shocked. What a huge sum! She doesn't have fifteen dollars and doesn't know when she ever will. Her allowance is only fifty cents. But Grampa tells them that they don't need to pay him until they sell their calves, and then they can pay him out of the profit. He also writes in the cost of the feed. He says they must feed their calves twice daily, and keep them and the stalls clean. If someone else has to care for the calves, they must pay that person wages. Jackie doesn't really understand all this finance, but is relieved that no one expects any money right now. It's never occurred to her that calves cost money. After all, they just come from cows. And how would you go about selling one? She sticks the booklet somewhere. She doesn't want to be reminded of her debit to Grampa.

Morning and night Jackie and Craig tend their calves. Jackie names hers Princess, and Craig's is Perry. Craig has read somewhere that if you lift your calf every day your strength will increase as the calf's weight increases. At first he lifts Perry up every day, but as the calf gets bigger he begins to skip days, and finally he quits altogether. It's not worth it, he says.

Down in the barn Jackie fills Princess's water bucket and feeds her her ration. She climbs the ladder to the loft and pitches hay down the chute. She's used to doing all this from tending her goat, who's in a box stall across the aisle from the calves. Princess likes to be rubbed where her horns will be,

and is mildly friendly, but a calf personality isn't as interesting, Jackie decides, as a goat personality. Calves aren't always trying to do something, like get out of their pens and jump places they're not supposed to. Sometimes at night, alone in the barn, Jackie perches on the top board of Princess's pen and sings to her. She practices her new voice, putting the grown-up quaver in it. She doesn't dare sing that way around the family, especially since she and Craig jeer at Joan for the vibrato in her singing voice. Jackie likes the quiet barn, with the calves, her goat, and two horses who stamp and whuff a bit in their stalls at the end of the aisle. There are about twenty cows in the barn, too, still heifers really, for they aren't milking yet, but they're in the back section that's closed off from the boxes and horse stalls. Jackie sometimes opens the door into that section, turns on the light, and contemplates the cows a while. They lie quietly in the straw and manure, close together to keep warm. Some chew cuds. The only sounds are their breathing and chewing.

Winter passes; spring passes. Jackie and Craig go to the 4-H meetings every month. They don't get to know anyone much better, even though there are games.

Summer comes, and the family except for Daddy moves up to a small cottage on Pleasant Lake, thirty miles away. They've done this a number of summers: Mother feels it's safer for them there than out about the farm with all the machinery and animals and heightened activity. The goat comes along but the calves stay behind. A hired man puts them in with the heifers and takes care of all the stock at once.

Daddy takes his meals at the Big House with Grama and Grampa and the hired men while the family is gone. He comes up to the lake midweek for overnight, and fishes, and comes for Saturdays and Sundays. One Wednesday he says, "I'll take Jackie and Craig back with me this weekend so they can get their calves ready for the fair."

The fair! Jackie's stomach lurches. She'd forgotten all about the fair, she'd even forgotten all about her calf! Guilt smothers down over her head like a gunnysack.

"How do I get my calf ready?" she asks anxiously. "How many days do we stay there? Will we sleep above the pens in sleeping bags?"

"No," says Daddy. "We'll take the calves up the day you show them. You'll get them all cleaned up, and then take them in the show ring and walk in a circle, and the judges decide which ones get the first prizes, and second, and so on."

"Walk in a circle?"

"You've seen it. With all the other kids and their calves. You'll have a halter and a lead. Like your project leader's shown you."

Jackie had forgotten she'd seen it at the fair. At the time, she hadn't specifically noticed. And what project leader? Now she feels not only guilt, but confusion and dread.

She and Craig ride the thirty miles home with Daddy that weekend. Red Richardson, the hired man who's been tending the stock at Chez Nous, separates Princess and Perry from the older heifers and puts them back in their box stalls. Both calves have grown astonishingly; they're almost as big as their pasturemates. They act scaredy. They don't seem to know Jackie and Craig. They don't like halters on their heads.

Jackie snaps the lead onto the metal ring on the strap that goes under Princess's chin. She tries to lead her from the barn up to the lawn. Princess doesn't want to go. She pulls back. She digs in her hooves and acts like a goat.

"She's not used to it. You have to train her," says Red Richardson. "Every day for half an hour you make her walk behind you, and don't let her get away with anything, and make her stop when you stop and go when you go, and after a while she'll follow right at your heels, like a dog, just as good as gold."

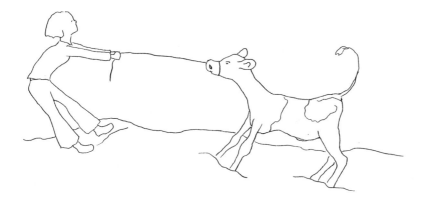

Drawn by Jackie Dougan when she was thirteen.

Jackie can't wait for after a while. She has just two days to train her calf to walk in a ring with other calves.

Craig isn't having any trouble with his calf. After a few initial bucks and pulls, docile Perry walks behind him wherever he goes.

All day Jackie practices with Princess. The animal shows little progress. She wants to go where she wants to go. She wants to stop and crop grass. She wants to head for the cornfield, and Jackie hardly has the strength to keep from being dragged behind. It's terribly frustrating, yet Jackie knows it isn't Princess's fault. She should have been being trained ever since she had her. She shouldn't have been abandoned all summer.

She works with her calf at half-hour intervals before she gives up, snarling, and either collapses, or reads, or stands under the hose to gather strength to try again. She envies Craig, who now and then takes Perry for an amble.

They tie the animals up and brush them. Their coats are scruffy. They've been running wild in the pasture all summer, among the burrs and velvet weed, and sometimes lying in cow pies. Lots of brushing and currying is needed, and on some stubborn places even soap and water. Jackie's guilt and dread are now joined by despair. These form a heavy thundercloud in her belly, with every now and then, around the edges, little heat-lightning flashes of panic.

Judging day comes. The two ride with Grampa in the cab of the farm truck up to Janesville. The calves ride in back. They're given a pen in one of the long barns. Jackie and Craig have never before seen the kids on either side of them; a sign on their pens say they're from the Lima Township 4-H Club. They have sleeping bags on the platforms overhead, and thermos jugs, and stacks of comic books. They're busy brushing their calves. Jackie and Craig brush Princess and Perry, and then climb up on their bare platform and swing their legs. They study the program that says the calf judging is at three o'clock. They listen to the loudspeaker that every so often calls out which group should now be getting ready to go in the ring.

By quarter to three everyone has a calf on a lead and is moving it toward the show-ring building. Jackie and Craig fall in line. Both calves step along tranquilly. Jackie feels a twinge of hope. Inside the building there's a wide sawdust area surrounded by bleachers. A scattering of people are in the bleachers. Jackie knows that Grampa is up there. He's not a judge today, like he often is, but she doesn't seek his face. She's too busy trying to keep Princess in line. Sheep judging is just finishing up; six kids and their sheep are facing the judges' stand. The sheep behave while the judges walk around them, looking over and under and feeling their fleeces. Princess gets tired of standing in line, turns around and starts to leave the building. Jackie jerks her back in place. Out of the corner of her eye she can see that Craig is having no trouble with Perry. She avoids looking for Grampa.

Now the sheep leave the ring. Different judges come to the stand and the grade calf line files in. For about a third of the circle Princess trots at Jackie's heels. Suddenly she surges ahead; Jackie wrestles her into place. Then

Princess slows down; Jackie pulls hard on the lead but this makes the calf buck and go slower. A gap forms in the line ahead of Jackie. She manages to make Princess speed up. Now they're in front of the judges' stand. Princess veers to the left. Jackie pulls; Princess suddenly crowds close and stamps on her toe. Jackie yips, pushes Princess off, drops the lead and grabs at her sneaker. Princess trots away. Jackie snatches at the trailing end of the rope, falls as she grabs it, stumbles up and pulls the animal back into line. People laugh. Jackie's face flames; her toe pulses.

They start around the circle a second time. It's hot in the ring; Jackie's face is all sweaty. Princess accompanies her erratically. Then they halt and the judges select several calves and their owners to come forward. They stand in a row and after a bit the judges give them blue ribbons. Then more are called forward and get red ribbons. Princess stands quietly. Jackie looks at the sawdust and her eyes swim, as if she's under water. She imagines that she's swimming in the lake, free, blowing bubbles, twisting and turning like an eel. She blots out the humiliation of the ring.

Then someone is handing her a ribbon. It's a red second place. The circle reforms and the line leaves the building. Princess trots behind her as if she'd been trained to a lead from the moment she left her mother.

Grampa meets them back at the pen and admires the two second-place ribbons. He tells them they did well for beginners. He doesn't say anything about Jackie's fall or her animal's behavior. Craig is cheerful; he says he thought being in the show ring was fun. He says everyone who didn't get a first got a second-place ribbon. "That's so nobody will feel bad," says Craig. Jackie feels bad anyway.

They go out into the fair and look at the pigs and chickens and horses in their various buildings, and at the quilts and jams in the Home Ec building. They ride the merry-go-round and Ferris wheel. Grampa buys them cotton candy. Then they load the calves in the truck and go home. Jackie's humiliation doesn't go away, but it fades. It's over, the ordeal is over.

But not quite. Back at Chez Nous, Grampa asks for their record books. Craig finds his. Jackie rummages in her room and finally finds hers. She takes a quick glance into it and feels so uncomfortable that she closes it immediately. They take them down to the dairy. After supper they sit at the Big House dining-room table, and Grampa looks at their booklets. Neither of them has anything recorded but the beginning fifteen-dollar and feed-cost entries.

Grampa shakes his head. "Didn't you show these to your project leader?" he asks.

Jackie and Craig look at each other. What project leader?

Grampa opens a large farm ledger and locates a page. "Here is what your calves have cost to raise," he says. "You must copy these figures into your records." He tells them the cost of the grain that went up to Chez Nous, and the dates. He gives the cost of the straw for bedding, and the hay the calves ate in the winter. He gives the cost of the calves' innoculations.

"Now Craig," he says, "you went to Y camp, and you both went to the lake, so here are the days that a hired man had to tend your calves. Since he was feeding all the other stock at the same time, the cost of his labor for your particular animals is very little, but it must be included."

He carefully checks the figures Jackie and Craig write in the columns provided, and has them add them up. Jackie's debt swells to $43.27. She abandons all hope.

"Those figures," says Grampa, "are what you each owe the farm for the cost of your calves and their upkeep. But now the farm is ready to buy your calves from you, and add them to the herd. They are good stock and we'd like to keep them. We'll pay you each fifty dollars. Will you accept that?"

Jackie can't believe it. There's a catch somewhere. But she nods quickly and so does Craig.

Grampa shows them where to write the sale price in the booklet, and make the subtraction to show the profit. Then he goes to his desk and writes them each a check on the long tan farm checks out of the ledger-checkbook. Jackie has never had a check before. She's not sure at this point what it's for, and what she's done to earn it. She's quite sure that she hasn't learned everything she was supposed to learn from 4-H, although she knows she's learned a whole lot about something these last few days. But that's too hard to explain to Grampa, even if she did understand. She takes the check.

The calves, now heifers, return to the pasture. Jackie and Craig return to the lake. "Did you know anything about a project leader?" Jackie asks her brother. "Weren't we supposed to have a project leader?"

"Oh, him, whoever he is," says Craig. "I've got that all figured out. He probably thought we didn't need him because we had Grampa and Daddy to tell us everything, and Grampa and Daddy thought we didn't need them because we had him."

When she can bring herself to, Jackie studies over the booklet and discovers it tells about raising a calf, and the things she should have been doing right along, such as keeping a weekly diary of her calf's progress. There's a place for a final essay and she writes a very brief one.

In the fall she and Craig turn in their booklets and get certificates of achievement. They don't rejoin 4-H.

32   WHY A ROUND BARN?

Jackie is twelve. It's late morning; the cowbarn is clean and empty. She stands looking at two handprints in the concrete floor. They are on the edge of a stall, near the gutter, near the doors out to the horseyard. Her father made the bigger print when he was nine. The smaller print is her uncle's, made when he was seven. She sets her tablet and pencil on the walkway, kneels, and places her right hand in the larger print. Ever since she can remember, she has fit her hand into Daddy's handprint. He always seemed like such a big boy, until her hand caught up with his a few years ago. Now hers is larger.

She pictures Daddy as a little boy, kneeling in this same spot, pressing his hand into the wet concrete, while Trever crowds to be next. The sun and blue sky are above them, and no round barn on top yet, except maybe scaffolding. The bones of the barn. The inside silo is here, though; it was built first, and then the barn around it. The silo would have been a mammoth

The round barn under construction, summer 1911.
The silo is almost finished.

lonely column, like silos she's seen after a barn has burned down. But unlike them, not really lonely and abandoned, for there would have been a beehive of building going on around it. There's a picture in an old album of the silo, nearly constructed, and you can see all the activity.

She's never been interested in pressing her hand into Trever's handprint. Her own handprint, and bare footprint, too, are beside Craig's and Patsy's and Joan's, in a foundation in one of the many extensions of the milkhouse. Maybe her children will someday come and fit their hands and feet into her prints.

The Big House and round barn as one faces north.

Jackie picks up her tablet. She's been writing an essay for school. Her teacher is new to southern Wisconsin and drove past the round barn one Sunday. Now he wants to know, why did your grandfather build it *round*? He says he'll give her extra credit. Back at Chez Nous she's completed a composition that explains the advantages of roundness. Daddy gave her some help with names and facts and figures:

When my grandfather bought the farm in 1906 there was just the side barn. It held nine or ten cows. That wasn't big enough for the kind of dairy that he wanted. He went up to the University of Wisconsin and talked to the agronomy professors at the Ag School, and other people interested in dairy farms. Professor Franklin King thought a round barn was ideal for a dairy barn.

You can do all your work in a circle, your feeding, your milking, your cleaning, and end up where you started. That makes economy of motion.

All the cows stand in a circle facing the silo in the center. The silo puts silage right in front of them. Grain and hay from the upper barn can come down chutes alongside the silo and end up in front of the cows, too.

The design is economical. A barn braced on a concrete pillar for its core will not blow over in a tornado. The strong center means the rest of the barn can be of lighter materials. The side barn, which was built probably around 1850, had to have huge, square-hewn beams. The round barn needs only two-by-fours and two-by-sixes.

Then look at a cow's shape. From the top she looks something like a violin. She has a slender head (with ears, and sometimes horns, sticking out like the pegs). She has a moderate neck, rather skinny shoulders, and broad hips. She is rather wedge-shaped. Anyone who has cut an angel food cake knows that the pieces will be wedge-shaped. In the same way a round barn with the stalls in a ring will have each stall a little bit wedge-shaped. A cow fits comfortably into such a stall. On account of her natural design she doesn't need much room by her shoulders, and she needs even extra room by her broad flanks, for milking and cleanup. It's an efficient use of space.

Even the feed depressions, the mangers, sunk into the concrete in front of each cow's stanchion, are slightly wedge-shaped. The larger end is closest to the cow, where she can best reach with her tongue. It is really surprising that more barns are not round barns.

That's really all her teacher has asked for. But Jackie decides to give overflowing measure. She has written how the barn is white, not red like most barns. She has told that it's divided into the upper barn, the loft, and the lower cowbarn. She's described the green shingled roof, starting steep, then making a bend and sloping more gently to the top, which Daddy and Grampa call a "hip roof." She's described the two ventilators on opposite sides of the roof, like decorations on a giant's cap. And then—although she knows the barn as well as the inside of her own mouth, but if someone were to say, "How many teeth do you have?" she'd have to count them with her tongue to be sure—she takes her pencil and tablet and rides her bike from Chez Nous down to the dairy to take a close look.

She's recorded the upper barn details, the skylight windows and the windows directly under the eaves, in the hay section; the people-height windows in the other part. Two huge barn doors stretch from floor to eaves and are on a track. When opened, they hang against the outside barn walls. From the foot of the ramp you can look through the open doors and see "The Aims of This Farm" framed shadowy on the silo.

If you walk into the barn from the ramp, ahead of you is a huge open space, all the way to the silo, large enough for a team of horses and a hay

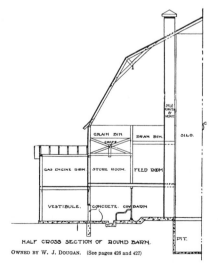

From Hoard's Dairyman, *April 11, 1913.*
The half not shown contains the hayloft.

wagon. On your right you'll see an incredible wall of hay, clear up to the roof if haying is just over. It stretches around behind the silo. The part of the loft that isn't hay and open barn floor has the feed grinder, usually with mounds of oats and unshelled corn beside it, the milking machine motor, and grain rooms with full and empty gunnysacks, and heavy paper sacks full of protein supplement for the pigs. Above the grain rooms are huge grain bins, stretching from silo to wall and almost to the roof; their broad wooden fronts are golden with age.

That is the upper barn. Now Jackie has come down the narrow inner staircase and, after the handprint ritual, is ready to record the cowbarn.

The silo, of course, is the center, with the hay chutes coming down alongside but stopping at the ceiling, letting the hay fall free to the floor. The smaller grain chute, with its paddle to shove in or pull out, hangs over the grain cart. The silage cart stands close to the silage chute, which is also a

The barn as one faces east, showing the cow entrance with overhead flytrap windows, the manure trolley, and outside silo, and side barn.

ventilator shaft. This area close around the silo is where the barnhands work, feeding the cows, who stand in a wide circle facing them.

Jackie counts. Forty stalls, each separated by a curved metal bar. At the head end is the stanchion; it's like a wooden safety pin that opens at the top and can be snapped shut after the cow sticks in her head. She's happy to do this because her grain is waiting in front of her when she comes to be milked. The stanchion swivels at top and bottom, so the cow can turn her head comfortably when she tries to reach the silage and grain from her neighbors' mangers. Alternating between every stall hangs a water cup or a salt dish, at cow-mouth level. A scaredy cow can swivel the whole stanchion around and with rolling eyes stare over her shoulder at Jackie, or a dog, or whatever is distracting her.

At intervals, walkways interrupt the stalls, sloping up from the sidewalk behind the cows to the area in front of them. Behind the rear quarters of the cows is the gutter, where the pee splashes and the cow pies mostly fall, and then the walkway from which the barnhands clean the gutter and do the milking. Finally come the thick whitewashed walls.

Jackie follows the walkway clockwise. Twenty-one windows set close together all the way around: they make the cowbarn a light and airy place. There are also five doors. The people entrance, which goes through the washroom with its sinks and hoses to meet the sidewalk from the milkhouse. The Dutch door wide enough for a cow to go through into the passageway to the side barn. The double doors that reach from walkway to ceiling, which open into the vestibule to the barnyard and are flung wide to let the cows in for milking. The cows crowd through these, led by the head cow, and mill and stamp and find their stalls. The fourth is the manure trolley door. The trolley is pulled or pushed on its overhead track through this exit and its load dumped onto the manure pile at the edge of the barnyard. The final door, again cow-sized, opens onto the north barnyard, which is flanked by the horsebarn and calfbarn.

The main cow entrance is especially interesting. The vestibule is a porchway, a couple of cow lengths long, and has no windows. The light is dim. Near the middle a blanket the width of the entrance hangs down, low enough that a cow has to duck to pass under it. All the flies on her head and neck and back are swept off. They buzz around in the dimness, spot a bright slit overhead, fly up through it, and find themselves in a closed, empty room. It is full of windows. They haven't the wits to crawl back down through the gap they entered from, so after a while they die. A barnhand eventually sweeps them up by the bushel basketful.

The vestibule flytrap is Grampa's invention, to keep the fly population down around the cows and milking. Its only moving parts are flies and cows. Grampa says of his flytrap, "I succeeded by thinking like a fly!"

There's another interesting feature in the cowbarn that is also Grampa's invention. In between almost every window, up against the ceiling, is a hole

The round barn as one faces west.

about a foot square with a sliding wooden shutter. On the outside of the cowbarn, down between the windows, each square has its corresponding screened square. The two have a passage between them through the thick walls; they form a kind of periscope for air, and are part of Grampa's ventilation system for keeping the barn cool in summer and warm in winter. The other part of the system is the two tall wooden shafts that run alongside the silo, up through the upper barn to the fans on the roof. When the ventilator fans turn, they pull hot air up from the center of the cowbarn to the roof. Then, to replace the hot air, cooler air enters through the little low outside windows and flows up the wall passages into the barn, entering at the ceiling-level square. The cool air sinks to the floor. The hot air, meanwhile, is flowing toward the center of the barn and up the big ventilator shafts to the outside. There's a continual current of warm leaving the top, and cool coming in the bottom.

It's one of Daddy's favorite tricks, when visitors come to the round barn, to demonstrate these ventilators. He takes his handkerchief and holds it under the shaft, and the wind going up nearly pulls it out of his hand. With this system it takes a terrible heat wave to make the barn anything but pleasant in the summer. In the winter, the shutters are closed and the cows' bodies heat the barn; the thick walls hold in the heat. The roof fans need change the air only once in a while.

Sometimes a sparrow manages to get into one of the ventilating passages in the outside wall and is trapped. Jackie or Craig discovers it beating its wings against the screening, and reports it. Then a barnhand loosens the screening and lifts the exhausted little body out.

Jackie goes through the washroom entrance to the outside and checks to see if there are any stray sparrows in a ventilating window. She follows the narrow concrete sidewalk around the barn to the horseyard. Because the barn is built on a slight slope, the sidewalk gets gradually lower while the windows remain the same height. By the time she gets beyond the horseyard, the windows are almost too high to look into. On the barnyard side, she knows, they'll be far too high.

There are no sparrows. And she has plenty of material for extra credit. She must remember to list "The Aims" when she describes the upper barn, but she knows these by heart. And at the end, to say how impressive the barn is, and that people often drive out on Sundays to see it and watch the milking. A good last line can be: "W. J. Dougan's round barn is a landmark in southern Wisconsin."

She goes into the Big House to get a sugar cookie from Grama, and to tell her about the essay, before riding her bike back up to Chez Nous.

Grampa in the hayloft.

33   BILLY BEADLE

Jackie is just thirteen. She's in love with Billy Beadle. She's never been in love before and she doesn't expect her love to be requited, for Billy is nineteen and going to the Ag School at the University of Wisconsin. She is content to follow him around the barn, where he's working for the summer.

Jackie at twelve or thirteen.

There is nothing about Billy that is not beautiful. She admires his jaunty whistling, his joshing back and forth with the other barnhands. She admires the way he slaps the cows around, not hurting them but making them step to. She admires the even rhythm he keeps up as he jabs the manure brush along the watery gutter, and the rhythmic ripple of his shoulder and back muscles under his white T-shirt. She admires the easy grace of his jeans clinging low on his hips, and the worn leather belt that holds them there. She admires his big rubber boots. She marvels at his strength when he pitches great waffles of hay into the chute, or, down by the crick, slings the milk cans of slops for the pigs up and over the fence as effortlessly as if he were pouring out a half-pint of chocolate milk. She loves to hear him sing the theme song of the band he stays up so late every night to listen to on the radio:

> Welcome all you listeners
> And here I am once more;
> It's quarter-past-eleven time
> And I'm knockin' on your door.

She knows every delineation of his profile. His haircut is perfection.

Billy is kind to Jackie. Sometimes he says something directly to her and she glows all over. Sometimes he asks her to run an errand, for a pitchfork or a missing tit cup, and her feet are winged. Sometimes he teases her and she is filled with joy. He names the littlest and homeliest cow in the barn, the one with bob ears and bob tail from frostbite, "Jackie-cow," and Jackie is honored. She gives Jackie-cow an extra scoop of grain when she's allowed to go around with the grain trolley and feed the cows their ration.

Jackie follows Billy on his work around the farm like a devoted puppy dog. The other farmhands kid Billy about his shadow. Billy laughs and says, "She's learning! Some day she'll grow up and marry a hayseed like me, and then she'll be able to run the barn single-handed!"

Billy's father, Leonard, is Grampa's farm manager and the best Duroc man in the county, if not the state. When he came to the farm from teaching Ag at Beloit High he brought his Duroc expertise, and the farm went whole-hog into raising Durocs for breeding stock. Billy is a good Duroc man, too, and teaches Jackie a lot about pigs when she rides along with him in the farm truck as it clanks over the ruts in the lane down to the back pasture. She laughs when he flips a pig out of the trough where it's gobbling milk up to its ears, keeping other squealing pigs from getting their share. There is always at least one pig that scrambles right into the trough at feeding time.

But Billy is more interested in sheep than hogs. There weren't any sheep on the farm until Billy came along. Now there is one. He keeps his prize sheep, the one he's grooming for the state fair, in the orchard across the road. This way he can give her special care each day.

Jackie loves to go with Billy to tend his sheep. He plays with the little animal, tussles a bit. The sheep trots along behind Billy when he goes to pick up a windfall, just like Jackie does. Jackie loves the feel of the soft fleece, loves to bed her fingers in it, to test its depth. She loves the creamy whiteness under the grimy surface of the wool.

One day Billy has to go away for a week. "Will you take care of my sheep while I'm gone?" he asks Jackie. There is nothing she would rather do. Every day, after corn detasseling, she brings her her rations and fresh water. She pulls grass and lets her nibble from her hand. She loves the soft breath on her fingers. Jackie has had goats, but there is a gentle nature to this sheep missing in her willful, sassy goats. She names the sheep Demi, after Demi in *Little Men*. She prints "DEMI" on the sheep's back in neat letters by every day embedding her fingers in the wool and then parting it, so that the separated wool gets used to staying separated and spells out the letters. She doesn't miss Billy as painfully as she thought she would; tending the sheep for him fills in the hollow.

Billy returns and thanks her. She prickles all over. He likes the name Demi better than the real one on the pedigree papers, and says he'll keep it for her nickname, but that he'll have to erase it from her back before the judging.

That's okay with Jackie. He cleans Demi snowy white and takes her to the state fair. She wins a blue ribbon. Then he sells her. Jackie cannot see how he can do it.

"That's the way it is with livestock," says Billy. "You can't let yourself get too attached."

Inside, Jackie knows she will always let herself get too attached.

William Leonard Beadle.

Fall comes; Jackie goes back to school, Billy goes back to college. On December 7 bombs fall on Pearl Harbor. Billy enlists in the Army Air Corps. When he wins his wings, his picture is in *The Beloit Daily News*. Jackie cuts it out and puts it in her wallet, where it's not visible to her friends. She is now in love with the boy who sits across from her in English class, the one who held her hand in the darkened bus on the church choir trip, but her first love will always be in an enshrined place in her heart, and now in her wallet.

At the back of the First Methodist Church is an honor roll. There's a long list of names on it. Each serviceman has a green star before his name. When

Jackie reads the names she can picture many of the faces, from seeing them growing up in the church, always as big boys much older than herself. Billy's name is there, with its green star. Every Sunday she stops and reads it.

The war goes on. Billy goes to England and is co-pilot on a B-17 bomber plane flying over Germany. One day Grampa comes into the kitchen at Chez Nous. Jackie is modeling a puppet head out of glue and sawdust. Grampa's face is heavy. He sits down slowly, says to Mother, "The Beadles just got word. Billy's plane is missing. It was on its seventeenth mission. It never returned to its base." He shakes and shakes his head.

Jackie's heart stands still.

There is a chance that the plane's crew parachuted down over Occupied Europe. There is a chance that Billy is a POW. On the church honor roll, every so often a gold star replaces a green one, and from the pulpit the minister talks about the young hero. Billy is missing in action. His star stays green.

The war years go by. The tide turns toward the Allies. They push across Europe. The POW camps are opened, one by one. Billy does not come home. Finally the war is over. Billy and his crew members are not found; there is no record of the plane. The government notifies the Beadles that it went down in the North Sea. But, maybe, something else happened, and the crew will still turn up.

Time goes on. Jackie knows Billy will never come home. Everyone must know it. She waits for somebody to change Billy's star to gold on the honor roll. Nobody does. The minister does not ever talk about Billy from the pulpit.

More time goes on. Jackie is grown up and has moved away. The war's been over many years. She's much older now than Billy was when she loved him, she's much older than he was when he died. The old First Methodist Church has been torn down and a modern one built in its place. On a visit home, Jackie stops in one day to look over the new church.

"What ever happened to the old World War II honor roll?" she asks a secretary she's never met. The secretary doesn't know. The new minister doesn't know. Finally, the new custodian remembers seeing it in a storeroom. He offers to find it for her.

"No," says Jackie, "just unlock the door." She goes and buys a box of small gold stars, the kind her piano teacher used to put on a piece when it was finished. She returns to the church and finds the storeroom. She pokes around. The honor roll is tilted in a corner. Its glass is dusty. She wipes it clean with her hand and unhooks the lid. She licks a gold star and presses it over the faded green one in front of the name of William Leonard Beadle. She closes the case again and stands for a minute, remembering that thirteenth summer, and Demi-sheep in the orchard, and Jackie-cow in the round barn.

"There, Billy," she says, and leaves the storeroom.

34 UNBUTTON

Jackie is fourteen. She changes into her jeans after school. Her horse doesn't want to go, but she rides him from Chez Nous down to the dairy. She sees the vet's old Buick near the cowbarn door. She tethers Paint to the elm, goes down the step to the barn washroom, and into the barn. Whenever the vet is around it's interesting. She's known Dr. Knilans ever since she can remember.

The cowbarn is empty except for Jackie-cow and Dr. Knilans. The vet is naked to the waist; his coat, tie, and white shirt are draped on a stall divider. He's busy on the walk behind Jackie-cow, with his doctor's kit. A vet has a large doctor's kit.

Jackie-cow is a funny-looking, who-knows-what-breed cow. She's one of the best milkers in the barn. Jackie likes it that she's called Jackie-cow. But now she's concerned about Jackie-cow's rear end.

Jackie has looked at cows' rear ends all her life. It's the major view in the round barn, forty cows' rear ends. But Jackie-cow has a lot of grayish tissue hanging out of hers, below her anus. It hangs in folds and loops halfway to the gutter. It's a little bloody. The cow seems unconcerned.

"What's the matter with her?" Jackie asks.

"It's the afterbirth," the vet says. "It didn't come out when she calved. I have to clean her. Unbutton her."

Jackie is astonished. "Unbutton?"

Dr. Knilans makes a fist. "See this fist? A cow has knobs sort of like that on the inside of her uterus."

Jackie nods.

Dr. Knilans cups his other hand over his fist. "This is the placenta, the sac the calf grows in. It grows around the knobs."

Jackie nods.

"Now, take your hand and peel the placenta off the knob. Gently."

Jackie carefully peels Dr. Knilans' hand off his fist.

"There," says the vet. "That's how you unbutton a cow. Nature usually does it, but when nature doesn't quite manage, we have to help."

Dr. Knilans gets out a long rubber glove, the sort Amos wears when he inseminates a cow. He dusts his arm with talcum powder.

"Is this cow a friend of yours?"

"Yes," says Jackie. "She lost the ends of her ears and tail from frostbite, before Grampa bought her. They call her Jackie-cow. For fun."

"Would you like to unbutton Jackie-cow? She's small enough—your arm might reach. And you have a gentle touch."

Jackie considers. "Yes," she says.

Milking in the round barn.

Dr. Knilans talcs her arm. He puts the rubber glove on her. It comes up and over her shoulder. He fits the fingers. He soaps all over the glove and arm. "Now," he says, "put your arm down and feel around for one of the buttons." He moves the hanging afterbirth and shows her where to insert her hand.

She makes her fingers into a point and pushes her hand gingerly into Jackie-cow's vulva. Her arm slides easily down the vagina. The passageway holds it snugly. She's surprised how warm it is inside the cow, it's like a warm bath. She's amazed how far the passageway goes. She reaches down, down. Dr. Knilans holds the tail aside. Her shoulder is right against the cow's anus.

"Are you there? Can you feel any buttons?"

Jackie gropes around. She feels a fleshy knob, like a mushroom. She nods.

"Now feel if there's anything to unbutton. Some of the knobs may be free already."

She feels something over the top of the mushroom. She works it gently with her fingers, feels it loosen.

"It's come off!" she says, grinning.

"See if there's another."

She feels around. It's working in the dark, by touch only. It's very warm. She unbuttons another knob. She feels further. She can't find any others. She pulls out her arm.

Dr. Knilans puts on the glove and reaches down. "One more, I think," he says.

He works around a bit. Then he pulls his arm out and all the afterbirth comes with it. "There," he says, dropping the gray mass in the gutter. He takes a tablet of medicine, big as a bar of soap, puts it deep in the vagina, and then peels the glove.

Jackie watches till he's done. Then she washes up in the barn washroom, and waits while Dr. Knilans washes up and puts his clothes back on. She walks out to his car with him and watches him stow his equipment.

"Do people have buttons?" she asks. "Women, in their uteruses?"

"No," Dr. Knilans says. "The placenta sticks without them."

He leaves to go to another farm.

Jackie goes to the milkhouse and gets a bottle of chocolate milk from the cooler. She drinks it, climbs on Paint, and rides back home. She tends the horse, practices her cello, takes her turn to set the table.

At supper she says, "I unbuttoned a cow this afternoon."

"Many's the cow I've cleaned," says Daddy.

"What's unbuttoning a cow?" Joan asks.

Jackie starts to tell her.

"Oh, not at the table!" Joan says. "Mother, make her stop! I can't stand to hear it!"

Mother asks Jackie to tell about it later.

Jackie explains after supper.

Joan is revulsed. "Honestly, Jackie, how can you stand to *do* those things?" she asks. "Why do you *want* to?"

"The cow needed it," Jackie says. "And I'd never felt a cow's buttons before. It was interesting."

35 MISS GLENN

For reasons not wholly fathomable to Jackie, her father—and sometimes Trever—occasionally lived at Aunt Ida's on Bushnell and attended Strong School directly across the street. High school was one thing, but why grade school with the district schoolhouse just across the East Twenty? Trever even attended Strong for long enough to be on the eighth-grade basketball team. To prove it there's a large picture of him with his teammates and coach, framed in oak and hanging on a wall at Chez Nous. The basketball in the picture is lettered "Champions—1918."

Miss Glenn, principal of Strong School and coach of a champion basketball team. Trever is in the front row, left.

The coach is the principal, Miss Frances Glenn. She stands behind the boys, a regal six feet with bulk to match, clad in long dark skirt and soft white blouse. Her brown hair is swept up to increase her height, and there is the faintest hint of a smile on her dignified face. She plays basketball herself, but Ronald never sees her move beyond a sedate walk. She never raises her voice.

Taylor Merrill, a boy several years older than Ronald, has printed up an elaborate blueprint newspaper, which Ronald greatly admires. He gets Taylor to instruct him in the technique. Ronald and Trever decide to publish a Strong School newspaper. They blueprint it in Aunt Ida's kitchen and sell it around the neighborhood after school for a few cents a copy. The first issue, besides short articles and bits of Strong School gossip, contains various jokes and this syllogism:

> We go to school to improve our faculties.
> Our teachers are our faculties.
> Therefore we go to school to improve our teachers.

Miss Glenn suggests to Ronald that the *Strong School Scoop* be discontinued.

By the time Jackie starts Roosevelt Junior High School in 1940, Miss Glenn has long been principal there, and has become a legend. She is stern, strict, and scrupulously fair. A wrongdoer quakes when sent to the office. Miss Glenn needn't reprimand. She just looks down from miles above, through her rimless glasses, listens to the charges, and metes out punishment. A look from Miss Glenn is worse than any lecture.

Twice Jackie goes to the office as a wrongdoer. The first time isn't her fault. It's Daddy's. The 1940 election is coming up; Wendell Wilkie is running for president on the Republican ticket. Wilkie is a man of stature and the author of the important book *One World*. His campaign train is making a whistle-stop in South Beloit at eight o'clock in the morning. Daddy thinks his children ought to see the man who might be next president of the United States. He takes them all, and they, along with a moderate crowd, shiver in a field where the train is going to pause. Eventually it arrives, shakes to a stop, and Wilkie, his face and smile familiar from newspapers and the *Time* magazine cover, steps onto the back platform, waves, and says a few words. He and his wife are both in their bathrobes. The crowd claps and cheers, the train pulls out, and Daddy drives them all to their respective schools—Craig to Todd, Jackie and Patsy to junior high, and Joan to high school.

"What will we say to Miss Glenn?" worries Patsy, for she and Jackie will both be late.

"If she gives you a hard time, tell her she's a damn Democrat," says Daddy.

At the office, Patsy explains to Miss Glenn where they've been and why they are late. Miss Glenn listens silently. Then she writes out a detention for each of them. These they accept meekly, and of course don't deliver Daddy's message. One would rather be struck by lightning than say anything impertinent to Miss Glenn. Daddy stops by to remonstrate with her, but Miss Glenn runs her school by the book, and stands firm.

After this, it's all the more surprising that the next year Jackie is hauled into the office for impertinence. She wasn't impertinent to Miss Glenn, though, but to the music teacher, Miss Groffman.

The war is going on. Food is being rationed. Many mothers are working and many students besides the country kids are now bringing their lunches. It seems to the school that it would be a good idea to begin serving a hot lunch; the idea is spearheaded by the cooking teacher. There has never been a school cafeteria in any of the Beloit schools, nor are there facilities for them. Cafeterias are conveniences of the future. Jackie has always eaten her lunch outside, or in cold weather in a classroom with the other country kids.

But Roosevelt Junior High teachers and staff begin preparing huge pots of macaroni and cheese, and other such menu staples—never any meat—up in the home ec room, which has stoves. They serve the food at long tables crammed into the back end of one of the downstairs halls, by the gym door.

Jackie finds the arrangement distasteful. The macaroni and cheese is never particularly good, and the back hall is dark, dingy, and depressing. The stink of gym and locker room seeps out to mingle with the smells of food and body and wet mittens. The students who take advantage of the hot lunch are crowded too close together and are mostly kids she doesn't know. Some are boisterous and messy. They fling food and wadded-up napkins and scramble around on the folding chairs. Teachers take turns being on lunch duty, trying to keep order. They patrol the dismal hall from the lunch area all the way up to the front of the building.

Pretty soon Jackie starts bringing her own lunch again, and eating it separate from the crowd. She's wandering up the hall one noon, munching her sandwich from her lunch sack on her way outside, when she runs into Miss Groffman near the front doors. Miss Groffman has a huge bunch of grapes in one hand and is using the other to stuff grapes into her mouth. Around a gobful she says sharply to Jackie, "No eating in the halls." Says Jackie, "Why don't you practice what you preach?" Whereupon Miss Groffman turns scarlet, grabs her by the collar, and marches her to the office. All the way Jackie hears about how Miss Groffman has to eat in the halls because she has to patrol the halls, how she'd rather eat anywhere but in the halls, and what gross, gross impertinence Jackie has displayed. In the office, under Miss Glenn's stern eye, Jackie hears all over again what she said to Miss Groffman and what Miss Groffman thinks of it. And hearing it, it does sound to her like the grossest impertinence. Miss Glenn shakes her head almost imperceptibly, looks hard at Jackie, and writes out a double detention. She adds, "You will apologize to Miss Groffman."

Jackie does. The unbelievable thing—Jackie can't even believe it herself in later years—is that she hadn't meant to be disrespectful. All those grapes popping in had somehow just made her words pop out.

When Craig gets to junior high he has his own innings in the office. Once he's running down the hall with a water pistol, shooting at a friend. Miss Glenn confiscates the water pistol. Craig begrudges her its loss—it was a new one.

When Jackie is in high school the war ends. The new superintendent of schools believes that the main jobs in the school system shouldn't be held by women. It's all right for them to teach kindergarten and the lower grades, but when it comes to principals, men should have the authority. He fires all the women administrators. The Dougans and a good many towns-people deplore what he has done, but it's in the years before the drive for equality and nobody does anything except bewail it privately.

The new superintendent is a coarse and bloated man, given to ungram-matical speeches. The students despise him. Craig and his high school bud-dies, all of whom had Miss Glenn for principal in junior high and respected her, in spite of the water pistol and other such episodes, get a measure of revenge on Halloween. At sunset Craig goes out to the pasture and scoops a juicy cow pie into a double paper bag. In the after-supper dark, they place it in the middle of the superintendent's porch, set fire to the rim of the dou-bled bags, give the doorbell a determined ring, and run. Out of sight in the shadows they have the satisfaction of seeing Mr. Dawald fling open the front door, go right through the screen, and stamp out the fire in his bedroom slippers.

Some of the administrators, like Miss Glenn, have been in the school sys-tem over thirty years but are still too young to retire. They are now too old to be considered for new teaching jobs, or for jobs anywhere. Miss Glenn's pension is too small to live on. She finally manages to get work at *The Beloit*

Daily News as a proofreader. The pay is low, the hours at night, and the print hard on her eyes. She suffers from headaches. It's a sorry comedown for someone of Miss Glenn's intelligence, abilities, and years of distinguished service to the community.

It's quite a while before Daddy discovers that Miss Glenn is working at the *Daily News*. He thinks about it and consults with Mother. Then he goes down to Miss Glenn's house. "Miss Glenn," he says, "come work for me."

Miss Glenn does. She sits in the office up over the milkhouse and is a regal figure working on the books. Even though there are two other women in the office, there's a lot of detail when taking care of upwards of 1500 customers and their accounts. Miss Glenn is a splendid accountant and does much more than secretarial work. She writes collection letters, organizes the advertising, sees the things that Daddy needs help doing, and does them. Jackie, now in college, feels glad whenever she comes into the office, but always a little strange, too, to see this woman who was Daddy's and Trever's principal, was her and Joan's and Patsy's and Craig's principal, and whom she still holds in awe, busy with a pencil behind a Dougan desk. Her presence elevates the office.

Daddy dusts off the picture of Trever and his basketball team with Miss Glenn as coach and hangs it beside his desk. When people exclaim over it, Miss Glenn glances up and smiles her little enigmatic smile. And once, when she's late to work on account of a snowstorm, Daddy hands her a detention.

Miss Glenn stays with Daddy ten years and finishes her working career in respect and dignity. The relationship is a mutually happy one. Toward the end she only comes out two or three days a week, balances the books, tends to any loose ends. After her retirement she moves to an apartment.

Miss Glenn and Daddy and Mother keep up their friendship. This is mainly through an interest of Miss Glenn's that over the years she's stimulated in Mother and Daddy—bird-watching.

"What did I know about birds before Frances Glenn came?" Daddy says.

"Anything bigger than a robin was a crow, and anything smaller than a robin was a sparrow."

It's an understatement, of course, but Miss Glenn is a knowledgeable and ardent bird-watcher, and active member of the Ned Hollister Bird Club. Daddy and Mother join the bird club, and go on bird trips, participate in the yearly bird census counts, haunt the bird-banding station south of Beloit, lie out in the bush to hear the woodcocks peenting far overhead, or watch the prairie chickens strut on their booming grounds. They, too, become knowledgeable and ardent bird-watchers.

They attend picnics and fish fries. Once, at the Hill Farm woods, they host the potluck supper that follows the New Year's Day bird count; the minutes one year read that the group gathered at the Dougan cabin "for hot chili and cold facts." On many a summer field trip, they complement the "hot facts" with cold milk and orange drink. And for several years running they give a pheasant banquet at Chez Nous, following Ron's annual hunting trip to South Dakota. Though they've always known Susan and Carl Welty, they now see much more of them through the bird club. Carl is an eminent ornithologist and author of the most widely used text in the country. Craig says Dr. Welty's class is one of the best he ever had at Beloit College, even with—*especially* with—its predawn field trips and crawling around in sloughs. Jackie strongly regrets that she never took the ornithology class.

When Miss Glenn begins to fail physically, Mother and Daddy become wheels for her and her close friend Miss Andrews. Miss Andrews taught with Miss Glenn in the Strong School years and has also been a lifelong bird-watcher. Mother and Daddy drive the elderly pair out into the Sugar River area or the Hononegah preserve, or even up to Horicon Marsh, where, armed with field glasses and Roger Tory Petersons, they all add to their life lists. Daddy always holds the strands of bob wire apart while Miss Glenn and Miss Andrews crawl through, and Mother helps steady them as they get back to their feet.

Miss Glenn and Miss Andrews on a bird club outing.

Miss Glenn and Miss Andrews make a striking pair. While Miss Glenn is statuesque and seldom wears a scarf over the billow of white hair that crowns her six feet, Miss Andrews is small-boned and under five feet, the stoop of age adding to her diminutiveness. And she invariably wears a brimless black hat resembling a muffin, which fits snugly down to her ears. The one is a great snowy owl, conspicuous on its rock or post; the other a sparrow that scrabbles almost invisible under dry leaves.

Miss Glenn and Miss Andrews always treat each other formally. Mother and Daddy never hear them call each other by their first names—it's always Miss Glenn, Miss Andrews. A few bird club members call Miss Andrews an affectionate "Andy," but no one presumes to nickname Miss Glenn. And even Miss Glenn doesn't know Miss Andrews's age, for Daddy has asked her, and Miss Glenn says she certainly wishes she knew. Actually, the whole bird club would like to know. Is it Miss Glenn or Miss Andrews who is the senior member? They haven't been able to acknowledge a senior member since Mr. Wendling died, and it has been their habit to have a special program honoring the oldest member.

On one of the Sunday birding jaunts, Daddy stops the car suddenly just over a small rise. He halts in the middle of the road. "Look!" he says. "What sort of birds are those, and what are they up to?"

All binoculars rise to focus on the pair on the branch. Daddy realizes that they are black-billed cuckoos, and what they're up to is copulation. There is silence from Miss Glenn and Miss Andrews in the back seat.

At that moment a car comes over the rise, slams on its brakes, but rear-ends the Dougan vehicle. No harm is done to either car, but everyone is shaken up, and Miss Andrews is unconscious for a few moments. A township policeman comes, and then Daddy and Mother drive their aged charges to the hospital to be sure they're all right. At the desk Daddy stands close on one side of Miss Andrews as she is signed in, hoping to catch her first name. Miss Glenn hovers on the other side; Daddy is sure she is alert to catch how old Miss Andrews claims herself to be. At just the crucial moment an attendant comes up with a wheelchair and insists that Miss Glenn sit down. Both Daddy and Miss Glenn miss the information that was almost theirs, and Daddy hears Miss Glenn say, "Oh, shucks."

The bird club eventually solves its problem by paying joint tribute to its two senior members. Mother writes the verse for the occasion:

Dear Miss Andrews, Dear Miss Glenn,
O do forgive our awkward pen.
To honor you with fervent rhyme
Gave us, indeed, a trying time.

If we were birds with gift of song,
To make you happy all day long
We members of N. H. B. C.
Would sing on every bush and tree.

We all agreed we should not sing;
That we would rather do our thing.
Often, on love, so much depends.
Our thing is loving you, dear friends.

Miss Glenn eventually loses a leg to diabetes; Daddy arranges for the bird club to meet now and then in the common room of her apartment building so that it's easier for her to attend. And even then the outings continue. Daddy gets Miss Glenn to the street, they fold the wheelchair into the trunk of the car, and the four go combing the byways for birds. Miss Andrews's eyesight fails, but she becomes adept at identifying songsters by their calls.

When Miss Glenn dies, Daddy and five other Ned Hollisters are her pallbearers. The club raises enough money for a memorial. Mother suggests that rather than a book on birds for the library they plant a tree on the Roosevelt Junior High grounds. They plant a little burr oak, and it thrives. Daddy visits Pete Halverson, who has a foundry and brassworks; his father, Harold Halverson, is in the Strong School basketball picture of 1918. Daddy requests a plaque for Miss Glenn and asks the cost. Pete says, "For Miss Glenn there is no cost." He makes a brass plaque, anchors it onto a block of cement, and buries the block at the foot of the burr oak.

Miss Andrews outlives her friend by several years. Despite her poor eyesight, she tended Miss Glenn considerably in her last illness, eventually moving into Miss Glenn's apartment to do so. She stays on there till she finally goes to a nursing home. Daddy and Mother are out of town when her death occurs; they don't hear about it until the next meeting of the bird club.

"What was her name, and how old was she?" Daddy asks.

"Her name was Bernice," says Susan Welty. "But the paper never gave her age."

"Oh, shucks," says Daddy.

At the start of the milk business, in 1907, Grampa thinks no one is capable of delivering milk but himself. Every day he takes the buggy and delivers the bottles to all the customers and to his sister Ida. The route grows and he purchases a milk wagon. It has brass trim and a glass front with a place for the reins to come through the glass. There's a well for him to stand in when he drives, and a space behind that big enough to hold many milk cases. The driver's side is open, so that a milkman can hop in and out easily. Grampa has his name and slogan painted in brown and gold on the cream-colored side, "W. J. Dougan, The Babies' Milkman."

Ronald sometimes rides with him on the route. As Grampa heads toward town, with the horses trotting at a brisk clip, he holds the reins and sings over the racket of the horses' hooves and iron wheels, "Rock of ages, cleft

Graham McCoy, a milkman in 1916.

for me, Let me hide—myself in thee!" It's the only time Ronald ever hears his father sing.

One day Grampa is on the route alone. He's returning home. Something startles the horses and they bolt. The wagon tips over. Grampa is caught between the wagon and the road, and dragged for a distance. The accident lacerates his legs and knees so badly that he's laid up for several weeks. He directs activities from a bed downstairs in the southwest room of the house. One of the hired men, Ross Martin, takes over the milk route. He thoroughly enjoys delivering the milk to the customers. When Daddy Dougan can finally be up and about again, there's no talk of his taking the route back. Ross Martin is, after Grampa, the first Dougan milkman.

No one can remember the name of a somewhat later milkman, only the story about him, which is that he never actually made it to a route. He was groomed for the job by accompanying an experienced driver, and before

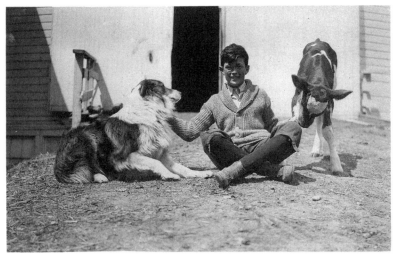

Ronald, age fourteen, with Bob and a calf on the ramp to the round barn loft.

long was pronounced ready to solo. But when the morning arrived he was sick. He recovered, another morning rolled around, and again he was sick. It became apparent that the prospect of delivering milk was too much for him. Grampa left him at his job in the milkhouse and trained someone else for the route.

Daddy has a milk route at various times in his life. The summer he's fourteen he drives on the east side with a wagon and team of horses. The horses know the route so well that they'll stop in front of the proper house without bidding. This lets Ronald read a page or two of his current book in between stops. The streets in the Keeler and White Avenue area aren't paved, and when it rains the horses have rough going. It takes them longer, plodding through the ruts. Ronald has it so timed that in bad weather he can drink a quart of milk and eat the packet of cookies his mother sends with him for a morning snack, between the stop on White Avenue and the stop on Keeler.

Once, in fair weather on Keeler, Ronald gets left behind. He's a sociable sort and enjoys talking to the customers. He talks so long at one back step, with the mother of one of his schoolmates (the schoolmate much in evidence in the yard, hanging up wet curtains on stretchers), that when he returns to the street whistling and swinging his empty carrier, the horses have tired of waiting and gone around the block to the next stop. After that he always loads enough milk for both houses, gives the horses a giddyap, chats at the favored back porch, then jumps the fence, drops his order at the other door, and meets his team on the street as they arrive. That timing pleases him, too.

He's glad not to have been the driver when Foxy and Happy, the mules, run away with Tim Pedley on Wisconsin Avenue. The rampaging animals climb the curb, one on either side of a telegraph pole, meet themselves head on, and knock each other out. Milk is all over the street.

During the years when Jackie is growing up, Daddy fills in many times on different milk routes for two or three days, even a week or two, when someone is sick and there's no one to take his place. But during the war, in 1942, when so many men volunteer or are drafted, Daddy has to have his own route for six months. He leaves the house at two in the morning, takes the whole River Road route, then puts in a full day's work at the office. He's always tired. That's why he fails for so long to catch the new milkman who is embezzling route money. Besides having no expectation of being cheated, he isn't alert to discrepancies in the books. When Walter Abbot comes along willing to take the job of milkman, Daddy is grateful, even though Walter is a Seventh-Day Adventist and will under no circumstances deliver milk on Saturday. Daddy is glad to be a route man only one day a week.

Jackie's experience as a milkman is in two segments, the first in winter. She is fourteen. It's the start of Christmas vacation. Daddy is upset. One of the route men has slipped on the ice and developed housemaid's knee. He isn't allowed to walk for two weeks. There's no one to take Roscoe Ocker's place, least of all Daddy, who is still on a daily route.

"It's not as if he's really laid up," says Daddy at the supper table. "Even though he can barely get his pants on over the swelling, he says he can drive. He just can't do the running."

"I'll do the running," volunteers Jackie.

Daddy contemplates her. "*Grâce à Dieu*," he says. "Better get to bed as soon as you can. I'll call Roscoe."

The next day Jackie leaves Chez Nous with Daddy at two in the morning. The stars are brilliant in the black velvet sky and it's bitter cold. She's bundled up with coat, boots, and snowpants, mittens and scarf and wool cap. At the dairy the yard lights are on and the trucks backed up to the loading dock. The milkmen are slinging cases into their trucks and arranging them. There is much chatter of milk bottles, and over it the banter of the men. Lester Stam, Howard Milner, Oscar Berg, Earl Bown—she knows them all. Roscoe Ocker is sitting on an upended milk case, directing the loading of his truck.

A milk wagon converted to a bobsled (1916). The Little House is in the background.

"There's my buddy," he calls cheerfully when he sees her. "I hear you're going to ride with me for two weeks."

Jackie nods and grins. She's always liked Roscoe.

The men cover Roscoe's load with a large gray quilted blanket to help keep the milk from freezing. They fix Jackie a niche up front to sit in. Roscoe swings into the driver's seat and warns her to be careful of the small kerosene stove that stands upright close to the dash, throwing off heat and a bright glow. Then they're off, out the farm driveway and down snow-covered Colley Road to town.

Roscoe explains that he's the swing man, the relief man, that every day he takes the route of one of the others who has the day off, and so Jackie will cover all of Beloit and South Beloit with him twice. That pleases her. Because of his leg they won't be going through the factories, though, when they take Howard's route. Ockie Berg will do those on Howard's day off, since Ockie's daily route is lighter right now on account of school vacations.

Roscoe Ocker.

Today they are on the west side. They thread the dark streets, McKinley, St. Lawrence, Moore, lit only by streetlamps at the intersections, and by an occasional mid-block house whose Christmas tree lights, left on, cast a diffuse and many-colored glow out onto the snow. Roscoe explains the route book, how every month each customer has a page with the usual order of milk, and then what is actually taken on any given date. Even though Roscoe runs six routes, he knows most of the orders by heart and doesn't often need to refer to a page with his flashlight. He instructs Jackie what to put in the carrier and, with rueful warnings about ice, where to deliver the milk—into the front porch entryway, or on the back step in one of the insulated boxes that Dougan's provides, or into the kitchen—opening the back door and putting the bottles on the floor. When she gets to do that, Jackie sometimes slips inside and stands very still for a moment, breathing in the warm air, hearing the furnace rattle and the hum of the refrigerator. She feels strange as she listens to the sleeping house.

Roscoe gives information about the customers. This family has a new baby and her photograph has already been in a Dougan ad. This one's had a recent wedding; this family has a great-grandmother living with them whose hundredth birthday was in August. Her picture was in the paper.

"She didn't say she attributed her long life to drinking Dougan's milk, though," he adds.

Jackie calculates. Since the dairy began well after the great-grandmother was born, she'd have been able to drink Dougan's milk only during her last thirty-five years. But it could have contributed.

One family recently lost a son in the Pacific, and has two other sons in the service. "These are hard times," Roscoe says, and she is solemn as she crunches up the snowy driveway and leaves the milk on the back porch.

The hours go by. Jackie's arm aches from the heavy carrier. She's tired all over from getting up so early, and in spite of the heater in the truck her feet are frozen and her fingers numb.

Houses begin to light up as people awaken. Day will come late. It's close to the longest night of the year. Now kitchen windows make yellow patch-works on the driveways, and Roscoe instructs her to knock and give the milk directly to the housewife. This will ensure its not freezing. He tells her whose house it is, so that she can greet the customer by name. The house-wife, sometimes in a bathrobe and curlers, sometimes with a baby in a high chair or scooting on the floor, sometimes with a husband in work clothes, bent over his coffee, or an elderly father, bent over his, is surprised to see her, but always welcoming. Now Jackie gets to stand in a kitchen for a few minutes, invited, and warm her hands and feet over a hot-air register and explain why they have a different milkman. They laugh, but sympathetical-ly, about Roscoe's housemaid's knee, and they are always interested to learn she's Ron Dougan's daughter. Most of them know Daddy and Grampa at least a little. At one house she is given a slice of bacon, at another, a cup of hot chocolate and a doughnut, and she carries a mug of coffee and a doughnut out to Roscoe in the truck. Her energy revives with warmth and food.

"At this rate we won't have any room for breakfast," says Roscoe, finishing his doughnut. It's daylight in another hour, and he and Jackie stop at the Subway Café on Third Street. Geneva Bown, the owner of the Subway, is an old friend of Jackie's. She used to work on the farm and her husband Earl still does, delivering milk—he was at the loading dock this morning. Geneva serves them a full breakfast of sausage and eggs and flapjacks, and leans on the counter to exchange gossip and news. Earl comes in for his breakfast just as Jackie and Roscoe are leaving to return to the route. They finish it up and are back at the farm with a truck full of empties by late morning. Daddy, also back, runs her up to Chez Nous.

"Have a good time?" he asks.

"It was interesting," says Jackie, "but it's hard work." At home she's exhausted but fights taking a nap so that it will be easier to fall asleep right after supper.

The days go by, every one different, but with the same basic routine. The best day is Christmas, for she and Roscoe can scarcely get through their route, so many customers have cards and gifts for them—Christmas cookies on a colorful paper plate, or a jar of jelly, a box of candy. She keeps being invited in and dragged by the children to see what Santa brought, and then the adults have to get on their coats and come out to the truck to wish Roscoe a merry Christmas too.

"I'm not even their regular milkman," says Roscoe. "Look at all this stuff! And Stam's been bringing home presents from this route all week."

"They like you, too," says Jackie. She knows Roscoe is pleased.

The family saves opening its presents till afternoon, when Jackie and Daddy are home. The evening before, at the Big House party for all the help, Grampa tells her he's proud of the job she's doing. It's her turn then to be pleased. Grama says, "Think of our poor little Jackie doing all that running on a milk route!" Jackie doesn't think of herself as either poor or little.

The very worst day, and one of the worst days of Jackie's life, is the day after New Year's. It blizzards all night. In the car, she and Daddy slough down to the farm through a sea of drifts, unable to tell where the ditches are, the snow blinding them as it drives through the headlights into the windshield. When they finally make it, Jackie finds she has been holding her breath.

They find the farm alight and alive with activity. Grampa has a team out, breaking up the drifts so that the trucks can get through to town. Erv has the snowplow on the front of a farm truck, following up the team. Farmhands are helping with the plowing and shoveling and loading. Some of the milkmen came out the night before, when they realized it would be bad, and have slept in the Big House. Others have ridden out together, a lucky thing since they had to shovel and push more than once on the way. Ed Pfaff is getting chains on the trucks that don't already have them.

Everybody is late getting started. Today Roscoe's route is the River Road, stretching halfway to Janesville. The houses that fall between the highway and the river are often on little lanes, five or six to a lane, and the lanes are choked with snow. With all the drifting Roscoe doesn't dare take the truck down them, even with chains. In the dark Jackie mushes to the houses, often the ones at the very ends of the lanes, dragging her heavy carrier, and groans out loud when her stiff fingers unfurl a note stuck in a bottle and she finds the regular order has been augmented, making her take the trip twice. She has broken a path, but by the return the wind has already filled her tracks. The gale howls off the river and she can't feel her cheeks. The truck also can't get into Burrwood Park, a riverside shantytown of decrepit trailers, tar-paper shacks, and rickety summer cottages arranged haphazardly on a grid of unpaved streets. She makes trip after trip, leaning into the blizzard or, blissfully, being buffeted from behind as she returns to the truck for another load. It's worse delivering to Burrwood Park than to the snug bungalows on the lanes, for she's acutely aware of how cold the people must be who are crowded into those insufficent houses. She's never really noticed such things, till this winter on the milk route.

But worst of all is delivering to the big houses high on the hills on the other side of the River Road. Each of these has its own driveway—its own long, drifted driveway with the snow-laden wind whistling up and down and around it—and there's no way the truck can go up these, either. She has to battle her way uphill, step by laborious step, churning and floundering through snowdrifts. She's icy, yet sweat runs in rivulets down inside her clothes. Her eyelashes cake and her breath gasps until her throat is raw and aching from cold and exertion. Her carrier is lead, pulling her arm from its socket, for she brings along extra milk as insurance. But then if the order is the same or diminished, she has to carry it back again.

In the truck Roscoe keeps chocolate milk hot in a little pan on the kerosene stove. It's always ready for her when she staggers back. He's sympathetic and supportive, but doesn't apologize for his inability to help further, or smother her with praise. Jackie's glad of that. They are two people doing a job together. Their parts are defined. But midway along some of the long driveways she remembers Grama's words and indulges in a tear or so of wrathful self-pity.

The snow lets up by mid-morning and the county has the River Road plowed to two of its three lanes, but drifting continues. Conditions are too bad to run back into town for a Subway breakfast. Before dawn Roscoe had produced two peanut butter sandwiches, and now they stop at a small grocery where they leave a case of milk and buy candy bars and apples. They warm up while discussing the weather with the elderly proprietors, who regale them with stories of much worse blizzards past. Jackie sits with her stockinged feet on the radiator and is gratified to find her toes gradually returning to her, red hot and itchy and full of needles and pins. She is reluctant to leave.

After the northernmost customer and longest driveway, Roscoe says, "Well, we've done it. It'll be easier from now on."

Jackie knows this from her previous River Road day, for now they'll turn inland and work their way back to town through more level and sheltered residential districts. She and Roscoe grin at each other in triumph. The harrowing day has firmly bonded their partnership.

Still, it's mid-afternoon before they finish the route and head back out Colley Road. Jackie has never been so worn out, but her fatigue is countered by a feeling of strength and accomplishment, of rising to a situation, battling through, getting done a job that had to be done. It's an exhilarating feeling, and turns the worst day into a best one. Nonetheless she falls asleep before suppertime.

The two weeks end. Roscoe's doctor permits him to use his leg, and Jackie returns to the routine of school. She has liked spending her vacation on the milk route.

———

Her second stint of delivering milk comes the summer she's sixteen. She and Craig both want summer jobs, other than the usual detasseling. They want to team up on a milk route—Jackie can quickly learn to drive and get her license.

Daddy says it's not a good idea. He has enough route men, and he'd have to carve a route for the two of them out of others' routes, then give the pieces back to the regular drivers in the fall. Besides, he needs them for detasseling—they're experienced and conscientious. However, Stam is slowing down and could use a boost this summer, and Roscoe, still the relief man, would probably enjoy his old partner back for a month or so. This wouldn't be make-work, for they'd both be learning the business. He could also use them after detasseling season for fieldwork. They'd receive detasseling wages throughout.

It's not what they'd hoped for, total responsibility and going together, but they see the problems. They accept Daddy's offer. Lester Stam agrees to teach Craig the ropes. And Roscoe is indeed pleased to have Jackie back as runner, though he will do his share of running, this time. She assumes her familiar spot at the front of the truck.

Delivering milk in summer turns out to be vastly different from delivering in winter. There are still the early hours. She and Craig bicycle the mile and a half from Chez Nous down to the dairy in the dark. But dawn comes soon, a faint graying of the black and gradually a lighter gray, followed by pinky fingers and gold-lined fleece, and finally the rim of the sun, piercing a sudden beam into Jackie's eyes and pinning her to the truck.

It's often rather chilly, predawn and dawn, and she starts out with a sweater, but soon after sunrise the day begins to warm. By noon, when they are returning to the farm, it's usually hot. The gray insulation blanket is now used to slow the melting of the ice that Roscoe shovels over the load. The running is easier with no snow or bulky clothes, though the carrier still strains her arm socket. People are out and about more, doing yard and garden work, hanging up the wash, painting their porch rails. Children are all over. Small ones in sandboxes. Middle-sized ones riding their tricycles and bicycles up and down the sidewalks. Bigger ones playing ball or kick the can in the streets or vacant lots.

Now, instead of putting the milk inside to prevent its freezing, Jackie often has instructions to come right into the kitchen and put it in the refrigerator to keep it from going sour. This happens in houses where everyone goes out to work, and they don't want the milk sitting all day even in an insulated box. Jackie loves to go into people's kitchens, see what they eat, how they live. She's always curious and takes a quick and searching look around, sometimes even darts into the next room or down the basement

Jackie at fourteen.

stairs to see what the cellar's like. At one house there's a genuine-looking treasure chest sitting on the basement landing. Jackie can't resist raising the lid. It's a disappointment, of course. It contains only old issues of *Popular Mechanics*.

People are just as friendly in the summer, probably more so. She gets cookies regularly, or a sample of whatever's baking. Once she has to stand and stir a pudding so it won't stick while a housewife answers the front doorbell. Once she watches a baby in a high chair while the mother rushes to respond to a minor emergency with an older child upstairs. She gives the baby a spoonful of something sloppy out of the dish the mother was feeding him from and is gratified when the baby, never taking his eyes from hers, eats it. And once, on Olympia Boulevard, she catches her jeans on a sharp edge of the truck and they tear, exposing a generous amount of underpants and thigh. Roscoe drives her to old Mrs. Carabini's house, where she sits with a towel around her middle while Mrs. Carabini's deft fingers sew up the rip.

Friendliest of all are the dogs, even the unfriendly ones who somehow stop their growling or snarling when she stands perfectly still and speaks to them in a conversational voice. They change their minds and come crawling up on their bellies, wagging their tails apologetically. The ones behind fences or on chains make little whiny noises, wheedling her to come pat them. Never once does she get bit. There is every size and shape and age and breed of dog that exists, and Jackie figures she knows them all, a lot of them by name. She also knows many cats.

She goes through the shoe factory again, as she did once when she requested the experience for her ninth birthday, and this time through the other factories as well. They deliver to the service entrance of the hospital. They deliver to the Subway Café and have breakfast with Geneva. On Lester Stam's route they have a morning snack and gossip with Grama at 647 Milwaukee Road. The work at the Big House became too much for her, and she and Grampa are now living on the edge of town, close to the start of the road to the farm. Grampa is never there. He's still working all day in the fields and the barns, even though he's retired. Aunt Lillian and Hazel are also on Stam's route, and Jackie decides that some of Lester's slowness isn't due to age.

She covers every street in town and in South Beloit. She has more leisure and comfort to ponder the differences in neighborhoods, the grand houses on Sherwood Drive and Turtle Ridge, the old streets of substantial houses near the college, the streets of smaller houses to the north and west, the Athletic Avenue and Race Street area where almost all the Negroes in town are crowded because they aren't allowed to live anywhere else. The street name, "Race," is ironic. The street wasn't named to point up the segregation, but because it ran along the now dry and shrub-filled mill race off Turtle Creek.

And she delivers to Burrwood Park, on the river, its littered streets unpaved and without sidewalks, swarming with scantily dressed little white children. Some of the shanties have flowers and paint and flat stones leading up to the doors. Others resemble derelict chicken coops. Old people sit on sagging porches, weary-looking mothers balance naked babies on one hip while they fill a bucket from an outside tap and their other children plash in the muddy water under the spigot. The farm has now gone to every-other-day delivery, on account of the war. It saves fuel and rubber to deliver twice as much milk to half a route one day and the other half the next, rather than to cover the total route every day. Burrwood Park, however, still gets every-day delivery because so few of the houses have refrigeration.

There is also little plumbing. At one house Jackie knocks and a small boy dressed in only an undershirt comes dancing out, holding a Dougan pint bottle half full of yellow liquid. "See this?" he shouts at her. "That's pee-pee! That's what it is, pee-pee! Pee-pee!" And he capers in again. Jackie delivers her bottle, collects two empties, and is glad that the caustic cleanser in the bottle washer is as strong as it is.

Near the end of the River Road route they deliver to an old farmhouse. There's a stake in the yard, and fastened to the stake is a long rope trailing over the grass. Beyond the end of the rope is a dirt path, circling all the way around the stake.

"See that?" says Roscoe. "The man who lives here had an accident and went blind last year, and that's the way he gets his exercise. He holds onto the end of the rope and walks."

The stake and rope and path haunt Jackie. In her mind she keeps seeing the man holding the rope and walking and walking, nowhere, like a bull on the bull sweep at the farm, or on the treadmill bull walk. In the several times they deliver to that house she never sees the blind man.

Detasseling time comes, and Jackie and Craig shift jobs. Jackie has enjoyed the milk route. She can see why most of the milkmen have been with the farm a long time. It's a worthwhile job, delivering clean milk to people. It has variety. It's as sociable as you want to make it. It's personal. You're directly in touch with your customer—a bottle of milk is not like a can of soup on a grocery shelf. You're up early, in the freshness of the morning, and usually through by noon. It's pleasant work with lots of exercise, but not as taxing as pitching bundles or haying or even detasseling, except when the weather is grueling. Then it can match anything. But terrible weather has its satisfactions, too, in the challenge of battling the elements and the sweet fatigue of victory.

All in all, milk delivering is a good occupation. She understands why Grampa was reluctant to give up his first milk route, and feels a bit sorry for that nameless near-milkman who never got up the courage to try.

37 BIRTHING PARALYSIS

Jackie is fifteen. It's a bitter cold night, more than twenty below. Before bed she hurries down to the barn to give her goat extra straw and to put the horse blanket over her horse. Before leaving she glances around at the other animals. In the last box stall a shadowy form is lying down. It doesn't look quite right. Jackie peers closer. It's a cow, and now she knows something's wrong. She's never seen a cow lie flat on her side; cows recline with their heads up and their knees tucked under them. She opens the stall door so that the single bulb can shine in. She sees two little hooves protruding from the cow's vulva. She runs for Daddy.

"Nice boss, good boss," Daddy soothes as he enters the stall. "Let me see." He looks at the hooves, and puts a hand here and there on the cow's body.

"What's happening?" Jackie asks.

"Nothing, that's the trouble. The calf is coming backward and upside down. Head first, those are the easy deliveries. Besides that, she's down. I'll have to help her. I'll run get something else on. Watch her, see if she tries to stand up, or if there's any sign of labor. No telling how many hours she's been this way—the stock man was here around four. The calf's probably dead."

Jackie watches. The cow's chest moves as she breathes but her lower body is passive. Jackie's eyes keep returning to the two little hooves. One sticks out farther than the other, and is curved down. Her throat contracts with pity.

Daddy returns in his old clothes, with a bull's-eye flashlight. "Here, keep this turned on her."

Jackie holds the light steady while Daddy works his hand in beside the little hooves.

"What we try to do is turn them around, bring them out right side to," Daddy says. After a few minutes he adds, "That's not going to work here. I'm trying to loosen it, draw it out. But it's not loosening."

"Shouldn't we call the vet?"

"By the time he gets here from Janesville this calf will surely be dead. I've delivered this kind before." He works his arm farther and farther in. He keeps trying to turn the legs, gently pulling. Jackie can see sweat forming on his face, even in the intense cold that has her doing a jig and her toes freezing. The minutes drag by. Daddy grunts and breathes hard.

"*Merde*," he swears. "She'll die too if we don't deliver it. Here, better give me some help."

Jackie props the light where it will continue to shine on the area. Daddy guides her hand to the leg above a hoof.

"Pull *with* the leg," he instructs. "We don't want any broken bones. If the cow were helping we'd only pull when she pushes. But now we want just long steady pressure."

Jackie gingerly gives a tug on the cold, wet leg.

"Harder. Pull really hard. Don't worry about hurting the cow—she's numb, maybe even unconscious."

Jackie pulls as hard as she can. Beside her Daddy grunts and pulls too. Nothing budges.

"Run get Craig," orders Daddy.

Craig is still awake, reading in bed. He flings on his coat and boots and follows Jackie to the stall.

The three pull—Daddy on the legs, Jackie on Daddy's waist, Craig on Jackie's. It's like the old folk tale of all the people hauling on the radish.

"It's coming," Daddy says finally. "Keep up the pressure. Easy now!"

And then, as in the folk tale, they all fall backward. The calf is out.

Jackie grabs up the flashlight and trains it on the small body. Daddy feels the chest. "No heartbeat," he says. "Stand clear!" He picks up the calf by the feet and swings it so violently that Jackie and Craig recoil in shock. Then he hunkers down and feels for a heartbeat again.

"That sometimes starts them breathing," he says, sitting back on his heels, "but this one's dead." He swipes his sleeve across his forehead, leaving blood and muck instead of sweat. "I'm not surprised. Too long with the umbilicus strangled."

"What now?" asks Craig.

Daddy stands up and moves the calf away from the downed cow. "We'll tend to it in the morning. But this cow needs all the comfort she can get. Go find some old blankets and rugs, kids, and newspapers. Lots of newspapers. They're good insulation on a night like this. I'll get more straw."

Jackie and Craig return with the bedding. The cow is too heavy to roll over, but they manage to get papers under her head and shoulders and to jam them in along her sides. They bank her around with straw and cover her with the rugs. She lies as if dead, but breathing. Daddy pulls back an eyelid and shakes his head.

"Will she get well?" Jackie asks.

"Dr. Knilans'll check her out tomorrow, deliver the afterbirth, try to get her to her feet. If she can get up, she'll probably be all right."

Jackie puts her manury, bloody clothes by the washing machine before going to bed. She takes a hot shower. So do Craig and Daddy.

The next morning the cow is still alive, but she hasn't moved. The dead calf is at the edge of the stall, stiff, frozen. Jackie doesn't touch it. When she gets home from school, the cow is still down and the calf gone. Grampa is in the stall. Jackie's eyes are question marks.

"Birthing paralysis," Grampa says. "There's a nerve that sometimes gets compressed at birthing, the obdurator nerve. If it's only injured slightly, she'll get up in a day or two and be all right. But nerves repair slowly. If this were summer, we could let her lie for a week, even two or three, feed her, turn her so she doesn't get sores. See if she'll recover."

Jackie takes off her mitten and spells:

S-T-I-L-L   T-W-E-N-T-Y   B-E-L-O-W.

"Yes. The cold is hard on her, even here in the barn. And the longer we leave her down, the more chance we take of losing value if we have to slaughter. We haven't the men to tend and turn her as often as she needs it. We could lose a whole quarter of beef, even a side. We'll give her a few days and see what happens."

Jackie looks stricken.

Grampa smooths and smooths the neck of the paralyzed cow. "Poor little lassie. Poor little mother."

Jackie checks twice a day but the cow doesn't get up. The cold snap continues in its intensity. She's at school when the cow disappears.

She sees Grampa the next day.

"Yes, we had to butcher her," he says. "Dr. Knilans was down three times trying to get her up, but it wasn't any use."

Jackie shakes her head. Grampa does, too.

"Where there's livestock there's deadstock," he says.

38 DETASSELING CORN

Craig is in Beloit High. He has to write a theme for his English class. He thinks back over the summer, and writes:

The Detasseler

On the hairy surface of the quack grass and velvet weed, the early morning globules of dew cling, glistening in the sun. The earth is a richer black than usual, made so by a recent shower, and the head-high corn stands silently in the windless July morning.

Into this lovely setting steps the detasseler. His orders are to pick all the showing tassels from the cornstalks as he walks between the corn rows. At sixty cents an hour, what could be easier? With a light heart the novice enters the half-mile-long field and slowly bobs out of sight, leaving a trail of soft yellow tassels behind him.

An hour later our hero appears. His countenance no longer bears the smug smile it possessed a while ago, and his pants are saturated to the knees with dew. His arms and neck are crisscrossed with welts obtained from the sharp thin leaves of the corn plant. His shoes are now samples of good Wisconsin earth, coated an inch thick in most places.

After considerable thought on the subject—and there has been much time for thinking in the corn row—he realizes that the job is more difficult than he'd anticipated. The foreman assigns him to a new section, telling him that he is leaving too many tassels, and after all, what is he getting paid to do? Fine thing, our hero glowers, but says nothing and begins once again.

The corn seems higher than before, and the sun's heat is emphasized by the lack of wind. "Gee, it's hot," he mutters over and over again. His hand closes on a tassel. He pulls. There is a sticky feeling when he lets go. Careful scrutiny shows him that that particular tassel was the pasture for an ant colony's aphids, or cows, and he has wiped it out. He rubs his hand on his trousers, but streaks of green remain embedded in his pores. "How the heck did I get into this job?" he wonders, raising his eyes heavenward.

Suddenly he appears at the row's end. His glazed eyes spot the water jug. He stumbles over to it and sends the lukewarm liquid into and around his mouth. It mingles with the sweat and dirt on his neck and makes little rivulets around his Adam's apple.

By the end of the day, the detasseler is no longer a novice. He has learned many things about corn he has never known before. He wishes he had never discovered these things. He teeters to his bike and slowly pedals home, eats, and drops into bed.

The early morning dew glistens in the sun. The head-high corn stands silent in the hot, windless morning. Into this lovely setting steps the detasseler foreman. "Anybody know why that west-side kid didn't come today?" he asks. No one knows. "Damn kids—can't count on them," he mutters and hurries off to tell the boss.

Craig gets his paper back. On it his teacher has written, "A pleasure to read!" Craig glows. He takes it to show Daddy and Mother and Grampa.

Jackie likes Craig's story. She, too, has spent summers on the crew, starting when she was tall enough. She knows Craig's descriptions are accurate. There are details, though, that he has missed.

When it rains, for instance. She welcomes a shower on a blistering day. But the rain pelts her lifted face and blinds her. Her glasses are scant protection, and in addition they steam up with her body heat, and stream with rain. With or without them, she can't see the tassels. Corn cuts, too, are somehow sharper in the rain; the wet seems to hone the leaf edges. And the mud that sticks to her shoes fast becomes a heavy boot. Each foot must be slung forward with conscious effort. It does no good to go barefoot for then the mud clings over her ankles and up her legs, heavier by the step.

But in the early morning, on a fresh summer day, when the dew glistens on the hairy sides of the velvet weed, it's joyful to start off down a row. She is doing a vital job and being paid for it. The sun is not yet high. Its rays filter through the corn stalks. The air is cool. There is friendly shouting back and forth between the rows with the other crew members. Sometimes they throw tassels high in the air in an exuberance of good spirits. Then the individual paces of the other detasselers gradually leave her alone in the green world. Sometimes she stops detasseling and stands very still, to experience the solitude. Sometimes she makes up cheerful songs and sings them at the top of her lungs:

> Here we go a-tasseling, a-tasseling, a-tasseling,
> Here we go a-tasseling, all on a summer's morn.
> We tassel fast, we tassel slow,
> We tassel every female row,
> So hardly any tassels show
> Out in the Dougan corn.

Or she sings,

> Stand up, stand up for Dougan,
> You Hybrid 6-0-2!
> Stand up, stand up for Dougan,
> And show what you can do!

She sings, like Robert Frost's scyther, from sheer morning gladness at the brim.

After a while, of course, discomfort sets in. The sun rises above the cornstalks and pours down heat. No wind can penetrate the rows down where she is. Her clothes, saturated with dew, steam dry. So much sweat trickles down from her hair that it runs into her eyes if she's forgotten to wear her sweatband. And she develops her personal detasseling malady, a stomachache.

The reason is this. A tassel has many pollen-bearing fronds sprouting from a common base. To pull it, one must part the top leaves and grasp it firmly at the base. It must then be pulled *up,* with a sharp wrench, which snaps it. If the tassel is pulled down, it usually breaks off short, leaving the base and the start of the fronds hidden inside. These then are a time bomb. They will

Ron Dougan, second from left, admires hybrid corn with University of Wisconsin professors at a Corn Yields Field Day at the farm.

tassel out after the field is supposedly picked clean. Because she's short, Jackie's upward thrusts are not made with her arm muscles only. They also involve a tightening and jerking of her diaphragm and stomach muscles. One or two rows of work don't bother her. But as the hours of the morning go by, her stomach hurts worse and worse from the repeated jerking.

Added to this is the ache of her arms. The tassels are over her head. She progresses down the rows with her arms up so that her hands are ready for business. But hours of upraised arms is excruciating. Still, if she drops her arms between pulls, it takes forever to finish a row. Worst of all is when there's a field of very tall corn, too high even for tiptoes. Then she must not only jump for the tassel, but pull it out on the upward thrust.

Detasseling sections vary in difficulty. If the person the day before did a good job, the one who follows is lucky. If the predecessor was careless, it's another story. Hardest is when a new field comes into tassel all at once. Then there's a tassel to every stalk, three stalks to a hill, on both sides—for the detasseler covers two rows at once. Jackie can't just walk along, pulling here, pulling there. She must stop, make three individual jerks, swivel, make three more jerks, take a few steps forward to the next set of hills, jerk, jerk, jerk, turn, jerk, jerk, jerk. The tassels form a pale yellow carpet behind her, and the gray path ahead is interminable. Its end, with the milk can of tepid water, is the Holy Grail. As she tassels on and on she feels her stomach cannot last. She will lie down and die between the rows.

Compensation comes the next day, if she can manage to get a section she has thoroughly picked. Then she can gallop along the rows, catching the stray tassel here and there. This is the way it is at the end of the season, too. The crew is down to only a few workers, and they romp through the fields, finishing the day's work by nine or ten in the morning.

The west-side detasseler in Craig's story is afflicted with painful corn burns. Jackie is, too, until she learns always to wear a long-sleeved shirt, no matter how tempting it is to take it off and let the air in. Otherwise corn leaves, slashing at the same angle at the insides of her upraised arms, first redden the skin, then make it raw, and finally bring out thin lines of blood.

In the depth of a field there is no way to tell how far she's come, or has yet to go. She can only pray for deliverance. But at last she glimpses the fence, beyond the last two hills, and tumbles out onto the grass. She sprawls there for a few moments—water is only at the starting end—then gets slowly to her feet, takes her bearings, and starts back along two fresh rows. The bearings are important. Detasselers have been known to get mixed up and detassel the necessary male rows or to return in a wrong lane, leaving a female row in full tassel.

While she's detasseling, the crew foreman is policing the field, checking on the efficiency of each worker. Some years he rides the horse, and Jeff wears a muzzle like a kitchen strainer without a handle. It's ignominious to Jackie to have Frank Moore come up behind her and cast down an armload of tassels she's missed. She not only feels chagrin to be doing a mediocre job, she also knows what missing tassels means. To the kids who bicycle out from town, detasseling is just a job. If they're careless, so what? But Jackie has a vested interest in the work. If the state inspector finds more than a tiny percentage of female tassels pollinating in a field, that field is condemned. The work and cost that went into it isn't quite for nothing—the corn can be fed to the cows and pigs, as the male corn is—but it's worthless as hybrid seedcorn. Maybe Daddy should give everyone a simple lecture: That a corn plant is both sexes, the tassel male, and the ear with its silk hanging out to catch the pollen, female. Therefore a plant can self-pollinate. But if you plant a field with two different sorts of corn, and pull the tassels off just one sort, then that sort becomes female only, and is pollinated by the tassels of the other sort. The ears that are cross-pollinated result in hybrid vigor, result in much better corn, and that's because . . .

Jackie shakes her head. There's so much more to it; even the start isn't that simple. Better just to keep telling all the detasselers that a lost field is a major disaster for the farm, and they better not be the cause of it.

But, in her telling, she has left herself still in the cornfield, on the return trip. She tassels back down the section with dogged determination until finally she bursts forth near the spot she started. There sits the blessed water can, or occasionally a case of cold orange or chocolate, just brought from the dairy. She can empty a half-pint of orange in one long breath. Sometimes the foreman is waiting for her, to direct her to a new section. Sometimes the rest of the crew is lounging there waiting for the stragglers before they all head for another field. If the field is on one of the other farms, they pile into the back of the farm truck. Then the ride is a gratefully received rest, with the wind blowing through Jackie's hair.

And finally, when all the fields have been covered and the job is done for the day, comes the delicious shower in the back hall washroom, which rinses all the grime and sweat and tiredness away.

A detasseled cornfield.

From the knoll of the Chez Nous yard, Jackie has a view of the detasseled fields. The plumed male corn stands out clearly from the detasseled female. The even pattern of six green rows and two tawny, six green, two tawny, combs over the land. She takes pleasure in the sight. It's a satisfying job, she thinks, detasseling. She knows Craig thinks so, too.

39 SNAKES

From the very start, W. J. Dougan has held his help to lofty standards. In a 1927 article published in *Hoard's Dairyman* titled "What I Am Doing on My Farm to Solve the Labor Problem," he writes:

> I require men of high quality. They must be intelligent, of clean morals, loyal to their employer, and efficient. The farm requires men of intelligence because they have to be independent workers. They must take a job and carry it through to completion. They must be clean in morals and in person because they handle the most delicate and most easily contaminated of food. They must be efficient because there is no place on a farm for a droon or a shirk. I am able to keep men of this high standard. Many of my men are college graduates; all are men of alert intelligence. Even during the war I held to my ideals and had enough men to carry on. . . .

And when a potential employee is interviewed, standing on the red rug before Grampa's desk in the Big House, the agreement is not consummated until he signs a card saying that he does not drink, smoke, or swear.

Over the years the farm has a remarkable procession of employees. Although with human frailties, they are in most instances honest, conscientious, hardworking, clean living. Several, like DeWitt Griffiths and some of the milkmen, never move on to other jobs but remain with the farm their entire working lives.

Uncle Pat, though, once says to his brother, when they are talking about early gallants, "There *have* been occasional snakes in the garden, you know!"

Daddy responds, "Not to mention the slugs and cutworms!"

Jackie has heard stories about workers who could be classified thus, workers before her time. With others, she's been a witness. She asks Uncle Pat; she asks Mother and Daddy. She keeps her ears open. Eventually, she compiles a list.

A man is caught smoking in the barn and dismissed. Another keeps a bottle hidden in a rumble seat; at its discovery he, too, is let go. Swearers are harder to apprehend, for Grampa can't hear them. One once takes glee in using foul language in Grampa's presence. Mr. Griffiths and others are shocked, more by the insult to Grampa than by the language itself. They tell Grama, and the man receives a tongue-lashing he'll never forget. It's remarkable that Joan and Patsy, Jackie and Craig grow up on a busy farm peopled by a spectrum of workers, yet aren't aware of the more obscene expletives of the language until they hear them at school.

Pilfering at the gas pump occurs now and then, one spate by the teenage sons of a farmhand. The boys drive across the fields and up the lane from the pasture so they won't be noticed coming onto the place. But Ralph Anderson notices, and Daddy deducts the price of the gas from the worker's paycheck. The boys also substitute new tires from the farm for their own worn ones; Daddy discovers this, too, and makes them bring the tires back.

There is some thievery of dairy products, even though Grampa and Daddy's policies are generous: milk returned from the route is free for the drinking; men who live away from the place can even take it home. These same teenagers, until they are apprehended, switch the fresh milk and free day-old milk in the cooler and carry home the fresh.

Daddy catches and fires an employee who in his own car is plying a milk route after work with milk stolen from the dairy cooler—some fifty quarts a day. Another, who has a small farm and a few cows of his own, puts the raw milk into Dougan bottles and peddles them on his route at a lower price to certain favored customers. He then pockets the revenue.

A rare helper at Grama's or Mother's carries off produce in a large purse or shopping bag. One who had previously made off with blueberries, horse blankets, and a device for bottling root beer goes too far when she tries to smuggle a watermelon under her coat.

There are certainly thieves who are never spotted. Willis Morecombe is one. In 1929 he left the farm, Jackie learns, and headed west. The herdsman, Clair Mathews, is happy to see his back, for Willis has been sparking

Clair's wife. Several years later Morecombe writes that while employed he stole five hundred dollars from Daddy Dougan. Now he's got religion and been born again. He encloses fifty dollars and will send the rest as soon as he can. He never sends another nickel, yet Grama and Grampa correspond with him over the years, and on a trip to Colorado are entertained royally at his ranch in the mountains. Perhaps Grampa figures he has to collect his debt in trade.

At least one employee regularly filches tools and supplies. Daddy is aware but doesn't do anything, for the man is needed on the farm and his pilfering is not hurting the business too much.

During World War II there's a new route man who juggles his figures to his advantage and pockets the difference. He's caught, leaves the farm, makes restitution. Grampa and Daddy don't call in the law.

Of the sexual trespasses, most must be known only to the parties involved. But the advances to teenaged Esther by O. J. Miller and Walter Lake are found out, and Floyd Peters, apprehended climbing across the roof and into Esther's bedroom, is fired on the spot. Bobby Emmert, age seventeen, comes to the farm from a rural village up north and is seduced by a helper in the Big House kitchen, Frances, a woman perhaps ten years his senior. She herself is married to a hired man, Oscar; they live in the upstairs apartment at the Hill Farm. She leaves her husband a note on a paper bag, saying that she doesn't want him anymore, she has a new lover. He departs but starts watching. There's a wild scene when he comes roaring into the bedroom. Bobby, britches in hand, flees out the window, across the porch ledge, over the canopy, and slides down the column, gathering splinters the whole way. Frances tries to salvage the situation by urging Oscar to go after Bobby and beat him up. He replies, "Blame yourself; you shouldn't go after a young boy." He disowns his wife. She turns out to be pregnant, and when the baby—perhaps Oscar's, perhaps Bobby's—is born, Frances puts her in an orphanage.

When Ronald is eleven, he tells Jackie, he wanders into the horseyard and glimpses the visiting brother of a barnhand doing something very odd to the pony. The scene makes him so uncomfortable that he backs away without being noticed. Uncle Pat adds that not the brother, but the barn worker himself, lays a carnal hand on him. At nine he's ignorant of the man's intent, but wriggles away and runs. He avoids going into the barn from that day until the man leaves for other employment.

There are miscellaneous incidents. A group of first-day detasselers flatten a large area of valuable hybrid seed corn to let the breeze into the middle of the field while they play cards. A pair of farmhands steal a car in town and hide it in the calfbarn. A milkhouse worker fails to register for the draft. A farmhand beats a horse and is fired.

Occasionally a Galahad falls from grace. In his old age, Jim Howard, model herdsman in the twenties, confesses to having tied two cats' tails together with a length of rope and then slung the rope over a beam in the side barn. "I don't know why I did it," he says shamefacedly, "and I was instantly appalled, and managed to cut them down before they did much harm to each other." He shakes his head in bemusement at his young self.

Totally unregenerate, however, is Louie Kozelka. He comes from a poor family in Necedah up north and boards at the farm. Grampa and Grama have retired to the edge of town, and Pat Anderson is now in charge of the Big House. Louie is an indifferent young man as to intelligence and working habits, but at the end of the war it's increasingly difficult to get help of any sort, so he's kept on. He goes home frequently, and though his stays are brief, he always carries two suitcases away from the farm. He courts a girl in Beloit and announces their engagement. Her family is even poorer than his. They'll be married at the Janesville courthouse, but there'll be no subsequent festivities. Neither family will be present. Louie hints broadly that they would like to be given a reception at the farm.

Pat Anderson and her husband Ralph are good-hearted. So are the other farmhands, and Grampa and Grama, Mother and Daddy. They all chip in to pay for a dress for the thin little bride. Pat bakes the wedding cake. Mother makes sandwiches and favors; Grama and Grampa buy candy and nuts. The men bring in garden flowers to decorate the dining room. There's fruit punch in a punch bowl. A lace tablecloth is on the table, and the best china and silver. Everyone contributes to the wedding present: matched sheets and pillowcases, wrapped in silver wedding-bells paper and tied with a silver bow.

Louie is expansively pleased with the reception, but his bride speaks only in monosyllables. Pat thinks perhaps she's embarrassed by the modest affair, or by what may be the skimpiness of her wedding rings, for she keeps her hands clasped tightly behind her. The couple moves into the vacant first-floor apartment of the Big House, the southwest rooms that used to be the office.

Louie's wife is rarely seen. The shades are always pulled. There's no sign of housework being done: no sound of vacuum sweeper, no clothes flapping on the line, and only rarely smells of cooking. There are noises of a dog and cat, and the radio is on from early morning till late at night.

"She must never get out of bed," observes Pat, whose ears place the radio in the bedroom. "Those wedding sheets are getting good use."

But on Louie's day off they will both issue forth, dressed in their Sunday best, and with heavy suitcases head north for Necedah.

Several months go by. Daddy has called Grampa's attention to the suitcases. He's also told him that expensive hybrid seed corn has been disappearing from the storehouse. They both suspect Louie of stealing corn and selling it on his frequent visits home, but they're reluctant to accuse him without proof.

One day, after Daddy sees Louie enter his apartment from the outside door, carrying a laden gunnysack, he comes and knocks. Louie is a long time answering. When he finally does, Daddy asks if he may come in and look around. Louie wants to know why. Daddy says he wants to see the gunny-

A summer meal on the lawn, 1917. Ronald is standing; Grama, Trever (sun in his eyes), Grampa, and Esther are across the table. All seven of these hired men are good guys!

sack. Louie brings it to the door. It doesn't seem as heavy now as it appeared going in, and contains a few potatoes and onions. Daddy apologizes and leaves, but not before glimpsing the state of the apartment. He worries whether he should force a cleanup.

Two days later Louie asks Mrs. Anderson for a plumber's helper. She brings it to him.

"Are you having trouble with your toilet?" she asks. Louie says he is.

A day later Pat asks if the problem is solved. Louie is noncommital. Pat says if something's wrong it should be fixed, and he should see Erv, the farm handyman, about it.

The next day water starts backing up in the sinks and drains of the main house. Pat goes to Ron. He seeks out Louie in the barn, goes with him to his apartment, and insists on seeing the toilet. He picks his way through the darkened living room, through the darkened bedroom where Louie's wife, curled up in bed with radio blasting, and with dog and cats beside her, doesn't turn her head. He enters the kitchen. Crusted dishes growing mold are piled everywhere and dirty water and dishes brim the sink. In the narrow bathroom behind the kitchen the toilet is gurgling and overflowing. There's water on the floor. Daddy seizes the plumber's helper and applies it vigorously, but it produces no results.

Louie shrugs and returns to the barn. Daddy works and works. Finally he gives up and fetches Erv. They cut off the water to the Big House. They drain the tank and stool and remove it. With all Erv's tools they can't get to any obstruction. Finally Erv inserts an auger, sets it rotating, and the trouble begins to emerge: grinding back out of the pipe come swollen corn kernels, some of them even sprouted. They work out as much corn as they can, but the auger doesn't go far enough. The pipe seems to be filled solid.

They go down to the cellar. The pipe travels a long way under the floorboards, almost horizontally, before going through the foundation on its way to the septic tank. The men break the pipe and pull out corn from either direction. Outside, they dig up the pipe and break it again. They have to climb down into the tank and ream out the pipe from beneath. They have to deal with the other affected plumbing. It takes two days of nasty work to put things to rights. Obviously somebody has flushed a great deal of grain down the toilet, but because of the pitch of the pipe, along with insufficient water pressure for the job, it didn't flush through.

Louie vehemently rejects all blame. He doesn't know how the corn got there. On a final trip through the gloom of the bedroom Daddy tartly suggests to Mrs. Kozelka that she get up and clean house. She doesn't turn her head.

Grampa is angry. "You must fire that man, Ronald," he says. But Ronald doesn't. He has no one to take his place; even bottom-of-the-barrels are hard to come by. It takes another month and another crisis before he does.

The two have departed on Louie's day off. The animals are locked in the apartment as usual. But instead of returning the next day, the pair doesn't show up. The third day comes and they aren't back. The animals are frantic and scratching at the doors. That night Mrs. Anderson calls Daddy.

"Ron," she says, "Louie and Ginnie have been gone three days, and there are animals in those rooms—crying. I'm worried about them. And the smell—well, the smell is seeping out into our living room, and it's pretty bad."

Daddy hurries down. He pries open a window. The stench rushing out nearly knocks him over. He climbs in to find bedlam. A dog and three cats are there, starved, and worse, have no water. There's no catbox; messes from many more days than three are spread over the floors. The apartment is a filthy shambles. Ralph Anderson, and Daddy muttering unprintable things in French, tend to the animals, while Pat retrieves a waffle iron and dishes. She takes down her own curtains from the windows, her own sheets off the bed, and picks through piles of stinking laundry for towels, facecloths, and pillowcases belonging to the Big House.

"No wonder they never hang out the wash!" she exclaims.

When Louie and his wife return the next day, Daddy tells them what he thinks of people who treat animals and property as they have. He says Louie better find employment elsewhere. The two pack up and leave; Louie is in a rage. They take the dog but abandon the cats.

The farm is left with a cleanup that takes weeks. Pat uses gallons of Lysol. Layers of food and feces have to be scraped off the floors. The rugs are a total loss. The rooms must be fumigated, the walls repainted. Grampa looks in every day or so, and shakes his head. But when the job is done, the Andersons like the fresh apartment so much that they expand into it for their own use.

Two months go by. Pat goes to her seldom-opened jewelry box and discovers that her mother's wedding ring and her father's ruby ring, tied up in a chiffon handkerchief, have vanished. She suspects these are the rings that Ginnie was hiding at the reception.

Two years go by. Ronald receives a letter. It's written on tablet paper, in pencil, and every other word is misspelled. It's from Louie Kozelka. With some difficulty Daddy is able to read that Louie divorced his first wife, married a fine woman, has a fine baby, is farming a fine farm, and wants everyone to know that he is getting along just fine. The letter ends with a word that is three times misspelled and crossed out. Finally it's written in block letters, misspelled a fourth way, and followed by black exclamation points whose periods slam right through the paper. Ronald puzzles over all misspellings until the word suddenly comes clear.

Catastrophe! The last sentence, were it legible, reads, "But you RON DOUGAN are a CATASTROPHE ! ! ! ! ! !"

Daddy whoops and pockets the letter to show the family, and Grampa, and the Andersons.

"You always look to see where a compliment is coming from," Grampa observes.

40 CATCHING A CUD

It's 1944, a Saturday morning in September; Jackie has begun her junior year. She comes downstairs to find Dr. Knilans having a cup of coffee with Daddy. He's made an early call at the round barn, but on that farm he has to stub out his cigarette before he gets out of his car. He knows he can always smoke and have a lively chat in Ron's kitchen.

Jackie has missed this morning's chat. But seeing Dr. Knilans gives her an idea. She has an essay for English due Monday. As assignments go, she puts "My Trip" on a par with "What I Did on My Summer Vacation," but she's dutifully thought over trips she's taken. Nothing has grabbed her—till now.

"Could I ride with you today?" she asks the vet, remembering she's always wanted to do this. "So I can watch what you do and ask questions, and then I'll write about it for my English assignment."

Dr. Knilans readily agrees. He likes company. Daddy says he'll pick her up in Janesville whenever they phone from the animal hospital. She asks about packing a lunch, but Dr. Knilans says he always arranges his day to eat at home. She grabs her jacket and boots, in case of barnyard muck, and a notebook and pencil, and hurries after the vet.

She settles into the sprung seat of the familiar Buick. The car has a great many miles on it and is rusting out. It smells of medicine and cigarette smoke, manure and oil. But with the war, there are no new cars. However, Dr. Knilans's vet status gets him all the gas and tires he needs.

He turns east onto Colley Road.

"So, what are your questions?" he asks Jackie.

Jackie opens her notebook. "Well, cow stomachs. I've never really understood them, except a little about the first one that the grass goes into and the cud comes up from."

"The rumen. That's the storage vault. It can hold fifty gallons of fluid in a large dairy cow. No digestion like ours goes on there, but it's filled with bacteria that break down the cellulose in the plants. Makes 'em digestible. Then the cud comes up, and the cow chews it, and it goes down into the second compartment. The reticulum."

Jackie writes rapidly. "How does the cud know to come up? How does it know where to go next?"

Dr. Knilans strokes his cheek with one finger. "I guess it just knows. And when it goes down again, it's chewed up pretty fine, and there's a groove, I think, and it just goes on into the honeycomb."

"Honeycomb?"

"That's what they call the reticulum. Have you eaten tripe?"

Jackie knows tripe is cow stomach. "Not any more than I can help. But I've seen it, when they butcher."

"Then you know its honeycomb pattern. It's called honeycomb tripe. We eat the rumen lining, too; that's smooth tripe. Then the third compartment is the omasum and the final one's the abomasum—there's where true digestion takes place. The sort we know, with hydrochloric acid and pepsin."

"Wait, wait! And *spell*." Jackie writes furiously. "But what do they *do*? Those middle ones?"

Dr. Knilans strokes his cheek again. "You're sure this isn't for biology? Well—the honeycomb is for temporary storage, I think, and in the omasum, a lot of liquid gets squeezed out." He turns into a farmyard.

"It seems to me," says Jackie, "that a cow has about two more stomachs than it really needs."

"You may have a point. I certainly wouldn't mind two less to doctor."

The farm is a sprawling one, with many outbuildings. Jackie follows the vet into the barn. The farmer, along with a large dog and several mucous-eyed cats, meets them. She pats the dog. The ailing cow is in a box stall. The farmer reports that she's not eating and her milk's fallen off. He holds her tail aside while Dr. Knilans takes her temperature. Then the vet listens to her heart with his stethoscope, moving it all over her chest area. He presses under her ribs; she grunts. He presses again, the cow grunts again.

"She's filled up with fluid," Dr. Knilans says. "She's swallowed something sharp; it's in the reticulum and it's pierced the pericardium. She's hurting. But I can't do anything. You'll have to ship her."

Pulling out of the farmyard, Dr. Knilans shakes his head. "I do Caesareans occasionally, but I haven't begun yet to operate for hardware. Where my son Dick's in school they have a whole case of things found in cows' reticulums. Stones, bones, nails, forks and spoons, bob wire, shoes, sardine tins, things you wouldn't believe, everything but the kitchen sink. A whole umbrella. Probably closed when she swallowed it."

Either way, Jackie finds it hard to imagine. She consults her notes. "But why the reticulum? That's the *second* stomach."

"The rumen's smooth, things slide on through and lodge in the honeycomb. A cow can live with a stone or two; it's the sharp things that cause the trouble, they pierce through the stomach wall and the diaphragm into the lungs and heart. You have to be so careful. A cow'll eat anything in the grass. A pig won't. Now that we've begun baling hay the cows are full of baling wire. Binder twine never seems to bother them, though."

"Not like Henry King," says Jackie.

"Who?"

"A poem. He died from his bad habit of swallowing string."

"Reminds me of my cousin Earl," Dr. Knilans says. "I was visiting on his farm when I was a kid, and he took a long piece of string, and tied a chunk of ham fat to one end, and threw it among the geese, and one gobbled it up, of course. Well, the next day, three geese were all lined up on that string, beaks to bungs. Took a while to untangle that one!"

Jackie is hugely amused. "What happened to Earl?"

"He got away with it. He got away with everything. But he came to a bad end. Don't put all that in your English paper, now." He turns into another farmyard. "A quick stop, here. Twin calves, came yesterday. I need to check out the heifer."

In that barn Jackie discovers that most heifers twinned with a bull will never be milkers. They're almost always sterile.

"Nine out of ten," Dr. Knilans says, back in the car. "They're called freemartins. They get the wrong hormones, their reproductive tracts are all screwed up. And they pee straight up in the air. Now, if the twins are both heifers, *that's* a bonus."

The morning calls continue varied. In one barn, Jackie watches the vet give an enema to a newborn foal, and steps back when the foal defecates explosively. "They're born plugged," says Dr. Knilans. "If they don't move their bowels soon, they'll die. The stimulation of nursing usually does it."

In the next barn a farmer has lead-poisoned a cow. Dr. Knilans shows his exasperation. He explains in the car.

The cow had ringworm, a fungus. A fungus needs air, so treatment is with grease, or a salve like Petro-Carbo. But for many years, farmers would smear on crankcase oil drained from the tractor, and that worked pretty well. "But then lead got added to gasoline," Dr. Knilans says, "and lead gets into the cylinder rings and concentrates in the crankcase, and a lot of farmers killed their animals. But it shouldn't be happening now. They know better."

Jackie tells Dr. Knilans about some doctoring she'd done last year. She'd found a barn kitten with an oozing sore on its neck and had covered the spot with a thick coating of Petro-Carbo. The next day there'd been a huge grub poking out the hole like an obscene tongue, quite dead. She'd pulled it out with a toothpick. After that the sore had healed right up.

"Yes, you cut off its air supply. Vaseline would've done it too, even butter. That could've been a heel-fly grub. . . . Do you remember that there were a lot of mysterious calf deaths in the round barn when you were little? Those turned out to be lead poisoning."

"No, tell me," says Jackie.

"I wasn't your vet yet, but I heard about it. Well, first one would die, and a week or two later another one, and then two at once—they were kept in that shed for older calves, behind the barn. And your dad and grandfather knew it was lead, since they ran the bodies up to Madison. The state vet did postmortems. So the word kept coming back lead, but they couldn't find the source. They had all the feed tested, and buckets, and chips of paint from the walls and windowsills, anything a calf could eat or lick, and there wasn't any lead—and then another calf would die. Your dad told me he'd never known such frustration. And then one day he was hanging over the stalls, pondering, and the sun was shining through a window onto the bedding—it was wood shavings—and he caught a glint of red on a scrap of shaving. He picked it up and then rummaged around in the sawdust and found more red scraps—not enough to notice unless you were really looking—and then he went up to the big pile in the side barn—"

"We always played circus over that sawdust," Jackie says. "If you fell off the trapeze it didn't matter."

"Well, he found more flecks of red in the shavings there, and it was red paint. The farm had been getting sawdust free from the Beloit Iron Works, from the pattern shop where they made wood forms for casting. They dressed the form ends with red paint, and the paint got into the shavings. Apparently it had a salty flavor the calves liked."

"We must have quit using those shavings in a hurry!"

"Certainly for the calves. I think they still use it in the round barn, behind the cows where they can't reach no matter how much they try."

"We're coming into Janesville," Jackie observes.

"Yes, time for lunch."

Jackie has scarcely noticed their route, but sure enough, the vet has contrived to be close to home at the proper time. Mrs. Knilans has been alerted; there's a place set for a visitor. After eating, while Dr. Knilans is collecting his afternoon calls, Jackie wanders into the hospital. She's familiar with it, the caged dogs setting up a din when they see her, except the sickest who lie huddled and look up at her with dull eyes. She greets each one, but it's Bill the monkey she's looking for, in his end cage. She squats and hands him pellets. He reaches through the grille and tucks them one by one into his cheeks, the whole time surveying her with his little bright eyes.

Dr. Knilans finds her there. "We're giving that rascal to the Madison zoo," he says. "He gets out and raises Cain, into the kitchen and opens all the cereal boxes, into here and lets the dogs out, climbs up on the shelves and tips over the medicines, gets into the feed. I'm fed up."

Jackie is sorry. When they were younger, Bill was the major reason they always wanted to stop at the veterinary clinic when the family was near Janesville. He's still an attraction. Maybe Dr. Knilans's words are just a threat.

The first afternoon stop is an emergency. A cow is down and has lost consciousness. Dr. Knilans diagnoses milk fever and gives her an intravenous. While he and the farmer talk, Jackie looks at cows and calves, pats the farm dog, coaxes the wild barn kittens. When she wanders back, the ill cow is on her feet looking perfectly normal.

On the road again, Dr. Knilans tells Jackie the technical name, and she writes "Milk Fever—Hypocalcemia" in her notebook.

"Magic, isn't it? Ten minutes and they're cured. I gave her 500 cc's of calcium gluconate. Milk fever can come on as soon as a calf is born, no later than two, three days. It's a hormone thing, a lack of calcium and magnesium; it can kill in short order. They used to think lactation was the cause of it, and of course milking does take calcium out of the system, so they'd insert little tubes into the quarters and pump air into the udder with a bicycle pump. They'd tie off the tits, and the cow'd quit producing. That sometimes cured her, but she might well end up with mastitis or some other infection afterward."

"Mastitis," says Jackie, hastily writing. "That's garget."

"Yes, the common name, and that's our next stop. I'm treating some cows over near Carver's Rock."

Jackie tells how in the round barn, before every cow is milked, the tits are dipped in something—

"A chlorine solution, to kill germs," inserts the vet.

"—and then the barnhand squirts milk from each tit into a gauze-covered cup, for garget. If there are any flakes—"

"Or even blood, in advanced cases."

"—then they milk that quarter by hand, and give the milk to the cats that are all waiting. So what is it? What's an advanced case?"

"Well, it's an udder infection that enters through the teat canal. And if you really want the details"—Dr. Knilans ticks them off—"temperature, fast pulse, quick breathing, shivering, they're afraid to lie down, won't eat, hardly chew their cuds. They stand with their legs straddled, they make a funny paddling with their feet, their udders are swollen and painful—and there's a foul discharge. They might even get gangrene."

Jackie expels her breath. "How awful!"

"But we rarely see a case that bad. Most mastitis is chronic."

Dr. Knilans prepares to give a shot.

At the next farm the barnyard is deep in muck; the milling cows are filthy. The sick ones, three of them, are inside in stanchions. The farmer greets Jackie as a Knilans daughter.

"No, just a friend," Dr. Knilans says. "Learning to be a vet."

Jackie finds that an interesting idea.

Dr. Knilans examines an udder. He shows Jackie the inflamed quarter. "See how red and sore it is? A new infection." He gently strips the milk into a pail. Then he fits a small tube to the end of a syringe and shoots something up into the tit. From his bag he takes two large pills and thrusts them down the cow's throat. "Apply a little heat to the inflammation," he tells the farmer. He examines the other two cows, not just their udders, to which he gives nods, but peels back their eyelids, feels their stomachs. "Off their feed?"

The farmer nods. "They're not chewing much."

"We'll have to catch a cud," Dr. Knilans says.

Jackie is mystified. She once wrestled her goat down and forced her cud out, to see what it looked like, but it couldn't be that, not with a cow.

But it is, almost. The farmer supplies a tin cup and the men go to the barnyard. Jackie watches from the entrance. The cows back off but the farmer grasps the nostrils of one with a nose leader. She arches her neck, rolls her eyes, and opens her mouth. Slobber beads out. Dr. Knilans swipes his hand around her mouth, then wipes the drool into the cup. The farmer grabs another cow and Dr. Knilans repeats the performance. Then he returns to the barn, takes the slobber from the cup, and smears it around the two cows' noses and gums. Their long tongues lick it in.

"Repeat that, if you have to," the vet instructs. "Or get a cud and mix it with their feed." He gives the farmer a packet of the big pills, washes his hands at an outside faucet, and they drive from the farmyard.

Jackie's pencil-fingers twitch. "What was *that* all about?"

Dr. Knilans laughs. "Catching a cud," he says. "You know this morning we talked about the rumen, and bad and good bacteria? Well, if anything happens to kill the bacteria in the rumen, the good bacteria that's breaking down the cellulose, then the rumen shuts down. It has to have a drink of good-bug cocktail in order to get going again. We could actually take a cud from another cow and sometimes do, or even tube another cow; that irritates and she regurgitates, and we get her liquid down the sick cow. But it's easiest just to collect the slobber. Slobber's full of good bacteria."

Jackie is intrigued. "But what makes the good bugs die?"

"In this case, sulfa—sulfanilamide. A new wonder drug, 240 milligrams a pill, and I prescribe two in the morning, two at night. It kills the mastitis bugs—strep or staph or E. coli—but it can also wipe out all the others. What I injected just now was penicillin—that's our *real* wonder drug. But it's so scarce I can only get a hold of a little. Not enough to shut down a rumen, though it might help. I divide it into small amounts, use it sparingly. You know about penicillin?"

Jackie does; she's read about it in *Life* magazine, and how many soldiers it's saving.

"Mastitis is catching, and the cows really ought to be isolated, but it's hard in a herd."

Jackie studies her notebook. "Can people catch it?"

"We don't seem to. Though I can't imagine it improves the flavor of the milk. Mainly it spoils cows. You lose a quarter or two, and no farmer finds it profitable to keep a half or three-quarters cow. . . . Now at this next place," Dr. Knilans pulls into a tidy farmyard, "I'll deliver a calf that probably isn't here yet."

It isn't. The cow is still in labor, not making progress. Jackie can tell the farmer is relieved the vet has come. Dr. Knilans strips to the waist, pulls on a long sleeve, and reaches deep into the cow. Jackie settles onto her haunches to watch.

"This is her first calving, a tight cervix, that's why she's having trouble," the vet says. "But the feet are out." He reaches with his other hand into his bag and pulls out a length of chain. The farmer threads the chain through a link at one end and Dr. Knilans feeds the chain into the cow, up to his other hand. "This is an obstetrical chain," he tells Jackie. "I loop it around the front feet and tighten it like a slip knot. The calf lies with its front legs forward and the head cradled down on the legs. It should come out all in one piece. Now, pull with her labor, Mr. Jenkins."

They pull, then hold the gain, pull again, hold again. They keep up a steady pressure, working with the cow. In a few moments the calf's front hoofs and head appear; on the next labor heave the body is thrust out. Dr. Knilans catches it, all unfolding legs, and lays it gently on the straw. He runs his fingers into the mouth and nostrils, clearing the mucus. The calf takes a snorting breath and Jackie breathes, too. She feels such an unexpected surge of joy at the ordinary wonder that she blinks back tears.

Dr. Knilans unfastens the chain and pours iodine on the navel, nudging the mother's insistent head back until he's finished. They leave the barn with the cow roughing the calf all over with her tongue.

"It's a bit paradoxical how a wet tongue can dry a calf," Dr. Knilans says. He peels the sleeve at the car, rubs himself with a towel, and puts his shirt and jacket back on. "That licking both dries and stimulates. It won't be long before the calf's on the tit. She needs that first milk—it's full of protective antibodies. Even after a calf's been separated, they take the mother's milk to it for a while. And if a cow dies birthing, we get milk from another cow that's just calved, to protect the orphan."

Driving down the road again, Dr. Knilans lights a cigarette. Jackie watches a hen pheasant prowling at the edge of a cornfield and makes a few nature comments in her notebook. The wild grapes blueing in thick clumps on the fences, the black-eyed Susan clusters, a lone cornstalk standing tall in a ditch. Then she records the last visit. "What about the afterbirth? It didn't come out."

"It might come soon. Maybe not till tomorrow. If it's not out by the next day, I'll come back to clean her."

"Does the cow ever eat it?"

"It doesn't do her any good; they've never been meat eaters. But it's nature's precaution to keep wolves and such from knowing there's been a birth. Now, we have one more stop, over on County M—a callback on a sick cow. But the calves there have scours. You know scours?"

"When I was little," says Jackie, "maybe five or six, I followed Grampa down into the side barn. One of the newborn calves struggled to stand up and shot a stream of bowel movement clear across the pen, I bet eight feet. And then another calf did, not quite so bad. Grampa stopped stock still. He was so angry his voice shook. 'The herdsman should've caught this!' he said, and went up into the round barn, I suppose me right behind, and I don't remember what came next. All I remember is that powerful shot, it was so startling. And Grampa's anger, because he never gets mad."

"Yes, that was scours, diarrhea. It's the greatest calf-killer we have. It's highly contagious and caused by bacteria, but there's not a whole lot we can do besides keep them clean and try to slow the peristaltic action. It helps to keep them apart and move their pens regularly, like hogs, so they aren't infected from the ground. But the farmer can go out and buy medicine himself, astringents like bismuth, without paying a vet. . . . Some vets are dosing them up with lots of vitamins, see if that will help."

They enter the final barn, Dr. Knilans checks his patient, looks at the calves, chats with the farmer, and they head back toward Janesville.

"Any other questions?" Dr. Knilans asks. "Got enough for your paper?"

"Plenty," Jackie says fervently. "But, does it hurt to have your horns sawed off? They're not like hair or fingernails, are they? I was down in the side barn once—I was little—and they had a heifer with her head in a wooden frame, she couldn't move at all, and they were sawing her horns off and it seemed like it was hurting awfully. Her eyes were rolling and she was gasping and moaning—I couldn't move—and when the horn came off, it wasn't hollow like I expected, it was sort of spongy, and it bled."

Dr. Knilans lights a cigarette. "Yes, it hurts, and I'm afraid I don't anesthetize. There's an artery that goes only into the horn; I pull it out so the spot won't bleed. It clots inside. Some cows never get horns, it's been bred out of them—Angus, the whole breed is polled. Cows that do are mostly dehorned when they're calves. You cut the hornbud with a jackknife, or use caustic. I usually cut off the nubs and scoop out the base of the horn; that probably hurts some. But it's fast."

"And in the side barn again, there was a newborn calf and it had its legs on—well, *backwards*, it looked like the hoofs were put on the wrong way, and it lay there on the straw all alone, and the next day it was gone."

Dr. Knilans chuckles. "Didn't you learn to stay away from that traumatic side barn? Well, that was a genetic defect. Flexed pastern."

"And pigs!" Jackie's words tumble on. "This time it was in the Big House kitchen, and I was little, and they brought in a litter of just-born baby pigs in a cardboard box, and somebody—it wasn't Daddy or Grampa—somebody picked them up one by one and crunched off all their teeth with a huge scissors, like a pliers, and those little pigs squealed like they were being butchered!"

"How is it you always manage to be on hand? Did you watch chickens get their heads chopped off, too? Those piglets, they were only getting rid of their milk teeth, which are sharp as razors and injure the sow. It probably hurt them some, but pigs'll squeal at having their tails pulled. I have a clippers for the job, but they're rather small. It's a quick operation."

"And I saw a cow that had just been hit on the head; I walked into the garage at the dairy, not knowing slaughtering was going on, and there it lay, dead." She doesn't add that in the moment of death it had made a small cow pat that lay at its tail, and that that pathetic little pile had given her such a wrench she'd turned and walked out again.

"You have to realize that animals don't anticipate pain like we do. It's suddenly there, and then it's over. And we do try to be humane."

Jackie nods. "Except dogs. When we bring Boxie up for her shots, she smells the hospital and claws to get back in the car again."

Dr. Knilans laughs. "Dogs are always an exception. Here we are. And there's your car. Your dad's here."

Daddy has come to Janesville for a part for the bottle washer and is talking to Mrs. Knilans over coffee. They ask how the day was.

"She asks a lot of questions, but she can come along any time," says the vet. "Next time, I'll have her pull on the chains."

"We never ran out of topics," Jackie says.

"Did he tell you about schistosomus reflexus, where the calf is born inside out?"

"*What!*" cries Jackie, and "*Ronald!*" cries Mrs. Knilans at the same time.

"We hardly touched on freak births; she has her own horrors," Dr. Knilans says. "They never live, and it only happens once in a blue moon."

Jackie grabs her notebook and writes down, "inside out."

"How about hoof-and-mouth disease, then?" Daddy asks. "Ol' Doc here is an expert. When he was a mere broth of a boy he was down on the Texas border, booting the infected animals back into Mexico."

"We eradicated it down there," Dr. Knilans says, "and up here, too. We killed herd after herd, buried 'em in great trenches. The government paid for all the slaughtered cows." Over his coffee he launches into detail. Then Daddy tells about the last epidemic in the Beloit area, in the early twenties. Grampa had put a notice in the paper, stating that no stock had been recently bought, all the cows had been tested that week, everyone on the place checked, no visitors were allowed in the barn, and until W. J. told them otherwise, Dougan's milk was SAFE.

"He didn't mention hoof-and-mouth till the last sentence," says Daddy.

"Talking about no visitors in the barn, I didn't tell Jackie, either," Dr. Knilans says, "that *vets* are notorious for spreading disease. You can follow the vet right down the road."

"*Used* to be notorious," says Mrs. Knilans firmly. "*Used* to be."

"On that cheerful note, we'll depart," Daddy says.

Riding home, Jackie tells Daddy about the day. "What I can't see is how any animal can grow up when there are so many things that can happen, or how anybody can drink milk, or how any farmer can make enough money to live on, with all the expenses there must be, even just from animals. Not counting corn borers, or drought, or everything else."

"It's not the easiest life," Daddy says.

"But never dull."

Daddy agrees. "Can you get it all in your paper? Dr. Knilans would probably like a copy. And Grampa."

"Well, not *all* of it." Jackie remembers the freemartin, the colt's enema, the swollen udders, Earl and the geese. "Maybe not very much of it at all. Doctoring animals is so—well, *basic*. I guess people are basic, too, but we try to hide it, especially at school." She grins. "I'll have to ruminate. See what comes up."

"Got a title?"

Jackie writing.

Jackie reflects. "You know, that's what I've been really doing all day. Catching what comes up. Maybe I'll call it 'Catching a Cud.'"

"Good name," says Daddy.

41 CRAIG'S MINUTES

Daddy is secretary-treasurer of the Rock County Breeders' Co-operative from its founding in 1938 till it's sold in 1957 to its long-term inseminator, Amos Grundahl. One winter evening in 1945 he takes Craig with him to the Janesville meeting. He suggests that Craig keep the minutes for him. Craig, who is sixteen, agrees. He sharpens his pencil, looks around at the assemblage, and settles to the task, denoting his father as R. A.:

—Knudson and Dave late

—Secretary-treasurer R. A. attempted to write checks

—Conway announced when meeting would end (9:25)

—Conway announced that he likes duck hunting

—Conway finally threw away his very beat-up cigar

—R. A., Godfrey, and Stew discussed oats. R. A. is getting $3.50 bu. for Clinton oats

—Conway announced he was getting $2.50 (uncleaned)

—Godfrey wondered if the friend of Conway that Markham was talking about was Glassco

—Stew Barlass muttered something at the mention of Glassco

—Conway got up & went out the door & told R. A. that he had something interesting to show him.

—R. A. said, as he looked out the door, "I'll come if it has a label on it."

—R. A. went out

—Stew went out

—5 minutes later Conway came in

—Godfrey and Markham went out

—R. A. came in and went to the House of Parliament

—Duff and S. went out

—Godfrey and Markham came in

—Duff and S came in

—The meeting came temporarily to order

—Stew came in (saying he wouldn't need to go to Charlie's) with a new cigar

—R. A. read the minutes I have just finished

—It was suggested they be burned

—The meeting went on

—Amos is going to be married the 4th

—The meeting was adjourned by Conway at 9:43

—The question came up whether Stew was in order

—It was questionable

—Stew went out

—Stew came in with a lamp for Amos, a wedding gift from the boys

—Conway made a nice speech and he and R. A. made a motion (with Stew) that the Association draw from the funds $25 for Mr. and Mrs. Amos Grundahl. Amos was very gratified. Amos is nice. I like Amos.

—Conway left at 9:50

—Human nature was discussed

"So," says Craig on the way home, "how did I do on the minutes?"

Daddy laughs. "Fine, aside from putting all our important Co-op business into one line! What was it—'the meeting progressed'?"

"Oh, that," Craig says. "That part wasn't important. All of you guys going in and out, to look at the lamp and sign the card for Amos—that was what tonight's meeting was really all about."

"I'm raising too smart a son," comments Daddy.

42 MUSICAL BEDS

Mother is a good friend of Thor Johnson, the conductor of the Cincinnati Symphony. When the symphony comes to play in Beloit she invites all the members, along with the music faculty of Beloit College and other musical friends, to an open house at Chez Nous after the concert.

Everyone comes and has a good time. But the first cellist, Walter Heerman, is particularly charmed. He wanders the house smiling beatifically, he walks around the lawn in the moonlight taking deep breaths, he ventures a short way into a hayfield. The second clarinetist and the harpist also walk in the moonlight, hand in hand out by the asparagus.

When the party starts to break up, Walter Heerman makes a request. "Would it be too much imposition to stay the night? It's so beautiful out here, and fresh, and out of the city. How much more lovely to wake up to the singing of birds and the scent of lilacs than to traffic noises and a hotel room! I could take a walk in the fields before breakfast."

Mother is surprised but rises to the occasion. She has to leave on a 6 A.M. train; in her role as vice president of the National Federation of Music Clubs she'll be speaking to a music club in Chicago, but she thinks rapidly. She has plenty of bacon and eggs and coffee and orange juice, so breakfast is no problem, although others will have to prepare it. And there are spare beds. She graciously extends an invitation.

Thor Johnson overhears. "That's a beautiful idea," the conductor says. "Might you have room for one more?"

Mother invites Thor, too.

When the second clarinetist and harpist get wind of the house party, they become eager. They, too, would love a night in the country! Possibly, possibly, could the Dougans add them in?

"Well . . . ," says Mother, wondering how many more of the orchestra will ask to stay, and totting up eggs and bacon and beds again. "Miss Hardwick, you could sleep in my son's room, he's away playing in the dance band. But I'm afraid Mr. Brissum would have to sleep on the couch."

Mr. Brissum assures Mother that he'd be delighted to sleep on the couch.

The open house ends and the orchestra goes back to the hotel, all except the conductor, the first cellist, the second clarinetist, and the harpist. They all sit around some more and talk and laugh. Then beds are made up, good-nights said, and the house becomes dark and still.

At two in the morning Craig tiptoes into the back hall. He's come home unexpectedly. He goes up to his room, undresses in the dark, pulls on his pajamas, and starts to crawl into bed. He's startled to encounter a feminine form, smell a feminine scent, and hear a feminine murmur.

"Honey? Oh, you mustn't." But a feminine arm starts to embrace him.

"No, I mustn't," agrees Craig, and beats a hasty retreat to the hall. He stands and thinks. If someone has been given his bed, that means all spare beds must be full. He takes a blanket and pillow from the blanket closet and pads downstairs to the living room. He'll sleep on the couch. He unfurls the blanket, wraps it around himself, fumbles for the couch, and sinks down onto it. He sits on a body and leaps up quickly.

The body makes a grunt, and then sighs in a sleep-laden voice, "Sweetie? Is that you?"

"I'm afraid not," Craig whispers. "Go back to sleep."

Craig gives up. He goes over to the fireplace, arranges his blanket and pillow, and curls up on the hearth rug with Boxer.

The next morning Mother and Mr. Heerman are up at dawn. Mother makes her train; Mr. Heerman wanders around the yard, sniffing the lilacs, treading through the plowed fields, gazing across the valley toward town. He returns with a fistful of violets and lilies of the valley for the breakfast table. Patsy and Jackie fry bacon and eggs. When the second clarinetist and harpist show up for breakfast, they meet Craig.

Later Craig relishes telling the family of his nocturnal odyssey. "I felt like

Baby Bear," he says. "Everywhere I went I kept finding a Goldilocks—and the funny thing was, I seemed to be the only one surprised. And this morning when that second clarinetist and harpist met me, you should have seen their blushes!"

43 STUART PETERSON

Stuart Peterson is a slow-witted man who has for years been working for Ruby Obeck on the Obeck place across the road from Chez Nous. With instruction, Stuart can do most things. He's strong and burly and good-natured. On Saturday nights he goes to the Shopiere tavern. As the beer flows, some of the locals turn to Stuart for sport. He's always good for a laugh, for he takes their teasing literally.

"Tell us about that lady we seen you with, Stu," one starts.

Another builds on it. "That gussied-up blond, cheek-to-cheek with you, down at Waverly Beach last night!"

"I never was at Waverly Beach!" Stuart protests. "I never was dancing with no lady!"

"Oho," cries the first. "You admit it, she wasn't no lady!"

"I never been to Waverly Beach!" Stuart insists.

One winter day he's working in a snowy cornfield east of the Obeck farm buildings, across from the Dougan fields. The cornstalks have long since been cut, tied into bundles, and the bundles set into large shocks, fifteen or sixteen to a shock. The shocks make the field look like a village of Indian tepees. Every few days Stuart loads all the bundles from one shock onto a wagon and takes them to the animals in the barn. He's whittled away at the field; it's now half-empty. He pulls up alongside a shock near the road and pitches the first bundle onto the wagon bed. As he turns back for the second, he sees something and recoils. He looks again, carefully. Feet are sticking out from underneath the shock. Feet in worn brown work boots, and a bit of leg, covered with a ragged cuff. It slowly becomes clear to Stuart that there must be more of that leg, and another leg under the shock, and that the body attached to those legs is certainly dead and frozen. He makes a gar-

Corn shocks.

gling noise, wheels and scrambles over the fence, through the ditch and out onto the road, where he flails his arms at an approaching tractor.

Gilbert Gjestvang, Grampa's farm manager, stops. Stuart gibbers and points. "A dead man! A dead man under the corn shock!"

It takes Gilbert a few moments to digest the unlikely words. Then he says, "You're kidding!"

Stuart insists.

"Come show me," says Gilbert.

But Stuart won't return. He points out the shock and then paces agitatedly while Gilbert scales the fence and starts through the shallow snow into the field. Near the shock and wagon Gilbert looks back over his shoulder. Stuart urges him on.

Gilbert approaches. He, too, sees the feet. He feels a distinct jolt. He looks again at Stuart and nods affirmation, and Stuart nods vigorously back. Gilbert walks slowly around the shock. The snow is undisturbed. Nothing else is showing. A man, lying full length on his stomach as this one seems to be, since the feet are turned down, would have to have a head . . . right about . . .

Gilbert abruptly lifts a bundle and tosses it to one side. Nothing there. He lifts and throws another one, and a third. This last reveals the head, turned sideways so that he sees an ear, a cheek, the nose. He involuntarily turns away, bile rising in his throat. Then he forces himself to look again.

The body has been here for a long time, long enough for the rats and mice to find it. The ear is almost gone, the lower lip eaten away, exposing teeth and gum. It seems to be an older man, thin, with sparse, graying hair. Gilbert doesn't think he's ever seen him before. The mottled cheek and brow look dreadful, with the eyelid half open, but there doesn't seem to be much decomposition of the flesh. The body must have been put here after the freezing weather began.

Put here. . . . That means murder. Someone had to put him here. Or could he have been drunk, might he have crawled in here to get out of the weather and died? But his position isn't huddled up, a man trying to keep warm. Well, he could have died by some natural means, and a companion stashed him here, not wanting any problem with authorities. But that's not likely, either.

Gilbert doesn't remove any more bundles. He strides back to the road. "Is Ruby home?" he asks Stuart.

"She's gone to town."

"We'll call Ron, then," he says, "and he can call the police."

Stuart hurries after Gilbert to the Obeck farmhouse, whimpering all the way.

"You've found WHAT?" Daddy bellows over the office phone. "A *dead man?*"

Gilbert and Stuart scarcely make it back to the road before Ron races up in the Buick. Gilbert leads him to the spot, and he circles from head to foot and back to head, swearing under his breath in French and shaking his head. "The poor bastard," he finally says. Then he goes to the Obeck farmhouse to telephone.

By the time he returns cars are streaming up Colley Road from both directions and half the employees of the Dougan farm are clambering over the ditch.

"Go back to work, you ghouls," says Daddy, but nobody pays any attention. It's only a few moments more before the neighbors begin to show up, and a stranger from Walworth County who's just happening by and stops to see what's going on. Each new arrival looks at the face, makes an exclamation of revulsion, and says that as far as he can tell, he doesn't know the man.

Once it's established that the corpse is a stranger, the mood of the crowd becomes almost festive. Comments such as "Sorta chewed up, ain't he?" give way to crude jokes. Those on the edge of the group, where Stuart has come closer and is circling, start to rib him. "Hey Stu, how'd you kill him?"

"I didn't! I didn't! It wasn't me!" Stuart protests.

Two police cars and an ambulance roar up Colley Road, lights flashing and sirens wailing, and the crowd cheers. Daddy again orders all his people back to work, and the farmhands reluctantly disperse. The neighbors and the man from Walworth stay.

Everyone falls back to let the officers through. They survey the scene, confer, pull out tape measures, a photographer snaps picture after picture. Out on the road the ambulance attendants lean against the ambulance, waiting. The policeman in charge questions first Daddy, then Gilbert, then the cowering Stuart. They then begin stripping back the corn bundles, taking pictures as they go.

"Are we needed to stay and watch this?" Daddy asks the policeman in charge. He says no, and Ron, Gilbert, and Stuart walk back to the road.

"I didn't do it, Mr. Dougan!" Stuart protests. "I didn't do it!"

"Nobody thinks you did," says Daddy. "Take the rest of the day off if you want. Go to a movie. Tell Ruby I said so. Here's a dollar."

"But the stock's gotta be fed," Stuart wails. "And that shock—that shock—*nothin'* should eat that shock—"

"Gilbert'll get somebody to load one from the far end of the field and haul it to the barn," Daddy says. "In a couple of days, when the police are finished, you or somebody can make a bonfire." He then heads for the Hill Farm to tell Grampa, glad that his father has been working on fences there and missed the commotion.

For a week the sensation of the stranger under the corn shock dominates township conversations—who he could be, where he came from, how he'd gotten under there, how long he'd been there. *The Beloit Daily News* publishes an initial story, then a follow-up, but these are of little help. The man, though clothed, had no identification or money on him, nor anything traceable in his pockets. He fits the description of no missing person on file. Forensic experts find no evidence of foul play: no bullet or stab wound, no strangling, no head bashed in. There's not a liquor bottle anywhere around. The autopsy tells nothing except that he hadn't eaten recently. He was probably under the shock two or three months. The verdict is: a person unknown, perhaps an itinerant worker, dying of causes unknown, perhaps illness or exposure or suicide, on a date unknown, and either crawling under, or being placed under, a corn shock in a field adjacent to Colley Road, Turtle Township, Rock County. If placed, it was by a person or persons unknown, and the death would have occurred in a place unknown, but probably near the field where the body was found. The police don't pursue the puzzle any further.

Nobody ever learns anything more about the man. Before long he's forgotten, except by Stuart and a small group of tormenters.

"Tell us about the dead man, Stu," someone says at the tavern. Others take up the game. "Why'd you do him in? Huh, Stu? Tell us! Why'd you kill him?"

"I never! I only found 'im!" Stuart insists frantically.

"Oh come on, Stu, confess! We know you done it. Nobody's gonna catch you now. You can tell us! Did he steal your girl?"

"I never done it!" Stuart sobs, and tears roll down his cheeks.

44 GRAMPA'S AND GRAMA'S INTIMATE LIFE

Grampa and Grama's intimate life is almost purely a matter of conjecture. It's a safe bet that it's not conjectured often.

Grampa calls Grama "Dearie," and if Grama calls Grampa anything, no one knows, because it's all on her fingers. It's obvious that Grampa feels tenderly toward Grama, and that she loves him. But she often gets impatient. Grampa writes to Ronald from the West, where he and Grama are visiting Trever and his family, "When little Karla sees Mother talking to me by hand she grows belligerent. She seems to think Mother is going to hurt me, I think because Mother emphasizes so vividly she thinks Mother is scolding me. Well, I think so sometimes myself."

And on the farm, when Grama gets all bothered toward Grampa and is carrying on with heat and passion, Grampa with a quizzical little smile will reach out a cautious finger, touch her knee, and say "Ssssssss!" That usually stops Grama short and makes her laugh.

All her life she saves Grampa's first letter, November of 1894, which contains this evocative paragraph:

> I have lived over again and again our summer at the camp. You know how much I said about forgetting the company as soon as we were separated. Well, I have changed my opinion. I have noticed that those I became attached to have been growing dearer to me. You know, too, that one of the reasons of postponing our correspondence was to test the genuineness of our affection for each other. Now my dear girl let me assure you that my affection for you has only deepened since our separation. We will not dwell on the events of the summer for when I begin recalling them the stream of thought is endless. There is one psycho-

logical phenomenon well illustrated in my thoughts of Geneva. I.e., that when we call up past experiences those that have impressed you most deeply at the time will be the first called up. When I think of our parting I do not think of the last trip over to Williams Bay as the last parting but rather the trip over on that foggy morning and our parting on the beach. Do you remember?

He ends the letter with the request that they exchange photographs, and signs it with an astonishing "Love and kisses."

Grama also saves the letters Grampa writes her when she's away for several weeks in the summer of 1914. These usually start, "My Precious Dearie," and, along with news, contain such lines as: "Everything is moving nicely this morning. But I do miss you. I was very lonesome last night. The cub-

Grama and Grampa at the Juda parsonage, early in their married life.

bies are lots of company to me and full of fun. Was sorry I got down out of the peak of the barn too late to bid you goodbye." And: "I am sorry you did not get my love letters while you were at Camp Byron. I have written to you every day." And: "Your nice love letters do me lots of good. I miss you so much. I cannot tell you all you are to me. Tonight my legs and arms are tired and nervous. I would just like to be with my strong sweet wife. She rests and consoles me."

Grama saves the letters, too, that Grampa writes daily in 1915, during the weeks that he travels around the state with Professor Otis, giving seminars on farm management: "I know my Dearie is thinking of me a great deal today and I am of her. I know she felt badly to have me so busy last night and to leave as I had to." "I love you so today I would give anything to see you for a little while." "Now a little love letter to your own self. I think of you with your anxiety and care for the cubbies and high ideals for the whole home life. I want to live up to my opportunity and be worthy of such a help-mate. Your loving Wess." "I am a little homesick tonight. I would like to be with you. Tell the cubbies to keep the envelopes and when I get home we will make a journey book from them. . . . You precious wife. I do love you more and more and I will try my best to be all you deserve. Must close and work on data. Your loving husband, W. J. Dougan."

There are also some letters from Grampa and Grama's old age. One is an anniversary letter from Grampa, when both are in their mid-seventies:

> This note is to remind you that you are as dear to me today as you were the day we stood on the little bridge and I placed the small dia-mond on your finger, or the autumn day we started our long journey of life together. It has always been a marvel to me that you had the faith in me and the courage to cast your lot with me. We have met the chang-ing scenes and vicissitudes of life together and surmounted disppoint-ments and difficulties: also garnered the joys and satisfactions of fellow-ship and service.

I have always regretted your losing the diamond but it was not a break in our love and devotion to each other. Today as a token of this sustaining love I want to take you to Mr. Brill's and have you choose another diamond bigger and better than the first one for our love is sealed with 45 years of experience.

Your devoted Husband, W. J. D.

Grampa himself saves Grama's appreciative response to his letter and gift. In it she apologizes for her impatience: "I don't mean anything when you can't get my message over the first time, only it is an effort when I am feeling run down to repeat a long sentence. Think nothing of it. I love you more than I can tell. . . . I dread the time when we have to be separated. I like to be in your presence more than anybody else's. So know as we grow older I love you more and more and you are dearer and dearer to me. Affectionately, Your Dearie."

Three years later, when Grama is in a Madison hospital for tests, Grampa writes her every day, describing the new trucks painted and lettered, the Golden Bantam sweet corn he's planted at Ron's place, and Effie's care for him. Effie is Grama's spinster niece, who keeps house for Grama and Grampa. "I stopped for breakfast. It was splendid, asparagus on toast. Fit for the king. And the king got it!" He ends his letters with how he thinks of her every hour, and "the usual love that has grown with the years." One, in its closing, echoes the "Do you remember?" of his first letter. He signs it "Yours," and adds, after his W. J. D., "I underline it—you know the rest."

A few things not contained in letters are known of Grama and Grampa's intimate life. Grama occasionally speaks on this subject to her next-door neighbor down the road, Mrs. Smith, who is Eloise Marston's grandmother.

Eloise, always quietly around, tunes in to adult conversations and stows them away for future pondering. At a young age she hears of Eunice's many miscarriages that lead to the bringing of Esther from the Sparta orphanage, to be the daughter that is missing in the family and to become her good chum. Later she learns that as soon as Eunice enters menopause, she moves out of Grampa's bedroom into the adjoining one, telling Mrs. Smith, "Well, there's no point in doing it once you're in the change, since the only reason you do it is to have a baby—and that would be wonderful, of course, but once you're in the change all that's over." Mrs. Smith's expression lets Eloise know that her grandmother doesn't agree with Mrs. Dougan, but Mrs. Smith stays silent, and Eunice doesn't notice.

Later yet, she hears Eunice tell her grandmother about a several-day conference she's just returned from. She'd gone along with Grampa, who was the main speaker, to write and spell to him what was taking place.

"And would you know, we were given a room with a double bed!" Grama exclaims. "Well, that really distressed me, but there was nothing we could do about it, we had to share the bed. But you know, Wesson kept himself so nice and clean, he was so nice and tender toward me, that it wasn't bad."

Golden Wedding portrait, 1948.

This time Mrs. Smith doesn't hold her tongue. "Well, of course it wasn't bad!" she retorts.

Jackie, growing up in a boisterous household of sisters and brother, is for a long time unaware of adult sexual life. At the Little House Mother and Daddy sleep together on the sleeping porch, but she and Craig sleep together in the next room, and Joan and Patsy sleep together in the third bedroom across the hall. It's a matter of space. Grampa and Grama, with all the space of the Big House, of course have separate bedrooms. Besides, Grampa snores.

The subject comes up when Jackie is more savvy about things, in her later teens. Mother says, "Gram told me that she and Gramp never had intercourse except to have children. I always felt so sorry for Grampa."

When Jackie hears this, she does, too. It seems mean of Grama, no matter how she herself feels, to deny patient, loving Grampa.

Mother also tells how Grama said to her once, over at the Little House, how disgusted she was when she'd be changing the sheets of the young hired men at the Big House, and find them wet. Mother says, "I said to her, 'You should approve. It shows they haven't been tomcatting around.'"

The topic of her grandparents' sex life doesn't surface again till years later. Jackie brings it up. By then she's read enough and learned enough to realize many of the forces that shaped both Grampa and Grama when they were growing up, from their births around 1870 to their marriage in 1898, and their subsequent life together. Both were children during the repressive Victorian era; both would have been protected from its hidden excesses. In addition, both were raised in strict Methodist households. Drinking, smoking, and gambling were the sins that were preached about. Desecrating the Sabbath was a pretty big sin, too. But the undiscussed biggest sin was sexual sinning. In all her years squirming in the long wooden pew in the Methodist church Jackie never heard a sermon that mentioned sex in any way. If it was referred to, the reference was so oblique that she missed it.

There was no public mention of sex at all, much less sex as a normal part of married life, a joy to the couple and a bond to the relationship. So if there was still this taboo two generations after Grama and Grampa's childhood, could they even have talked about it?

Daddy, who is in on the later conversation with Mother and Jackie, says he can't remember any birds-and-bees lecture from either parent, though Grama's letters to him at college are full of exhortations to stay pure. "I assumed she meant smoking, though. Nobody ever mentioned sex. But there's always so much sex on a farm that you never needed to be told anything. You could see the birds and the bees, and chickens and pigs, and you regularly had to take the cow to the bull. A farm is a synonym for sex."

"You told me," says Mother, "that your father told you when you went off to Northwestern that sex was a sacred and blessed thing, given by God to have children and to procreate the world."

"Did I?" says Daddy.

"And you told me that when you went off to France, Grampa said to you that before he and your mother went to bed together, they'd kneel down and pray at the bedside, and ask the Lord to bless their union with children."

"Did I?" says Daddy. "Now take me, I just hung my pants on the bed-post, and those four children came from somewhere!"

"And Grampa always loved children, wanted children, wanted a family," Mother persists.

"So I'm thinking," Jackie says, "that the same taboos affected Grampa as affected Grama. He must have been at least a little responsible for any lack of sex in his later years. It wasn't just the snoring."

"And I'm thinking," says Daddy, "of the old story of the census taker who asks the German woman how many children she has. 'Six boys,' says the woman. 'Oh, every time a boy!' says the census taker. 'Ach, no!' says the woman. 'Thousands of times and nothing!'"

45 GRAMPA'S GLORIOUS DAY

It's spring of 1948. Grampa has been working alone in a field all day, and has gone on home to Grama and Effie in the house on the edge of town. Daddy has been out of the office, doing discouraging work on the milk-house plumbing. Close to six o'clock he stops by his desk. Two little scraps of memo paper are laid across the day's work, so that he'll notice them. He recognizes Grampa's familiar pencil scrawl.

Ronald: I had a glorious
good time today.
The sky and clouds have
    been grand.
The team responded to every
touch & were so strong &
    willing.
The machines were good if

they are old. That wonderful
field of No. 1 grass is such
a satisfaction—we have been
preparing for that for the
past ten years.

"Dad"

Daddy reads his father's note twice, grins, sticks the little papers in his pocket to show Mother, straightens his shoulders, and heads for home.

It's a sunny June day. Craig is eighteen, Grampa is seventy-nine. Grampa has retired, but still works all day, every day, on the farm. Craig is working on the farm, too, before starting Beloit College in the fall. Daddy has teamed him up with Grampa, to be Grampa's man Friday on whatever project Grampa wants to do. Today Grampa's project is to make water run uphill.

Craig and his Model T Ford.

They are down in the pasture where the Chicago–Milwaukee–St. Paul & Pacific (or "The Milwaukee Road") railroad tracks go by. Alongside the railroad bridge over the crick there is a concrete underpass in the railroad embankment, for cows and machinery to go through to the fields beyond. The floor of this underpass has filled with water and sludge. When the cows come through it, they get muck halfway up their legs. Grampa does not like his cows coming up to the barn with dirty legs.

He's hitched a long scoop bucket called a slip to the one horse left on the farm, Barney. Barney is old, too, and blind, and retired, except when Grampa finds a job for him.

Grampa and Craig position the bucket in the muck. Each holds onto and presses down a handle; there is one on either side. Grampa speaks to the horse, old Barney plods, Grampa grunts, Craig wrinkles his nose, and mud

Grampa.

and water are scooped uphill. But the grade is a long one, and when they dump the bucket, midway up, muddy water flows back down into the underpass.

Craig can't see how they are any ahead. The next rain will fill the under-pass up again anyhow, no matter how clear they get it now. He can think up a dozen ways of doing the job better than Grampa's way, most of them more ambitious than he feels: siphons, drains, canals. His main thought is, why do the job at all, why not just let the cows have dirty legs? He and Grampa, after several hours at this job, have much more than legs that are dirty.

Gradually, however, the underpass clears. Enough water soaks into the hill that after repeated trips the end of the job is in sight. Craig and Grampa sit down on the bank of the crick for a well-deserved break. Barney lowers his head and crops grass. Grampa takes out his blue farm bandana and wipes his face. The sun shines warm. The crick swirls and eddies beneath their feet.

Craig has been thinking ahead to college, to life. He's been active in the Methodist Youth Fellowship at church. Now Reverend Krussell has been urging the ministry. Craig motions for Grampa to hand him his pencil and paper.

"I have often heard," Craig writes, "how you left the ministry for the farm, but I've never heard how you decided to be a minister in the first place."

Grampa studies the paper. Craig rolls onto his elbow and nibbles a grass stem. Grampa folds the paper and puts it back in his pocket. He ponders before he talks.

"My family were religious people," he says, "and I was raised to be God-fearing and Bible-reading and church-going." He goes on, telling Craig about what it was like to be a boy on the farm at Lowell, about his father's death, and his mother's hopes for him. He tells how he felt drawn to the ser-vice of the Lord, but that he was uncertain that this was God's plan for him. He had had to drop out of high school, and already he was older than other college students. He spent much time in thought and prayer as he worked the land, wrestling with the problem.

"And finally one evening," says Grampa, turning and twinkling at Craig, "I went up on a hill, and I stood there, looking at the sky, communing with the Lord. And I shouted out loud, 'Lord, what am I to do? Give me a sign!'"

Craig is strongly interested. He indicates this by his face and eyebrows, and asks with his voice, "And did He?"

Grampa nods and chuckles. "He did. There in the clouds I made out the letters P C, 'Preach Christ!' That was my sign. I knew now what it was that the Lord wanted me to do. And so I left the farm and went to the university."

Craig sits up and reaches for the paper again.

"How awful for you, then," he writes, "when you finally got to be a minister, to lose your hearing and have to leave. For the Lord to take away from you the very thing he'd told you to do. Didn't it make you doubt Him?"

Grampa studies Craig's words, almost imperceptibly nodding and nodding his head.

"Yes, it was hard," he says at last. "And I spent many months thinking and praying and agonizing. And finally in great torment I went up on another hill, and I stood there looking at the sky, and I shouted out, 'Lord, what am I to do? Give me a sign!' And there, in the clouds, I again made out the letters P C!"

Craig looks puzzled at Grampa. Grampa's face breaks into laughter. He laughs so hard he can hardly talk; his eyes disappear.

"And it came to me," laughs Grampa, "it came to me, that I'd perhaps misunderstood the Lord the first time, and that all along He'd been saying to me, 'Plant Corn'!"

Craig and Grampa whoop. Grampa rolls back on the bank and kicks his feet in the air like a colt.

47 A SOWER WENT FORTH

It is late April, and Grampa has gone forth to sow. He's doing it in the old-fashioned way, almost like the picture illustrating the parable in Grama's big Bible, or the painting on Grama and Grampa's wall of the French peasants, by Millet. He has a bag of seed fastened at his waist and a box hanging on his chest; he walks along cranking a wheel on the box and it sprays the grass seed in a wide arc around him. His arm goes back and forth as if he's playing a fiddle.

His walk is more of a stumble. This is partly because Grampa's usual walk is something of a stumble, slanting forward and going fast; it's partly because Grampa is old, almost eighty; and finally because a blanket of snow covers the ground.

"This is a thousand-dollar snow," Grampa had said to Jackie as she'd stood on his porch with him the night before. They'd watched the fat wet flakes drifting down. Already the lawn was covered with white.

"It is not cold enough to do any damage," Grampa had continued, "and the moisture will water all the seedlings in the most gentle and gradual way possible. A spring snow like this is a benediction of the Lord."

They'd watched some more, and Grampa's throat made its little droning, thinking sound, like a chicken. "There's a field at the Hill Farm," he'd said after a bit. "It's due to be seeded, but we can't get the machinery on it now. The seed would do splendidly in this snow. I shall have to sow it by hand."

The field is a large one. Grampa finishes. He's tired. While he was sowing, the pain returned to his chest. It's the familiar burning pain that he's had off and on for some time now, but has told no one about, except Dr. Thayer. He knows the name. Angina pectoris. Today the pain is strong. He climbs in his car and drives back to town, not stopping at Ron's place or the dairy. At home he kisses Grama on her couch, goes to the kitchen, and says to Effie, "Please call Dr. Thayer and tell him I should see him. I have some pain."

Effie delivers the message and reports, "He's at the hospital. He says to come over there."

Grampa goes upstairs and takes off his heavy work shoes. He takes off his overalls, his work shirt, and his one-piece long underwear. He takes a bath. He puts on clean underwear, a clean shirt, a good suit. The pain stays with him. He gets in the car and drives to the hospital. He asks for Dr. Thayer. They take one look at him and rush him to the emergency room. He has had a heart attack.

Dr. Thayer calls the farm. Daddy and Mother are in Colorado with friends, on a vacation trip. Nobody knows how to reach them. The state police are put onto the job of finding the car.

Jackie is on her bicycle near Beloit College. Patsy swoops up to her in the car. "Grampa's in the hospital," she shouts out the window. Jackie veers and changes course. At the hospital Patsy is there, and Craig, and their cousin Jerry. Grampa is in bed with oxygen tubes in his nose. Jackie is startled and filled with foreboding. But Grampa is cheerful. He's not in much pain, he says. He makes them feel cheerful. They all chatter cheerfully among themselves and to Grampa.

"Will you rub my feet?" Grampa asks Jackie. "They're cold."

Jackie stands at the foot of the hospital bed and rubs and rubs her grandfather's feet.

The Colorado police flag down Daddy at Pike's Peak. He rushes from Pueblo to Denver and catches a midnight plane. He leaves Mother to pack and follow on the train. The friends will continue the trip with the car.

When Daddy gets to the hospital the next morning, he finds Grampa sitting up in bed, thinking about his plans for spring. He has his farm books and maps around him. They are starting a new enterprise; the contour plow and other machinery are coming on May 10, Grampa's birthday, to terrace all the fields at Chez Nous and the Hill Farm. The fields, on Grampa's maps, are marked out in the flowing lines of the contour levels. Grampa reviews the work with Ronald.

A redheaded nurse comes in at frequent intervals to take care of Grampa and chat for a moment. Grampa can't praise her highly enough. She is Betty Beadle, daughter of Grampa's former farm manager, Leonard Beadle. Grampa and Daddy have watched her grow up from a baby.

Trever arrives, and Grampa speaks of his life to his two sons. He says it's been full and rich and happy, and filled with every blessing. Were he able to do it over again, he would do things pretty much the way he's done them.

"If it's the Lord's will to take me now," he says, "I am prepared."

To Ronald it doesn't look as if this is the time. His father is much too active, too vital. In a vibrant voice Grampa recites from memory Tennyson's "Crossing the Bar":

> Sunset and evening star
> And one clear call for me,
> And may there be no moaning at the bar
> When I put out to sea,
> But such a tide as moving seems asleep,
> Too full for sound or foam
> When that which came from out the boundless deep
> Turns again home.
>
> Twilight and evening bell,
> And after that the dark,
> And may there be no sadness of farewell
> When I embark.
> For though from out this time and place
> The flood has bourne me far,
> I hope to meet my pilot face to face
> When I have crossed the bar.

When he finishes, Ronald and Trever's eyes are wet. Grampa's are wet, too. He prays with them.

Throughout the day Grampa has many visitors. Craig and Jerry come again. At one point they are alone with Grampa. He recites "Crossing the Bar" to them, too. They talk about life and about death. "Cubbies," says Grampa to his grandsons, "I do not know how I know so surely, but I know that I shall live forever."

Jackie comes again, too. She brings a painting she's just finished in art class. It's of a straddle-legged calf ducking its head and sucking on its mother. The pair are standing by a golden strawstack, and she's painted the sky a rich brown. Grampa laughs silently at the picture. Then he critiques the anatomy of the cow, but he doesn't object to the brown sky as her professor had. He has her place the picture on the window ledge where he can see it. Then Jackie rubs and rubs his cold feet some more.

LaBerta Ullius from the Big House sits with Grampa into the evening. She and Grampa have a special bond. When LaBerta's young daughter was killed several years before, Grampa was a strength and comfort. And every morning, when he comes out to the farm to work, he stops in to the Big House kitchen for a chat. He calls LaBerta "Cookie." He says to her from his hospital bed, "Cookie, I feel that I shall live forever and ever." There is strength in his voice.

The next morning Daddy gets up and goes to meet Mother's train. Grampa had been so well the night before that it doesn't occur to him to call the hospital first. Craig and Jerry come from Craig's early clarinet lesson to the hospital. They walk in jauntily, and stop. Betty Beadle is bending over Grampa. They catch her eye, questioning her, and Betty nods. The grandsons stand crying while Grampa gasps his last breaths.

Daddy is paged at the Northwestern station. Jackie hears at college, leaves her class, and pedals over to Grampa and Grama's house. Everyone is there when she arrives. Grama is sitting on her couch rocking back and forth, wailing and wailing. "Daddy is gone! Oh, my precious Daddy is gone!" Her sons sit on either side of her, holding her. Mother greets Jackie with brimmed eyes. Daddy acknowledges her presence; his eyes have tears, too. So do Trever's and everybody's.

Jackie feels cold and numb and sick at heart. She's never seen the family like this before. There have been only a few deaths, Aunt Ida and Aunt Della—but never a death when Grampa was not here. There has never been a time in her almost twenty-one years when Grampa has not been here.

"Daddy's gone!" wails Grama.

Jackie can't stand it. She goes out and climbs the big pine tree in the back yard until her weight will let her get no higher. She sways there amid the new needles. She's in shock.

Scenes with Grampa flood her mind. Grampa last Christmas, reciting for the family not a Christmas or new birth poem but "Crossing the Bar." Grampa coming back from the dentist last week, shouting, "Don't worry! You won't have to grind up my feed! These old teeth will last me the rest of my life!" Grampa last fall in his living room, reading aloud an essay he was sending to his old friend and longtime employee, DeWitt Griffiths, who was dying in a Madison hospital; it was the last of several letters where he was comparing life to the seasons. Grampa saying, "This one is so hard for me to write because I, too, am in the late autumn of my life. Winter cannot be far off."

Jackie sees now with clarity what she had refused to recognize then—that Grampa wanted to talk about his essay with someone. He wanted to talk about the winter, the end of life, the end of his own life. Grampa wanted the comfort of talk and acknowledgment of death. But she hadn't done it. She was afraid to think about Grampa dying. No one in the room had done it, for Grampa was always the comforter.

She's glad she went to the hospital both days, that she brought the picture, that she touched him. She's glad she was able to do something for him, to rub his feet. She realizes that was another sign of death that she hadn't recognized—Grampa's feet cold from lack of circulation.

And she sees Grampa in his chair, reading the page she wrote to him while she twists his hair into a Kewpie-doll curl, Grampa pleased and laughing and saying, "Yes, the round barn has a lot to say!" She should have grabbed a pencil then and there, and found out from Grampa the things that only he could tell her, the things she knows just bits and pieces of, the things she doesn't know at all. Now it is too late. Too late.

And it's too late to tell him in words everything he's meant to her. She has just assumed he would always be here. She hasn't faced the fact that life will stop, even for those you love, for those who are always here.

She hugs the trunk of the pine tree and weeps till she's exhausted. Then she rests with her head against the bark, her eyes closed. She feels blank and empty.

After a while a picture creeps into her mind. It's not one she has ever seen, yet it's as clear as if she had. Grampa is walking over the snowy field by the Hill Farm woods. The April sun warms his sparse hair and makes the snow glitter with a million diamonds. A meadowlark is singing on a fence post. Grampa has a bag like the ones in the Bible pictures, and he is rhythmically casting alfalfa seed ahead of him so that it dusts the snow. His footprints and the seed on the snow mark where he has already been.

Words accompany the picture, the words of the parable. A sower went forth to sow. A sower went forth to sow. Over and over the words go through Jackie's mind as she watches Grampa going back and forth over his last field. Grampa is the sower, she knows. He has always been the sower. If he had to die now, it's fitting that he died sowing.

And the seed has not fallen on the rocks or the wayside or among the brambles, at least not much of it, but on good earth that he has prepared, Waukesha-loam-over-gravel earth. The seed has sprung up, and it is the barn and the silo and the Aims; it is the cows and pigs and chickens; it is the alfalfa and Vicland oats and hybrid seed corn. It is the milkmen and the barn-hands and the farmhands, the Tri-Y boys and the 4-H-ers. It is all the children all over town who have grown up on milk produced by The Babies' Milkman. It is the people in his early churches at Juda and Oregon and Poynette, and the people in the Church that has been his whole life—everyone whom he has shown by his example how to love, how to have life as well as a living. Most of all it is his family: Daddy and Mother and her aunts and uncle, and the grandchildren—her cousins, and Joan and Patsy and Craig and herself. They are the seed springing up on the good soil.

Jackie stirs and opens her eyes. She feels bleak but no longer quite so forsaken. Grampa has sown, but what will the harvest be? She can grow true, if she will, and become a sower herself.

She climbs stiffly down from the top of the tree. The shining snow and the solitary sower are still in her mind's eye as she goes back to her people in the fullness of the empty house.